Steinar

by

Mary Morgan

The Wolves of Clan Sutherland
Book 3

Steinar

Cover Art by *Lisa Dawn MacDonald*

The Wild Rose Press, Inc.
PO Box 708
Adams Basin, NY 14410-0708
Visit us at www.thewildrosepress.com

Publishing History
First Edition, 2024
Trade Paperback ISBN 978-1-5092-5332-6
Digital ISBN 978-1-5092-5333-3

The Wolves of Clan Sutherland, Book 3
Published in the United States of America

She gestured to her gown. "Can you honestly tell me I look like a woman who is a leader of men on the seas?"

Steinar's expression stilled. He wiped the back of his hand leisurely across his mouth. "Nae," he rasped out.

There she witnessed the invitation in the smoldering depths of his eyes—dark with desire luring her forward.

Her heart hammered against her chest. Inga's mind ordered her to leave—escape the temptation to feel his arms around her. But her body betrayed and overrode all thought. Slowly, Inga removed the jug from his hand and pressed it against her lips. Tilting it back, she drank deeply of what remained. After tossing aside the jug onto the ground, she smiled fully. "Then I am correct."

Steinar pushed away from the wall. "You think to claim victory?"

Her breath rose heavily with each rise and fall. When did she become the prey and he the predator? "Always," she whispered, determined to grasp any shard of control or sanity.

In one swift move, Steinar clasped his hands around her waist and turned her around with her back against the wall. His body towered over her, trapping Inga. Escape not an option.

She gasped. Fight or surrender?

For the first time, Inga lessened the strings binding her to an oath moons ago.

An oath to never let a man control her.

An oath to never let a man touch her.

Oaths be damned! She craved to have this man kiss her.

Praise for Mary Morgan

"If readers have not yet read a book by Mary Morgan, jumping in with "Magnar" is like plunging into a raging river of pure writing force." ~InD'tale Magazine, November 2020 Issue, 5 stars and Crowned Heart Review (*Magnar*)

~*~

"A beautifully written Viking paranormal romance, Rorik is a must-read this summer. Highly recommend!" ~ N.N. Light's Book Heaven (*Rorik*)

~*~

"Dark suspense and sexual tension ripple across these pages from the very first chapter. Mary Morgan brings ancient Scotland to life in vivid and pulse-pounding detail. It's brilliantly and masterfully done." ~ InD'tale Magazine July/August 2021 Issue (*Rorik*)

~*~

"I loved everything about this story - the plot, the beautiful scenery, the holiday theme, the chemistry between Alex and Aine, as well as the full cast of characters. Would I highly recommend this masterfully written book…Aye!" ~ Still Moments Magazine (*Wishes Under a Highland Star*)

~*~

"The author has taken her knowledge of the Irish legends of fairies or fae along with the Scottish legends of dragons and used them well in creating this wonderful story. This light-hearted romance catches the reader's imagination from the first page to the last page and will have them smiling and even crying in places." ~Readers' Favorite (*Wishes Under a Highland Star*)

Dedication

To all my readers throughout the world, thank you for your continued support for my stories. I'm honored and grateful for your encouragement and praise through the years. I shall strive to always give you the best tale—the best happily ever after story.

With love,

Mary

Glossary of Old Norse Terms

Āsgarthr – Home of the Norse Gods
Hamnavoe – Current day town of Stromness, Orkney
Hnefatafl – Viking chess
Kærr – dear, close, beloved
Kirkjuvágr – Kirkwall
Njörd – God of the winds and sea
Orkneyjar – Orkney
Rán – Goddess of the sea
Skald – Norse bard/poet
Skinnleikr – Viking skin throwing game
Völva – Wise woman

The Nine Noble Virtues of Wolf Lore

1. Learn to control the beast within. If not, the man will cease to exist.
2. First lesson for the wolf: the man is always Alpha.
3. Scotland is our home. *Orkneyjar* calls to our soul.
4. When conflicted, follow the path of the stars. Odin will shine his light upon you.
5. Keep your weapon as strong as Thor's hammer.
6. Discipline your beast to honor the code of the Brotherhood.
7. Honor the Gods. Do not beg at their feet for aid.
8. When All Father calls you to His table, storm proudly across the void.
9. Remember your ancestors and honor their wisdom.

Prologue

What began as a magical, whispered thought deep within a dark forest between a druid, a raven, and a Norse Seer, eventually took shape within the minds of seers and druids who belonged to five ancient clans that carried blood from both the Norse people, as well as the Picts.

While feuding clans and marauders continued to ravage the Scottish realm, the blood of their victims seeped into the land, and the people wept as they cried out for vengeance. Despite the pleas for war from their people, the chieftains, after seeking counsel from their druids and seers, sought another plan to ease the conflict tormenting the clans.

These chieftains called for an order of guards to protect their current king and those who would follow to reign over Scotland. Though these ancient clans had ties to two different countries—Norway *and* Scotland, they deemed the strongest king should rule over both.

After much debate, they came to a settlement. If the King of Scotland were to govern over both countries, he would require strong men to protect, serve, and even spy on his behalf. Men whose bloodline would be filled with the magic of the Norse God Odin and the Pict God Dagda—a bridge linking all the people's beliefs.

The runes were cast on a stormy night, and the men were chosen. 'Twas on a Moon Day within the Black Frost month on *Orkneyjar*, that the blood of a wolf and an eagle were mixed with powerful magic.

Each selected man from these ancient tribes entered the stone chamber—to be one with the bones of the wolves. What emerged was dominant and commanding—feared by those who witnessed the pairing of each man with his wolf.

And as the centuries bled into the next, within the boundaries of Scotland, the wolves became more of a myth—one told by bards on a cold winter's night.

Especially for the one they called the Pirate Wolf. His ruthless tactics on the sea were feared by many, and those who dared to steer a path onto the waters made certain to avoid him.

Though his soul belonged to the depths of the bitter sea *and* to his wolf, the man's loyalty remained steadfast to the King of Scotland and the God Odin.

Yet on his quest to seek the ultimate treasure for Scotland—a prize valued by both Norse Gods and Kings—the Pirate Wolf confronted his greatest challenge against an enemy more powerful than he imagined.

And the sea gave no mercy to the Pirate known as Steinar MacDougall, descended from the great Lord of the Isles, Somerled.

This is his story.
The MacDougall Wolf Saga.

Chapter One

Western coast of Scotland—Late Spring, 1207

"You are an angry siren threatening me with your thrashing waves!" Steinar's laughter rang heavily, competing against the might of the thunder overhead.

And the sea responded to his outburst. Another wave crashed against his body with the force of Thor's hammer, knocking the breath from his lungs and filling his nose with the salty brine of the sea.

A great spasm filled Steinar, and the wolf within him howled in fury—giving him the air to breathe. On a thunderous exhale, Steinar emptied what the sea had delivered into his stomach over the edge of the ship. The taste of bitter bile, fish, and ale soured in his mouth while he took in gulps of air and steadied his stance.

Resuming his position, Steinar heard the strain of the mast as the sail flapped furiously in the wrath of the storm—a storm that appeared without warning when they sighted another sailing vessel with an unfamiliar design on their sail. With their path unclear, he chose to ride out the storm near the head of the wolf on the bow, keeping his feet planted on the wooden steps carved down its sleek back. Within moments of the dark clouds descending around their ship, he gave orders for his men to row faster and wrapped a long rope around the wolf's back and his hand.

Secured, determined, and curious, Steinar led his crew toward the other ship. An hour later, the storm continued its vicious assault.

When the ship pitched forward, a barrel of fine mead flew past his right shoulder, grazing him on its way into the murky depths of the water. Ignoring the pain, he blew out a curse. Steinar slammed his fist against the wood, angry at the loss of precious cargo.

"'Tis the second barrel we have lost!" shouted Ulrik.

"Aye, *aye!*" he bellowed in return to his friend. "Have the men make another attempt to bring down the sail!"

Steinar did not dread the fury of the sea. Yet he pondered if the God, Loki, had a part in this tempest. "I do not fear you," he spat out into the icy torrent of water.

His tight grip on the rope burned into his palm, and Steinar dared to glance at his knuckles. They were clenched so tight, the stark whiteness reminded him of the creamy thighs of the last woman he took to his bed. He smiled inwardly and cast his sight outward again.

The wind howled mightily around him, mocking Steinar. "Am I not gifted with the power of the seas? They are a part of me!" He shook his head in an attempt to free the water lodged within his ears.

Hear me, Odin, part the storm for me to see who dares to venture with us. Steinar's thoughts were more a plea than a prayer.

He sucked in a breath, bracing for another angry blast from the sea.

Instead, lightning seared the sky in a brilliant flash causing him to hold his breath. A gift from Odin? *Thank you, All Father.* He exhaled fully.

Though he sensed the intruder nearby, his sight

remained blurred from the salty seawater. Steinar eased back, allowing his wolf to come forward within his eyes. Within moments, another arc of lightning seared the darkened sky. This time, the light remained longer, as if Odin held up a torch within the storm-filled skies.

A snarl escaped from Steinar as the ship appeared before them. Disbelief warred with his vision. Nevertheless, there was the proof he required. "The ship is under the Olafsson serpent banner!"

Ulrik moved with unsteady steps toward him. "Are you certain?"

"Aye," snapped Steinar. He pointed a finger in the direction of their foe. "Wait for the light from Odin."

Wiping water from his eyes, Ulrik stared outward.

Seconds later, another bolt of lightning creased the stormy skies.

His friend dug his fingers into the wood of the ship. "Sword, shield, hawk, *and* bloody spear through the center of the sail."

Glancing at his friend, Steinar sneered. "Aye, 'tis their banner for the four Olafsson brothers!"

"I thought they kept near the shores of *Dubh Linn* in Ireland? Or sought to trade their wares in Dunnyneill for slaves? Why have they returned?"

Closing his eyes to another torrent of seawater, Steinar hesitated on his response. Though this group raided the seas without mercy, he thought they also started skirmishes near the outer islands, which put them near his own isle of Islay. Did they return to wreak havoc against King William on the mainland? Or to return to their home on Torvay? This isle had remained free of any son of Olaf for many moons. Peace between his own clan and Olafsson remained strained over the years, so were they on a quest to conquer more lands? Ever since his grandfather, Somerled, seized control of the other isles from Olaf's father years ago, tension warred between the two families, until the sons fled after the death of their father.

But these men could not claim any land once belonging to Olaf. They were the same as Steinar. Bastard-born without any rights to land or title.

Ulrik shifted his stance. "Do we tempt the Gods and go after them? They are near lands once belonging to your grandfather and now your uncle."

Steinar looked beyond his friend. *What would the great Somerled do? Would he tempt the Fates and a storm to capture an enemy's cargo?* His wolf padded closer within Steinar.

Uncertain, Steinar watched as lightning continued to shine a light over Olafsson's ship. When their foe altered their course to cross directly within their path, he narrowed his gaze. "Let us pursue them. Perchance they have decided to return to Ireland and have lost their way, or the storm has altered their course."

Ulrik raised his fist and spat out into the sea. "They control the seas as fierce as you! They are nae lost! Might I remind you Ireland is southwest, and the path they're traveling is *southeast*."

Arching a brow in amused contempt, Steinar knew his friend was correct. He leaned forward on the ship's wolf's head. He kept his focus on the west, intent on surveying their foe.

When another wave pounded with brutal ferocity over his body, he let out a roar, coughing out the salty water. "Is this the best you can deliver? Has Odin given me aid and then forsaken me?"

"Do not stir the wrath of All Father!" warned Ulrik. "Let us put aside this madness and seek out the nearest land."

After spitting out more of the seawater, Steinar glared down at his friend. "Nae! We do not turn away like frightened pups! The storm is a lesson to our enemies not to cross this path!"

Ulrik swayed with the ship. Placing a hand over his sword belted at his side, his gaze turned predatory. "Follow and attack?"

"Confront and wait for them to advance," ordered Steinar. "Tell the others. And get Haaken to fasten the cargo more securely. I do not wish to have more precious barrels tossed overboard. The God of the sea has nae need for mead, wool, and amber."

"Haaken will remind you we should have placed the cargo away from the horses," prompted Ulrik.

Steinar slashed his hand in the air. "There was nae room near the keel, and the man comprehends this!"

Ulrik gave a curt nod and moved slowly back to the others.

While the men steered a new direction toward their foe, the sea continued to strike without mercy. Steinar coughed out more water, yet he refused to relinquish his position to seek safety below on deck.

With the wind at their backs, their ship sailed along the waters with the force of the storm. When a giant wave threw the ship high, Steinar held fast. And with a resounding crash, the bow slammed back into the water. Keeping a tight grip, especially when the waves lashed across his chest, he roared, "Block the coast!"

A thunderous response echoed forth from his men.

The ship listed to the right and Steinar waited,

watching—allowing his wolf to witness their foe. As the other ship drew near, he could see the stark whiteness of the men's eyes peering back at him. Studying each man, his inner wolf snapped and shook his head in fury.

On a deep inhale, Steinar kept his focus on them. No fear could he sense, and he exhaled on the next lashing from the sea.

Steinar held up his fist. "Hold!"

All rowing ceased. Quick steps sounded behind Steinar, alerting him to the presence of Ulrik. The man most likely had his sword unsheathed in preparation for an attack.

And still Steinar waited.

One of the men on the other ship stepped forward. "Have the men of Sutherland lost their way?" The man's voice thundered over the storm.

Realizing their banner belonged to Sutherland, Steinar knew he had the advantage. Most feared the Pirate Wolf—a position he favored for the moment.

"Now why would you make such a declaration?" bellowed Steinar. He lifted his hand upward. "The Gods favor our journey."

The man raised a fist into the air. "As they do ours!"

"Then why do you journey near *my* lands?" Steinar studied not only the man speaking but those who had surrounded him.

The other men laughed and shifted their positions, some even drew their swords.

When lightning splintered the sky once again, Steinar realized how close they were to Jura. If they continued on their present course, both their ships would surely crash into the rocks guarding the bay. He swept his gaze back to his foe. "I have nae desire to have the sea claim—"

Steinar's last words lodged in his throat. A great howling filled his head from his beast. The wind knocked him forward, and he swung from the rope with the ease of a hawk. With a resounding snap, the rope that held him secure now plunged his body into the waiting bosom of the sea.

His arms flung madly about while his wolf merged his power with Steinar's to keep him above the water. Instantly, sharp talons seized his legs, and he cried out in pain. Shouts from his men consumed his thoughts, and the tempest of the sea drew him deeper. Fighting against the burning hunger for air in his lungs, and the pain in his legs, Steinar gave control to his wolf. Letting his body relax, he spoke the ancient words of magic within his mind. Long, agonizing moments drifted by, and Steinar repeated the words again.

Yet the shift from man to beast did not happen, and his power within the water began to swiftly leave him.

Steinar attempted to shake loose from the grasp of the enemy. Their steely grip kept him anchored below the surface. Searing pain traveled up his legs and into his back with a force that burned the blood in his veins. He battled the scream lodged inside his chest, threatening to explode forth. On one final effort, he tried to force his body upward with his arms, calling forth all the magic he possessed.

The struggle cost him, and his wolf's howls of protest echoed inside his mind. He found his body sinking farther into the dark watery abyss. The more Steinar battled, the weaker they both became.

Better to die at sea than on the land!

Twisting his arm over his head, Steinar's fingers

fought to take hold of his axe attached to a sheath on his back. If death was his destiny, he stood prepared to enter Valhalla with his weapon clutched within his grip. But pain slashed across his shoulders and down his arm, halting his progress.

Nae! A great spasm slammed into his body. His lungs were in burning agony.

Clenching his fist, Steinar raised his arm upward. *God of the sea, do not let me fail. Can you not save me from this wretched monster who dwells within the darkness?*

"Monster?" echoed the siren's voice from below him. "You call for the God of the sea but not the Goddess? You are the monster, Steinar of the house of MacDougall. Victory is mine this day! I have not only claimed the Pirate but his magical wolf who dwells within you—both shall become my slaves to do my bidding."

I am no one's slave! And Odin guides my oar and my blade over the seas!

The blow came swift and hard against his chest. Steinar bent forward on a gasp, drawing in a huge amount of sea water. No longer could he hear the cries of his wolf. Unable to withstand another moment trapped within the icy waters, he drew his fist over his heart.

May All Father find me worthy to enter the halls of Valhalla.

"Odin does not rule in the depths of the seas! You have forgotten the edicts here, and the siren's song of the waters. Once you have listened to the luring melody, I take what is mine."

Steinar did not fear the darkness surrounding him. Yet whatever held him firm within its grip sent icy tendrils of dread through his blood. He closed his eyes, prepared for death's embrace. However, the scream of another pierced his thoughts.

"Nae! Do not claim this man!"

He snapped open his eyes—scanning the murky depths for the voice who challenged the monster below him.

"You dare to challenge me?" demanded the shrill voice of the monster.

"Aye!"

The monster laughed harshly. "A life for a life?"

"*Aye*. A vow I give freely! Now release him!"

Unable to see who was speaking and with his determination to survive ebbing away, Steinar allowed his body to sink farther into the jaws of the seas. Whatever awaited him would be up to Odin. Not to the monsters of the deep debating over his continued existence.

Images of his life flashed in vivid colors inside his mind. Each one reminding him of a life—one filled with adventures on the seas, battles won, kinship with his other wolf brothers, and regrets with his father. Emotions within him swirled in a tempest.

Forgive me, Father, for not making amends before I entered the Brotherhood.

His body jerked once, then twice.

A great roar filled his head while being shoved with force upward. As the water broke around his head, Steinar let out a guttural cry, attempting to draw in air. Too weak to manage staying above the water, he felt himself start to submerge. However, strong arms wrapped around him, hauling him toward the ship.

Although the storm had lessened, the wind

continued to slash furiously around them.

Once on board, Steinar was dumped onto the rough deck. He immediately emptied the contents of his stomach. With a shaky hand, he wiped away the spittle from his mouth. He coughed, ridding the last of the water from his body.

"My thanks for saving me, Ulrik," he managed to choke out in a hoarse voice.

Gruff laughter greeted his hearing.

Again, strong arms yanked him to standing. Glancing outward, Steinar was not prepared for the sight before him. In a wry twist of fate, mercy had been granted to him by these men known as the Serpents of Olafsson. His captor released his hold and stood back.

Steinar kept his hands clenched by his sides. Instinctively, he sought out his wolf within him. *Are you alive?* Smiling inwardly, he almost let out a shout of triumph when the beast lumbered forward. Quickly scanning beyond, he prayed his own ship had survived the harsh storm and found safety.

"We should have let the sea take its prize," grumbled one of the men.

"Nae, Balder. The Pirate is not worthy," argued the largest man in the group.

"Then what do you suggest, Leif? Simply relinquish him back to his men?"

"Slay him where he stands!" shouted another man.

"And risk war?" Steinar snorted in disdain and shifted his stance. His wolf moved closer, eager for the chance to taste blood.

The one known as Leif roared with laughter. "We care not about any king."

His wolf howled in protest, and Steinar unclenched

his hands. "Did I mention any king? You would dare to tempt your fate with the Wolves of Clan Sutherland? Release me back to my ship, Olafsson. Now!"

Leif raised his spear outward toward Steinar. "I do not fear your kind. Nor do I take orders from a MacDougall."

Steinar swallowed the anger that flared from the man's insult and allowed the power of his wolf to flicker within his eyes.

A few of the men took a step back.

"Look at how his wounds are already healing," muttered another man. "'Tis not right. The Gods have marked him. We should toss him overboard."

"Be wary the next words you spout," warned Steinar. He fought to control the raging beast within his body. Blood was foremost on the animal's mind.

"Enough!" Leif bellowed. "Or I shall enjoy removing your tongue from your throat."

Steinar shook with power. Beads of sweat broke out along his brow. If he let his wolf have free rein, there would be no survivors. War would be declared, and King William would have more trouble battling another enemy.

Indecision plagued Steinar. Fight to the death or surrender to his foe.

"Nae!" ordered someone within their group.

Leif snarled and glanced over his shoulder. "Why?"

When the men moved aside, another warrior stepped forward. "He is far too dangerous. Take him near the barrels and bind him in chains."

Leif clenched his fist.

The action did not go unnoticed by his leader. "Do not challenge me. The Gods have spoken!"

Steinar almost laughed at the absurdity. No chains could keep his beast a prisoner.

Their leader made no move to approach. Intrigued, Steinar tilted his head, waiting for more demands to be issued from the warrior.

Confusion settled over him. Steinar dared to take a step forward. The warrior was cloaked in a hooded garment—from the steel helmet to the cloak covering most of their body. Eyes the color of a glittering sea, white with foam, stared intensely at him. Steinar's brow deepened further.

His wolf inhaled sharply and then let out a low growl.

Though this person wore trews, the intoxicating scent became undeniable. Steinar's lips curled in disgust at the shocking revelation. He spat onto the deck. "When do the men known as the fearsome Serpents of Olafsson take orders from a *woman*?"

Chapter Two

The MacDougall's words churned the fury within Inga. Her hand itched to unsheathe the sword at her side and teach this arrogant wolf a few manners. Did she not save him from the clutches of slavery within the deep water—an agonizing torture far worse than death?

"Aye, they take orders from a woman *or* suffer lashings by my hand," she explained, her voice heavy with sarcasm.

Steinar dared to take a step toward her. "Remove your helmet, woman."

The hiss of steel slashed through the air as each of Inga's brothers unsheathed their swords.

Though this man was now her prisoner, his smooth command left no room for challenge. He towered above all of them. For a brief moment, Inga almost consented to his demand. Almost. She gave a warning look to Leif when her brother dared to take a protective stance in front of her. Whatever plans MacDougall had for her, Inga had to be the one to show her strength. Or the wolf within the man would slaughter them all.

"I take nae orders from lowly beasts," she announced, gesturing to another brother to step aside.

The MacDougall arched a brow. "As I sensed. A woman with a face of a goat."

Balder leveled a blow to the man's jaw. "You will show respect to our leader and sister!"

Steinar appeared unfazed—barely moving against the strength of her brother's fist. The man rubbed his hand over his chin and gave Balder a scathing look. He quickly resumed his attention to her. "Then if you refuse to show me your face, can you share your name? Unless you fear I shall tell others about the infamous leader of this clan?"

Inga snorted. "You assume your freedom is forthcoming, MacDougall."

A smile twitched at the corners of his mouth. "Most definitely. Until that time, I would like to ken the name of my enemy." He dared to advance another step toward her.

Aware of his strategy, Inga allowed the man to banter words with her. She was no fool. He moved like the wolf inside him—stalking her with words and eager for the kill once he stood in range.

She steeled herself for the attack. "Be warned, I might change my mind and toss you overboard into the clutches of the sea."

"If death is my future, then there is nae harm in giving me your name."

Sweet Freyja's tears! Never had she encountered a man like this one—foolish and brave. His foolish demeanor came from the man, and his bravery spoke of the beast who dwelled within him. Inga had heard the tales of the fearsome MacDougall wolf pirate. A conqueror who took what he wanted. The sea was his home to rule and command.

She kept her focus steady on his eyes and her stance prepared. "I am known as Inga the Ruthless."

His hand reached out to her in a blur. Inga barely had time to evade the strike. She quickly ducked and landed a blow centered to his male parts. The howl of pain echoed all around her as the man slumped to his knees. In one swift move, she followed with a kick to his face, landing him backward onto the deck.

While his face contorted with pain, Inga took advantage and leveled a dirk against his throat. She bent forward. "Never underestimate your foe, especially a skilled warrior *woman*. Did you ken I was trained by the huntress women who are descended from the great warrior lady *Scáthach* on the Isle of Skye?"

Steinar grunted a response. Though he continued to struggle with pain, Inga noted the fury within his eyes—the black depths, etched with silver glared at her. The wolf had emerged, though the man remained in control of his beast.

"I do not fear your wolf, MacDougall," she whispered. When Steinar's eyes narrowed, she suppressed the shiver within her body.

Rising, Inga motioned to one of her brothers. "Bind him in chains around the barrel of mead."

Brant sheathed his sword. "What if he shifts to his wolf?"

Inga knew she risked her life and her crew by taking the man captive. But what they didn't know was she needed Steinar. Inga required his strength and knowledge of the sea around lands not belonging to their clan. The Gods had shown her a sign during the storm when he became trapped by the siren's song deep within the water. She'd only prayed the man had no desire to be thrown back into the sea, thus keeping his wolf hidden.

"Then may your aim strike with certainty across his throat," she responded with deadly calm, sheathing her dirk on her side, and stepped away.

Steinar let out a low growl and gnashed his teeth. His garbled words of warning were a mix of both—man and beast.

She kept her outward appearance calm. Yet her stomach roiled with uncertainty.

Brant blew out a curse and gestured for two other men to bring forth the chains.

Leif stormed to her side. "We might have evaded his ship, but you cannot control the beast lurking inside the man. Are you certain in your judgement, Inga? I fear 'tis unwise to keep the wolf bound on this ship."

Rarely did her brother—the oldest of their clan— ever question her rulings. But for the past several months, he challenged all her decisions. Keeping her focus on the rolling sea waves, she tempered her growing anger and own doubts. "Aye," she managed through gritted teeth. "Slow our progress onward until I consult the Gods."

Leif grumbled a response and retreated to the other men.

Inga crossed to the stern of the ship to check on the horses. Grateful the storm had lessened in its intensity, she took in their surroundings and exhaled fully. Even with her back to the MacDougall, she felt his penetrating gaze on her. Her skin prickled with awareness. Tempted to look over her shoulder, she kept her sight fixed on the rocks looming around them. They'd managed to slip through the first dangerous path toward the mystical Cove of Gríma hidden within the other isles. Without a clear direction, she feared the destruction of their ship by the jagged edges of the monstrous boulders.

She exhaled fully and rolled her shoulders to ease the tension humming within her.

"The man confounds me, Tove," she murmured, stroking her fingers through the glossy mane of her horse. "And why do they always challenge me? Must I continue to fight to prove my position as a shieldmaiden?" Her questions settled uneasily inside Inga. She quickly tossed them aside, blaming her uncertainty over lack of sleep and being at sea far too long.

Footsteps sounded behind her. Her hand stilled on the animal. "Do you wish to voice your concerns like the others, *Jorik*?"

Her brother reached over her shoulder and handed her an aleskin. "If you have discarded Leif's council, surely you will care nothing about my account."

Accepting the offering, Inga took a long swallow. She moved away from her horse and settled onto a bench. After giving her brother a brief glance, she noted the disapproval within his eyes. "So you are in agreement with the others?"

Jorik snorted, then wiped his mouth across his sleeve. "You have never sought my counsel, so why concern yourself with my opinion?"

"You ken I listen to *all* accounts." After taking another long swill from the aleskin, she regarded him for a reaction.

He narrowed his eyes. "As the youngest, I am always the last."

"Nae. I am," she countered, handing him back the aleskin. "Forsooth, the younger can be the wiser. Leif rules by the spear *and* blood. While your strength comes from the hawk—keen eye of observance. You ken I value all of my brothers' advice."

Jorik touched a hand to his chin in thought. "I am

wary of the wolf within the man. Our chains cannot hold the beast lurking within his eyes."

Inga opened her mouth to utter a protest, but her brother held his hand up to halt her words.

He shifted his stance. "Furthermore, I understand your need to take the risk in order to secure a path through these treacherous rocks in search of the Cove of Gríma near Jura. My thought is to consider Torvay. 'Tis nearer. MacDougall is a sound choice to grant us the direction. But what will you give him in return? What argument are you prepared to present in order to gain his trust?"

"Did I not free him from slavery?" she challenged, quickly dismissing any thought about landing on Torvay.

"And this is your argument for his aid?" Jorik shook his head. "Nae, Inga. As a warrior, the MacDougall stood ready to die. This is vastly different. You also denied the Goddess a worthy prize."

She arched a brow in disgust. "I have nae desire to incur the wrath of Odin. The Wolves of Clan Sutherland are his creation. I'd rather do battle with the Goddess than with Odin. In saving his precious wolf, I have gained favor in his eyes."

Jorik shrugged and cast a furtive glance over his shoulder. "Regardless, you must gain MacDougall's trust and aid soon. We cannot linger in these waters. Either we move forward or wait for another sign. Certainly, a few more months will not matter, given this is the year we can see the isle. We can return during the summer months. The longer daylight shall be in our favor."

Her fingers skimmed over the pouch hidden within her cloak containing the valuable map. Though her brother's words made sense, the time to act was now. "The runes disagree with you, Jorik. The sunstone brought us here. If we do not procure the treasure now, the winds will blow the mists down over the cove for another ten years. 'Tis time to reclaim the treasure. Have Leif await my orders to move forward."

Her brother gave her a curt nod and departed.

The eyes of another observed Inga with intensity from the opposite side of the bench. Though she happened to be blind in one eye, the seer's vision bested those who had both. "Are you certain of the runes?" the woman rasped out, challenging her.

Inga swallowed the biting words she longed to toss out at the seer. "Did we not see the vision together, *Helka*?"

The woman clucked her tongue in obvious disapproval. "Aye, aye, but my interpretation differs from yours. The treasure you seek is not what was shown to you."

"Have you not taught me to trust my first instinct? To open my mind beyond the visions?"

Helka shifted on the rough bench and closed her eyes. "When the heart is cleaved in two, then you shall find the treasure."

"Words *you* heard," Inga snapped harshly. "This journey is as much for you as it is for me."

A tight smile curved the wrinkled features of the woman. "So you keep reminding me."

Inga rose, tightening her cloak against the force of the wind. She cast her gaze to the man chained to the barrel. The eyes of the wolf regarded her with hatred and another emotion. *Curiosity*.

Inwardly, Inga smiled. With steady strides, she

crossed the ship, ignoring the questioning gazes of her brothers. Coming to a halt before the man, Inga fought the urge to place her hand over the hilt of her sword. "You can leave, Brant," she ordered. "I have questions for the MacDougall."

Her brother snarled at the prisoner but complied.

With slow movements, Inga removed her helmet and settled herself against one of the barrels of mead next to him.

"Often, the sea grants nae mercy, especially when the Goddess wants a prize valued highly by Odin. I saved you from a fate far worse than death—one where All Father would approve of my request for assistance from you." She paused to gage his reaction.

The wolf retreated and the man emerged. Eyes the color of sapphires pierced through her. Inga's heart skipped a beat, and she fought her reaction to the man.

"Continue," he ordered quietly.

She steadied her breathing. "I require your skilled assistance in steering passage around these rocks and away from the swirling waters of the black cauldron belonging to the Goddess Rán."

"For what purpose?"

"We are on a quest to find the Cove of Gríma on a mystical isle north of Jura. Nae one knows the name of this island, not even the Gods."

"'Tis a myth and folly to navigate in this direction," he argued in a muffled voice. "Many have lost their lives and ships to the tempest of the cauldron. 'Tis greater than the one near my own isle of Islay."

Inga hesitated. How much should she share with the MacDougall? She threw caution and her doubts to the winds circling around them. "I possess the ancient map of Āsgarthr—one which shows the mirror isles here on earth."

Mirth danced within his stunning eyes. "Even Odin does not ken its location."

Inga dared to lean down toward him. "Because he granted the treasure to the Northmen to find. His son, Thor, secretly placed the treasure in a magical cove within these isles. Legend told by the skalds spoke of a great feasting after a battle honoring Odin. The God appeared as a warrior in the great hall one night and granted the jarl the map to a treasure."

"I have heard the accounts," he snapped. "A treasure of a thousand gems made by Freyja's tears as she wept for those slain in a battle. They contain nae truth. Just another tale fueled by drink."

Inga would not be dissuaded. "How do you ken? Have you searched the surrounding smaller isles near your home of Islay? Or between Jura and Torvay? This is where the map has shown us this island."

Steinar looked beyond her. "My father spent a good amount of men and years searching for the treasure. They wasted time, and good men were lost in these waters in search of this mythical treasure. Many have been lured with song to the edge of the swirling cauldron and perished. Furthermore, Islay is nae longer my home. I belong to the Brotherhood."

"They did not have the map," she pressed, eager to secure his trust and help.

The man resumed his gaze on her—dark and penetrating. As if he could see to her soul and know all her secrets.

"For skilled warriors on the seas, I find your request amusing *and* annoying." When he lifted his arms, the chains rattled eerily. "You ask for my aid while I am in shackles?"

Inga tilted her head. "Until you make your decision, I consider you a foe."

Steinar lowered his arms, shifting closer to her. "Nae chains can bind the beast who dwells within me. How can you trust me?"

His words skimmed over her skin like warm honey. Inga kept her gaze steady with his. "I trust the wolf but not the man."

Shock registered briefly over his features, then swiftly vanished. "If I agree to your terms, what do I gain?"

Inga smiled inwardly. "Your freedom."

"Not good enough," he returned. "I demand a portion of the treasure."

Arching a brow in skepticism, she chided, "Now you believe in the treasure within the mystical isle?"

He shook his head slowly. "Nae, not completely. But I am curious. Furthermore, I have another request before I consider your offer."

She snorted and shifted her position. "I have not consented to your *first* demand."

"You will allow my ship to journey with yours on this search. With two crews, your chances are far greater. Do you not agree?"

Unable to contain her frustration, Inga muttered a curse and looked away. "I do not ken your men."

"And you ken me?" Steinar grunted a curse.

Securing his trust became her focus. "Aye," she confessed, returning her attention to the man.

"In our brief encounter?" he shot out in contempt. "From tales spoken around a fire about the Pirate Wolf?

Nae, you ken *nothing*."

Ignoring his censure, she continued, "You are dangerous, cunning, predatory—a wolf. You have not unleashed the beast to feast on his enemies. Though you have shown him to me and my men in your eyes, you've kept the wolf hidden. I sense his curiosity inside the man. I sense *your* curiosity."

His smile came slowly—sending a shiver down her back. Fascination over those full lips rooted inside her. Heat swelled uncomfortably within her. She fought the urge to wipe her palms down her cloak. Instead of arguing and glaring at her, he disarmed her with a smile, sending her heart spiraling overboard into the sea.

Furious over her lack of control, Inga stood abruptly. "I agree to your first demand—a portion of the treasure *and* your freedom."

Shaking his head, he challenged, "I require *my* ship *and* crew."

Inga smacked her fist into her palm. "Your assistance is on my ship. To steer a path through the rocks and around the bend to the mystical isle. We have nae need for another ship."

"My men can follow behind your ship. Ulrik is capable of steering a path and guiding my ship. You forget, I have journeyed these waters numerous times."

Uncertainty battled within Inga. Her fingers drummed uneasily against her thigh. The man asked for too much—demands she knew would not settle well with her brothers. She feared they'd toss him over into the sea once she released him from bondage. Before she agreed to anything, she required each of her brothers to swear an oath to do no harm to the MacDougall.

Her gaze traveled outward. *We are so close, Freyja.*

I cannot let one man control the outcome. Continue to guide me on this quest.

"Do you want the treasure or not?"

Steinar's question snapped her from her thoughts. This time, Inga showered the man with a beaming smile. "With or without your aid, I shall claim the treasure of Odin. For the moment, I shall consider your demands."

After giving her a curt nod, the man settled back against the barrel.

When Inga turned to leave, his words made her pause.

"Do not linger too long. The tides will draw you closer to the demon rocks hidden under the waters. Death's embrace will crush the ship into shards of wood and seize you all."

She shrugged. "Is not *death* the final adventure, Steinar? And a watery grave is one I choose over a bleak landscape."

Chapter Three

Steinar's gaze followed the movements of his captor until her brothers assumed a protective stance around her. They feared the wolf more than Inga, and this interested him. Why did the woman trust the wolf? He sought an answer within, but his beast remained silent.

Her skill within the waters surprised him along with the acceptance of leadership from her brothers. These men were whispered to have a brutal leader—one which all thought to be Leif the Bloody Spear. Tales of his victories were told by the skalds. The man thrust first with his spear and then asked questions later. A warrior whose blade remained tainted with the blood of his enemies.

Did your brothers kill for you, Inga the Ruthless? Or are the accounts of this clan's leader about your battles?

Then his thoughts returned to her proposal. Could this be the treasure his leader Magnar the Barbarian spoke of during their meeting many moons ago? A treasure even the other Gods craved to possess. Intrigued with this new direction, he looked to their leader shouting at the men gathered around her.

Another thorn pressed inside him was his fascination with the woman. She'd left him without breath the moment she'd removed her helmet. Burnished copper braids wove a crown around her head. And those eyes were gems any warrior yearned for in a woman—a radiant hue of the palest blue. As if the moonlight dusted her orbs with their brilliance. Did she lure her enemy to their deaths with her beauty? Or weave a song simply to remove their heart?

Steinar shook his head. *I shall not be swayed by womanly curves and stunning eyes.*

His wolf gnashed his teeth and retreated within Steinar.

Do not tempt me to toss us both overboard and into the arms of death. Though he uttered the warning to his wolf, he doubted the beast trusted his words.

Movement to his right shuttered all his previous thoughts, and he lifted his gaze to a man who had adorned most of his face and arms with the ancient blue markings of Odin. The man proceeded to sit beside him on the deck.

"Ale to remove the brine of the sea from your mouth? A fierce night we ensued on the sea. Yet the morning brings a threat of another storm." The man shoved an aleskin against Steinar's bound wrists.

With a slight nod, Steinar accepted the drink. After taking a long swill, he handed the aleskin back to the man. "My thanks."

He chuckled softly and scratched a finger across the bridge of his nose. "You are a brave man to attempt a battle on board a ship with countless enemies surrounding you. What did you hope to gain by such a reckless action?"

Steinar changed his position slightly to ease the tension along his back. "If I had not risked a chance, I would not have known *her* strength." He shrugged. "In truth, the woman had to prove herself to me."

A great roar of laugher belted forth from the man.

"A tale worth telling in the sagas of what I have witnessed," he announced triumphantly.

Arching one brow in skepticism, Steinar remarked dryly, "The battle has only begun. Do you plan to give the full account? Or will this be kept a secret like Inga the Ruthless?"

The man pounded his chest with his fist. "I am Snorri Sturluson, I have a duty to explain all I have witnessed. I sense a magnificent tale is forthcoming. As for this ship's leader, I leave that particular account to her."

Stunned, Steinar leaned back to study the man. "Snorri the *Icelander*?"

He belched before taking another draw from the aleskin. After wiping his mouth with the back of his hand, he remarked, "I prefer Snorri, the greatest skald to venture onto the seas!"

Steinar snorted in disbelief. "'Tis a name too long. Regardless, I am honored to be on this ship with you. I have heard how your arguments have swayed those to put down their swords to avoid bloodshed. Might you consider transferring your allegiance to me and my crew once I am set free?"

The man's lips thinned, though mirth danced within his eyes. "Are you certain of your freedom?"

Pointing to the group huddled in conversation, Steinar replied, "Inga is discussing my terms to her brothers."

"To pen the tale of the *Pirate Wolf* would be an honor," he mused, lifting his gaze in their direction. "Yet convincing her kin will prove difficult. Death is what they seek for you. Even I am unsure what I can offer to persuade them in your favor."

Steinar heard the warning in the man's voice. For the moment, he put his trust in the woman. "Your sagas have been told around the fires—ones heard by all within the Brotherhood."

"I am one of many skalds," admitted Snorri quietly.

"I'd prefer my tale woven by your hand," urged Steinar. "You would give an accurate account."

Snorri snapped his attention to him. Victory gleamed over his features. "If you are set free, I do have one request."

Intrigued, Steinar pressed, "What do you want?"

He tilted his head to the side while tapping a finger to his chin. "To see the wolf within you."

"Would you not fear the beast?" challenged Steinar. His beast growled low, but he ignored the animal. "'Tis not an *ordinary* wolf. Once I allow him loose, the beast might consider you his enemy."

A frown marred Snorri's brow. He took another draw from the aleskin, casting his sight outward across the expanse of water. "In Iceland, the skalds feared to tell the accounts of the Wolves of Clan Sutherland. Speaking aloud their names might bring dishonor *or* the wolf to their doors. All dread calling forth the magic of the beast or the wrath of their maker—Odin." The man returned his attention to Steinar. "I carry the marking of the beast over my heart. 'Tis a sign of my loyalty to Odin. If I am unfit to stand before the wolf, then All Father will allow the beast to slay me where I stand."

Nodding slowly, Steinar understood his meaning. "Then if I grant your request, with approval from my beast—"

"You do not control the wolf within you?" interrupted Snorri with exasperation. He dared to jab a finger against his arm. "Are you not the master of the beast? Is it not written in the Nine Noble Virtues of Wolf Lore?"

A low growl rumbled low in Steinar's throat. He did not need a reminder of the code. Magnar often argued the same with him when Steinar permitted his wolf certain freedoms during battles. He clenched his hands into fists. "Do not quote the virtues to me, *Icelander*. 'Tis a bond between man and beast. I do not order the wolf, nor does he make demands of me. Though there are times when I must reign over his beastly nature to prevent him from slaughtering those in his path."

The man frowned. "An interesting relationship. Knowledge I must task to parchment and soon." He lifted his palm upward. "I fear the storm shall present itself within the hour."

Sniffing the air, Steinar agreed. Another tempest continued to threaten from the west. "Your request is granted at a time of *our* choosing after my release, and when I am allowed to return to my ship."

Dropping the aleskin next to Steinar, the man stood abruptly. "Aye. You must discuss our terms with your wolf. And I have to present evidence in your favor."

"Certainly, Inga can order her brothers to consent to her plan," argued Steinar, growing weary of making bargains.

"Though the woman is their leader, all are required to vote as one for any decision to occur. Without my argument to spare your life, they will continue to banter words until the ship crashes onto the rocks." Snorri bent forward and lowered his voice. "A fault with this clan— their debates are lengthy, loud, and often lead to blows."

Steinar grunted a curse and watched as the man

dashed across the deck. True to his words, Leif had taken a blow to one of his brothers. Inga's voice bellowed for them to cease as she took a step back to avoid the clash of fists.

When Snorri attempted to thwart more fighting, he promptly got shoved aside.

Letting out a groan of protest, Steinar glanced outward. Narrowing his eyes, he probed the sea to the south. He didn't have to wait long. Heaving a sigh of relief, he smiled inwardly. His ship had survived the lashings of the storm and settled far back within the waters.

Unsure of the decision awaiting his fate, Steinar reasoned that another plan was required. After scanning the ship, he sought out the heavy ropes binding the largest sail.

Steinar sought out his wolf. *If they decree our death, then shift into your beast and run to the mast. Once there, I shall take over and destroy their sail.*

Furious with Steinar, the beast gnashed his teeth in protest.

Nae! Their blood is not yours! Do not seek vengeance! We must wait until our ship draws near before we attempt the angry seas again.

The beast paced angrily within Steinar, but eventually settled inside without another complaint.

Both man and wolf watched the brawl continue. Snorri had attempted once more to argue in Steinar's favor. And again, the brothers ignored his argument and pushed him to the side.

The wind shifted, and lightning fractured the dreary sky in the distance. Steinar inhaled sharply. Time had become his enemy. He'd hoped the woman would have been able to convince her brothers. Her offer intrigued him. But Steinar would not confess this to her. Instead, he offered conditions.

He glanced at the rolling waves. Risk the monster of the seas or battle the enemy until all were slain? When more men huddled around the brothers and away from him, Steinar knew he could not wait any longer.

As he stretched out his limbs preparing for the order to shift, the Icelander shouted a warning and held up his sword to the storm descending swiftly over the waters.

Steinar froze in his actions along with the others.

The skald's voice rang out. "Instead of accepting the gift Odin has presented to the Serpents, you risk death to all! Do you not see his fury with each flash of lightning? I suggest another bargain!" Snorri glanced his way. "Allow the MacDougall to steer us through these treacherous rocks. In return, Brant will take the man's place on his ship."

Enraged, Steinar shouted, "Those were not my terms!"

Brant raised his sword to the sky. "I accept!"

Within seconds, all the others gave their consent. Inga turned toward Steinar with a smile that froze the bitter words of disagreement on his tongue.

Partially raising his arms, he relented. "Accepted. Now release me!"

She gave a nod to her brother. Swiftly crossing the deck, Brant freed Steinar from his accursed chains.

"My axe?" he demanded.

"You have nae need of your weapon while on our ship."

Steinar flexed his hands. "Then you will have nae need of yours either."

A flicker of uneasiness passed over the man's features. His hand went to the hilt of his sword. Heaving a sigh, he conceded. "I would have thought your wolf to be your greatest weapon."

Pointing a warning finger at the man, Steinar declared, "If *we* die, I desire to enter Valhalla with my weapon clutched in my hand."

Brant swallowed. "Aye. But we shall not speak of death today."

"Agreed."

The man pointed behind him. "Your axe is on the other side of the barrels."

Before Brant returned to his brothers, Steinar grabbed his arm. "Do not forget your other weapon, Brant the Shield. If I am correct, your *shield* is more powerful than your blade. Nae?"

Brant stroked a hand over the braids of his beard while a smile curved the corners of his mouth. "When this task is completed and we have found the treasure, I shall enjoy sparring with you on the shore."

"In a game of *skinnleikr*?" suggested Steinar.

The man roared with laughter and then smacked him heartily on the back. "Aye! But many bones will be broken."

"I can assure you, the bones broken will be yours *and* those of your brothers."

Uttering a curse, Brant retreated across the ship.

After quickly retrieving his axe, Steinar joined Inga and her brothers.

Snorri nudged him. "Do not forget our bargain, MacDougall wolf."

Adjusting his axe into the straps which held his sheath on his back, Steinar countered, "You altered our terms."

"Did I not grant your freedom?" exclaimed the skald.

Steinar clamped a hand on his shoulder. "You resorted to a last attempt of reasoning before they took a fist to you."

The man shrugged. "A slight adjustment."

Steinar had more important matters to contend with. His ship sped rapidly toward the Olafsson's. Soon they would be upon them, and he needed to make his men aware of his safety and their new direction. From there, Brant would be able to transfer to his ship. Ulrik would not be pleased. Yet safety for both ships remained Steinar's focus until he had a chance to view this mystical map.

Without waiting for approval from Inga, Steinar bellowed orders to her brothers and the other men to certain positions on the ship. Crossing to the stern, he pounded a fist against the smooth wood. Waiting. Watching. Willing his men to see his stance.

When the ship swayed, Steinar held up his fist. "Keep her steady!"

"Thank the Gods! 'Tis Steinar!" shouted Ulrik, followed by the rousing cheers of his men.

As they approached, a frown creased his friend's brow. Ulrik raised his sword upward, prepared to do battle. "Are you their prisoner? What has happened to your trews?"

"Would the enemy allow me my weapon?" scolded Steinar. He glanced down, seeing the deep slashes in the material and shrugged.

When the ship drew alongside, Ulrik leaned against the side. "By the hounds of Odin, we thought you had died!"

Steinar smiled broadly. "Nae, the Gods favored me with life instead of death. Odin is not ready to claim me. This ship rescued me from the water and from a monster who sought to kill me. For now, Brant the Shield will assist you. I am to remain here to guide her safely through the rocks."

The man's elation shifted to fury. "Has the sea water addled your mind?" demanded Ulrik, spitting into the water.

Haaken and Alrek gave a nod of agreement as they glared with contempt to the men behind Steinar.

"Are you certain your men follow *your* orders?" snapped Inga, coming to his side. "They appear ready to strike us down."

Ulrik gaped at her. "They keep a woman—"

"I am their leader!" corrected Inga, turning away from his displeasure to consult her brother.

Steinar let out a groan when she appeared before his men and made her declaration. Ignoring the strained and stunned expressions from Ulrik and his crew, he bellowed, "We waste time with this discussion! I shall give my account once we are on land." Pointing outward, he added, "Do you wish to confront another storm so close to the rocks? You ken what awaits us!"

Ulrik hesitantly lowered his sword. "Send the man over."

Glancing upward, Steinar whispered, "Grant us safe passage from these waters and hold back the storm, All Father."

Steinar did not fear the oncoming storm. Nae, he had battled far worse between the isles and these rocks, as well as his men. They understood the risks when they ventured through these waters. His prayer to Odin was one he'd often sent outward. And the God continued to favor him and his men with victory through these waters and around northern Scotland.

Nevertheless, this time his whispered words left him with a sense of dread. Would Odin judge him—or Inga worthy of finding the treasure? Courage to see beyond the veiled mists into the isles depended on a warrior's honorable code within his heart.

Uneasiness settled like a hard knot in his gut when his thoughts dwelled on the leader of the Olaffson's clan. And he prayed she'd not shove a blade through his heart when she realized the destination he sought.

The Isle of Islay, specifically Finlaggan Castle. Once home to the great Somerled and now belonging to his Uncle Rangvald.

Will you forgive me, Inga the Ruthless? And will Odin forgive my deception to this woman?

Chapter Four

Fighting the urge to scream, Inga pressed her fist against her mouth. Her ship leaned far too close to the jagged claws of the giant rocks waiting to rip them all apart. With each sway or tilt, she held her breath. And what lay beyond those rocks frightened her even more. The wind brought the song of the sirens to their ship.

She swallowed hard. What possessed her to let the man guide her through these waters? Even now, her fear could not be quelled while she watched Steinar hold onto the serpent's head on the bow.

Magnificent in his stance, Steinar commanded the seas with each shout, slash of his hand for direction to her men, and muscles rippling with strength and power. Never before had any of her brothers attempted such an act of senseless bravery, and this intrigued Inga.

The fresh storm seized both ships with its savagery. However, the man gave no care for the lashings slicing across his body. When a bolt of lightning seared across his shoulder, the man laughed and raised a fist upward.

And Inga praised him inwardly. *Odin favors his warriors, and I deem you are one of his with the way he sheds his light over you, Steinar MacDougall.*

"Oars in!" shouted Steinar while wiping seawater from his eyes.

Instinctively, Inga wanted to halt the man's order. Should they not be shifting away from the rocks? She cast her sight to the mast, flapping furiously in the wind. As if the elements couldn't decide which direction to blow.

Clutching the sunstone beneath her tunic, Inga battled the urge to yank it free and search for a new direction through the threatening clouds over them. She resumed her focus on Steinar. He swayed with each movement of the ship, becoming part of the serpent. She sensed no fear from the man.

"Loki's balls! Will you doom us, MacDougall? I have nae wish to die today!" Leif's curse thundered behind her.

Inga swallowed and refused to meet his scorn, certain her brother would see the wariness in her eyes and demand he take over in guiding them onward. She gripped the sunstone tightly while holding her breath as the ship rose high upon the water and then slammed back down with the force of Thor's hammer.

When a wave crashed over her, Inga's steps faltered, but she remained rooted in her position. Unfortunately, a part of their cargo pitched overboard and one of the barrels of mead narrowly missed her head as it made its descent into the angry seas.

"Odin's blood," she hissed out, attempting to grapple with a portion of the rope that had snapped free. The coarseness struck against her hand, leaving red welts across her skin. Jorik and Balder came to her aid and quickly secured the rest of their cargo.

"'Tis madness!" shouted Leif, adding, "He means to crash us onto the rocks!"

The other men nodded or shook their fists toward Steinar.

Inga scanned beyond the grumbling of her men.

"Then explain why he would doom his own ship? They follow directly behind us, even after almost two days at sea!" Returning her attention to her brother, she continued, "Are you young lads experiencing your first sea voyage during a tempest?"

The other men swiftly looked away or lowered their heads.

Leif dared to challenge her when he put his hand over the hilt of his sword. "You were a bairn when I went on my first voyage, and my leader was not a MacDougall."

Glaring at her brother, she took a step forward. "And this *bairn* is now your leader. Stop questioning my decisions, or I'll throw you overboard. Or worse, I'll appoint Balder as my second in command."

Outrage flashed briefly in his eyes, but he remained silent.

Inga turned her back on him and the others. Glancing upward, she whispered another plea to Odin and to the Goddess Freyja to see them safely to land. She continued to view Steinar's position. He took no action to have the men resume their oars. Did the man command the elements of the sky?

With unsteady steps, she made her way forward to avoid any further debates with Leif. Even after all their time together, her oldest brother continued to challenge and defy her. Aye, he accepted her position—they all cast their votes in agreement. But Inga pondered if his arguments were to aid or hinder her.

Thunder rolled over them, its deafening roar sending the horses into a stomping fit of fear. Were the Gods angry? Never had she witnessed a storm's intensity as this one snaring them within its power. She blinked, attempting to discern their direction. But the storm would not give up its power.

Whispered words from long ago pushed through her anxiety.

"Who are you?" demanded her mother, holding the large golden shell outward.

"Daughter of Olaf—"

Her mother slammed the shell onto the rough table, shattering the sea gem into jagged pieces. "Nae! Who are you?"

Inga swallowed, keeping her hands clenched within her lap. Her anger seethed within, threatening to surge forth. "Who do you want me to be?"

Her mother wrapped her long fingers around the brilliant sunstone around her neck. Instead of anger, her mother's features softened. She turned and moved to the shore. "If you do not ken who you are, then I can nae longer aid you."

"Wait!" Worry infused Inga. Fear of failing her mother, once again, overwhelmed her. With each lesson, she overthought her response. Rising from the wooden bench, she ran to her side and grabbed her mother's cool hand. "I am a daughter of the sea."

Smiling, her mother traced a gentle path with her finger over Inga's cheek. "You would do well to remember your lineage. In times of great trouble, the words and training I have taught you will be of guidance. I shall not always be here to assist you. Nor will your father. Your path is carved alongside your half-brothers."

Inga squeezed her mother's hand. "I do not want you to leave."

Heaving a long sigh, her mother placed Inga's hand

over her heart. "This is why I have taught you these words of wisdom—they are how you came to be. Even Odin cannot undo what I have given you. Always remember, my daughter."

"So long ago," she mumbled. Brushing away the moisture on her cheek, Inga rested her gaze on the churning waters and leaned against the side of the ship.

Even though the storm's fierce power slashed around them, Inga allowed the tension to withdraw from her body. She drew strength from the sea. Trusting in the Gods and Goddesses and the blood which flowed within her veins, she closed her eyes.

"I am born from the sea. My blood was mixed with the waters from the fjords that formed my ancestors. My skin smeared with the brine from seaweed gathered along the shores of Norway. My hair has been washed and braided with seashells upon the rocks in Kirkjuvágr by the wise women. Hear me, Goddess, hear my heart beat deep within the water. With your guiding hands, steer us out of danger."

Inga loosened her grip on the sunstone and lowered her hand.

"You made me a shieldmaiden to have power over the seas, Mother. Give me strength, courage, and wisdom to follow a new direction with this wolf. Without his protection, the men shall succumb to the song of the waters."

With each inhale and exhale, her heart slowed its frantic hammering against her chest.

Within moments, the storm lessened in its intensity. Inga slowly opened her eyes. A shaft of sunlight streaked through the dark clouds, shining its light away from the threat nearby. The sunlight made their surroundings bright enough, in spite of the danger of more rain.

The men gave a cheer of triumph, including those of Leif's.

Steinar had led them away from the jaws of the monster, and her prayers had been answered. The sirens would not claim victory today.

Nae, not today.

Lifting her gaze, Inga sought out the man who continued to maintain his position. With steady steps, Inga advanced toward Steinar.

She halted before him, resting her hand on the serpent's tail. "I thank you."

He wiped a hand over his brow. "The Gods favored us today. Tomorrow they might not be so forgiving." Steinar pointed below. "We dared to mock the dark sirens within the abyss."

"You are correct," she contended. "But your skill on the sea is magnificent."

Steinar smirked. "Courage, and the right course kept us away from the tempest deep within the waters."

Inga snapped her gaze outward and took a step backward. Her stomach clenched. The shore of an unexpected land greeted her. Her right hand hovered over the hilt of her sword, eager to strike out at the man.

"In order to secure a safe passage around the cauldron of water, we are near the shores of Islay," announced Steinar, sliding down the back of the serpent and landing on the deck next to Inga.

"This is not Jura. You betrayed us," she hissed out, glaring at the man.

"Nae," he responded slowly, looming over her. "I led us safely through a storm and away from dangerous waters. 'Tis what you requested."

Her breathing became labored—more to do with the man standing so close to her than her anger over their new position. Inga's stubborn pride kept her from retreating. Was she not the leader on this ship? "Take us to the inlet within Jura," she demanded tersely.

"After I have concluded my business on Islay. I must meet with my uncle. His summons many moons ago has nae doubt left him in a foul mood." He pointed outward. "I am certain his men have seen our ships and have sent a messenger to him. Brant can remain on board my ship during my time on Islay. Will this be in agreement with you?"

The man's eyes bore into Inga. Challenging, mesmerizing, studying. Her men continued with their raucous laughter and discussion behind her. Did they not see the land ahead? Or had the storm blinded them all? She barely remembered the last time she and her brothers had journeyed to Jura. All their time had been spent on Torvay.

We were all so young, and I can recall the one time.

"Should I be prepared for chains or to have you strike me down with your sword?" His question appeared laced with mirth.

Inga shrugged, banishing memories from long ago. "Undecided. For now, I shall accompany you on your journey."

The man smiled, softening his hard features. "For what purpose, *Inga*?"

She would not be swayed by the smooth burr of his voice, nor the brilliance of his eyes. Frustration over her lack of control with this man continued to plague her. *I am a shieldmaiden, not a lass who swoons over men.*

"There shall be nae conversation about the treasure

to your uncle. If you so much as whisper one word, I will not be so forgiving as I am for allowing you to land on Islay."

His good humor vanished. Fisting his hands on his hips, his lips thinned. "I give you my oath, Inga, I shall not speak of this treasure or map. My uncle has enough power and wealth."

Curious, she pressed, "But does not your loyalty lie with him? Surely you are bound to him by blood—"

Steinar's lip curled in disgust while he cast a glance over his shoulder. "My *loyalty* is to King William and the Brotherhood." He swiftly returned his attention to her. "And now I am bound by my oath to you."

"Will you give your share of the treasure to your king, then?" she asked softly.

Before he had a chance to respond, Jorik came striding to her side. "We are not at Jura, Inga."

Ah, so you do remember our visit to the isle. She placed a hand on her brother's shoulder. "As soon as we land on the shore, prepare two of the horses for our journey. I'll see to Tove. You, Leif, and Helka are coming with us."

Ignoring Jorik's questioning stare, Inga turned to Steinar. "How far to your uncle's home?"

"Home?" Steinar folded his arms over his chest. "My uncle resides at Finlaggan castle. 'Tis a mighty fortress. Who is Helka?"

Dropping her hand to her side, she pursed her lips. "The woman is a trusted friend and seer to our kin." With the man's keen senses, Inga was surprised he had not noticed the seer during their voyage. But then, if the woman wished to observe, she would have remained hidden in her corner of the ship.

"Brant and Balder will not be pleased," grumbled Jorik.

Inga glanced at her brother. "Because we've landed on Islay or that they will be left behind?"

Jorik kneaded a hand over the back of his neck. "Both. You ken our brothers. Also, the Icelander is seeking permission to journey with Steinar. And why are we taking only two of the three horses?"

She waved him off dismissively. "I need their strength here to guard both ships. What cargo we have left cannot go missing. And I cannot order Snorri to remain behind. He must travel without a horse. His quest is his own. Helka can ride with me, and you can follow on foot. If there is trouble on either ship, one of the men will require a horse to alert us. I do not ken how many horses are on Steinar's ship. Now go tell the rest of the men."

He gave her a nod of acceptance and moved away.

"There is nae need to concern yourself for my ship," interjected Steinar, dryly.

"Why not? We are both on a quest. I have sworn an oath to you as well. You have led us away from a watery grave. Although, I suspect you kept silent about our destination."

Though the man remained quiet, Inga witnessed the truth within his eyes.

Tapping a finger against her lips, she pondered another idea. She swept aside a portion of one of her braids that had come unbound during the storm. "After the horses have been secured on land, I'll have Jorik open one of the barrels containing the furs and a pouch of amber. We shall trade with the other MacDougall for more horses and food."

The ship swayed, and Steinar turned away from her to lean against the side. "My uncle cares nothing about furs and amber."

"Even stones from as far as the Baltic?" suggested Inga, watching as they neared the shore.

"Perchance. Present him with a barrel of mead, and he certainly would be agreeable to your bargain."

She grew wary of the constant debate with this man. "Why would they wish for mead? And we have lost a number of good barrels during the storms."

Steinar slid her a sideways glance. His gaze raked boldly over her. "Because my uncle enjoys good mead along with his women. Go to his table bearing a bounty of goods with precious mead and your *beauty*, and he will surely grant your demands."

Inga gaped at him. He left her without words— stunned by his declaration. Before Inga had a chance to retort, Steinar slipped over the side of the ship into waist-high water.

Watching as the man strode with commanding strength through the strong waters, Inga pressed a fist over her heart. Confusion warred with her warrior side. Never before had any man attempted to call her a beauty. Most men feared her. Or worse, despised Inga. She traveled the seas with men, making her undesirable to any man she met. She'd accepted the truth many moons ago. But Steinar's words made her pause to consider the possibilities of being with a man.

Yet only for a brief moment.

Her fingers grazed along her matted, salt-brined hair. The sea clung to her like barnacles on stones along the shore's edge. "I am too tall, have a strange eye color, and can battle against any man successfully with a sword. Nae, I am not a beauty."

Letting out a heavy sigh, Inga lifted her face to the light breeze and sunlight gracing the sky.

"I may have trusted you on the sea, but I cannot do so on land, Steinar. For the first time, I fear you might be the mighty warrior proclaimed by the seer who will end my life as a shieldmaiden. And I will never, *ever* take you to my bed."

Even though she made the firm vow, Inga's words left a dull, hollow ache within her heart.

Chapter Five

After stomping his feet firmly on the shore, Steinar knelt on one knee. Scooping up a handful of the gritty sand, he brought his fist to his mouth. "Thank you, All Father, for giving us safe passage to Islay. The woman is favored by you and this I can feel inside me. I cannot fathom the reason, nor will I ask you to explain." With one final prayer, he tossed the mixture outward and stood. A chill crept over his bones while he waited for his wolf to draw away the cold from his body and into the animal's.

Shouts of anger reached his hearing, but he gave no care about their cursed argument at being led astray to another isle. Steinar's attention remained riveted above. He stared at the men positioned on the hill. No doubt his uncle's guards. And they did not look pleased. Granted, he had ignored the summons from his uncle in late winter, but they should not be so swift to pass judgement against him for arriving late. Even with the arrival of a second ship, the grim expressions and unsheathed weapons did not bode well.

"Your cloak and dry clothing from one of the trunks," announced Ulrik, appearing by his side. "And the man called Snorri demanded he come with you. Claims he is writing your saga."

Steinar snorted while adjusting the axe on his back. "I do not think my uncle cares in what condition I greet him."

Ulrik pressed the items into his hands. "Nevertheless, I ken you do. Have you seen the condition of your trews and tunic?"

He tucked the fresh clothing under his arm, and then Steinar nudged his friend. "More men have gathered along the ridge. Tell the others to watch their drinking. Inform those on Olafsson's ship as well. And have Haaken ready two horses. He shall accompany me, along with the skald."

Ulrik nodded slowly. He darted a glance over his shoulder. "Are you wary of your uncle's summons?"

"Always. His yearly demands to sway King William to grant more land on the mainland increases with each visit." Steinar swiped his fingers over his brow to rid the moisture trickling down his face. "He expects me to convince our king."

"Never an easy task," commented Ulrik, kicking aside a stone on the shore.

Steinar chuckled low. "Perchance with a beauty to distract him, he will not return to the same yearly argument."

"Be...*beauty*?" Ulrik choked on the word.

Arching a brow in curiosity, Steinar stared at his friend. "You do not think so?"

"Nae, nae." His friend scowled while shaking his head.

Steinar resumed his attention to the ridge. "Then I must make certain she is presentable before she greets my uncle, aye?"

Ulrik shifted his stance. "How do you propose to tell her your plan? Tell her she cannot see your uncle until she is clean? The woman appears as if she hasn't bathed in a year."

"Have you taken a look at yourself, Ulrik? Combined with your stench from the past several months at sea, 'tis a wonder any woman would embrace you."

The man wiped a hand over his face. "With my good looks, they seek what is beneath my trews."

"For the love of Thor!" Steinar coughed into his hand, almost dropping his clothing onto the ground.

The subject of their previous conversation strolled alongside them with her horse trailing behind her.

"I doubt any woman would fancy a look at what you have hidden beneath your trews." Effortlessly, Inga mounted the animal and reached for the reins.

Clearly insulted, Ulrik spat on the ground and stormed away.

Steinar tilted his head to the side, regarding the woman. "Are you always so blunt in your manners?"

Inga's brow furrowed as if she struggled with a response. She adjusted her position on the horse. "I have always spoken my mind. And what would you say if one of my brothers stated the same to Ulrik?"

He gaped at her. *You are a female I cannot fathom, Inga.* "Your brothers are men. My friend would have laughed or thrown a fist at their face. Yet the barb from your tongue—a woman—stung as deep as an adder's bite."

Narrowing her eyes, her frown deepened. She skimmed her hand over her horse's glossy mane.

"Have I offended you?" asked Steinar.

Inga glanced sideways at him. "Nae. 'Tis not the first time a man has given me a tongue lashing over my behavior and words. I travel the seas with men, spend most of my time in the company of men, *and* lead a group of men." Nervous laughter escaped from her rosy lips. "Nevertheless, I am expected to behave as a quiet and meek woman when I speak."

"Aye, you give a good argument," he managed slowly. "But have you considered learning from your other half—as a woman?"

Inga stared at him. When her full lips parted, she snapped them shut.

Silence reigned between them until a gruff sound intruded behind them.

Jorik thrust the reins of Steinar's horse into his free hand. "You have insulted my sister. Inga has learned to be a shieldmaiden from powerful women—"

"Enough! I do not need you to defend my actions," ordered Inga. "Steinar requires nae further knowledge of my training. As a man, he would not be interested."

After securing his parcel of clothing, Steinar mounted his horse and gestured to Haaken. "You are wrong, Inga. When you are ready, I would welcome hearing your account."

Haaken rode near his side. "Take up position and guard your back as we travel?"

Scrubbing a hand over his beard, Steinar nodded. "When we arrive at Finlaggan, inquire to any news on the mainland."

The man smiled slowly. "Aye," he muttered, retreating to the back of their group.

Inga adjusted her position on the horse. "We shall follow."

Curiosity spurred Steinar on. "We are not done with this discussion."

Inga arched a brow in challenge. "Aye, we are."

His wolf growled low.

Aye, agreed. She is hiding something, my friend. You can smell it within her blood, too.

What possessed Steinar to learn more about the woman? He grappled with the feeling, unable to untangle the strange emotions coursing through his body. But Inga had secrets, besides being the leader of the Serpents. *Soon, you shall divulge what you are hiding. You guard your fear of being discovered, but there is more beneath your shields.*

"Before we depart, I have a request," she announced, staring intently at him.

How Steinar enjoyed a good challenge. He gave her a long, cool study. "Depends on if I can grant your *demand*."

"Until we safely return to our ships, Leif will assume the position of leader when we meet with your uncle and his men." She looked at her brother who gave her a brisk nod of approval. Removing all but one of her blades, she handed them to Leif. Fastening her cloak more firmly around her shoulders, Inga waited.

"A wise choice," he agreed, taking the reins of his horse. Steinar wiped a hand over his nose, eager to rid the stench of months at sea from his body. "My uncle's men await us on the ridge. Once at Finlaggan, you will be shown to your chambers."

"Where will you be?"

He slid her a glance. "You do not trust me, Inga the Ruthless?"

She bit her lower lip. "Nae. 'Tis not true—"

"I need to wash the grime of sea and battles from my body before I greet my uncle. There is a stream that borders Finlaggan." Giving a nudge to his horse, they ambled along the shore leading to the hills.

53

Inga followed alongside him. "And what about us?"

"For the love of Odin," he mumbled. "I will instruct the men to bring the wooden bathing tub to your room. Your brothers can bathe in the stream."

The woman beamed a smile at him. "You have thought of a good plan, MacDougall. I shall welcome stripping free from my clothing and sinking into a hot bath."

Steinar's hands clenched the reins. The blood in his veins rushed to his cock. His tongue became trapped within his mouth as a vision of Inga bathing in the water flashed within his mind. Unable to respond, he fought the sudden wave of lust and shifted uncomfortably. He shook his head to rid himself of the image.

Leif grumbled a curse and maneuvered his horse into a light gallop on the other side of Steinar's. "Let us proceed." He pointed to Inga. "Follow behind me. Jorik and Haaken will take the rear. And Inga?"

"Aye?"

"Keep silent."

She snorted a laugh and dipped her head toward her brother. "As you command, my leader."

After regaining some composure, Steinar gave a firmer nudge to his horse, and they took off upward to the hills. As the journey led them farther away from the shore, an ache settled within him. The land did not bode well for the Pirate Wolf. His ears heard the faint crashing of waves, luring him back to the sea's embrace. He shuddered, fighting the despair that accompanied him whenever he ventured onto the land.

He dared not look behind him for fear he'd succumb to her heady song. The sea might be his mistress, but his uncle's demands were long overdue.

When they reached the ridge, Steinar kept his surprise hidden at seeing his uncle's right-hand man. Godred MacLean glared at him steadily as he approached. A mercenary for hire, the man soon became one of his uncle's confidants—securing trade, lands, and dealing with loathsome enemies.

Many feared Godred. But Steinar did not. And this became a challenge for his uncle's guard.

With each new meeting, Godred's insults increased, stirring the beast within Steinar, but not the man. If Steinar learned anything in his lessons within the Brotherhood, he managed to conquer the skill of keeping his fury maintained while giving an outward appearance of calm.

The man leaned forward as if to sniff the air around them. "Since when does the *Pirate* travel with the Serpents?"

Steinar's smile held no humor. "I do not answer to you, MacLean."

"Your uncle will not be pleased," argued Godred, glaring at Leif.

The current leader of the Serpents snarled while tapping two fingers over the hilt of his sword. "My blade has yet to feast on the blood of a MacLean."

Godred chuckled low. "I do not fear you, *Serpent*."

"Do not challenge their leader, Leif the Bloody Spear," warned Steinar.

Godred's good humor vanished, replaced by a stunned expression. Without another word, he snapped his fingers. Another guard approached by his side. "Ride ahead and announce to Rangvald his nephew has landed."

"And the others?" asked the guard.

"Steinar can explain to his uncle why he travels with those who are not trustworthy."

The guard gave a quick nod and galloped away.

Godred leaned to the side and looked beyond the men. His smile turned predatory. "Who is the woman?"

"My sister," answered Leif, tersely.

"Interesting…" The man turned to his men, giving out orders to maintain a position on the ridge. No others were permitted any farther along the shore without his approval.

Steinar frowned, and his wolf gnashed his teeth. Fighting the urge to take his fist to the man's face, he moved his horse away from him. Without waiting for Godred to take the lead, Steinar gestured for the others to follow him. They took a well-worn path, leading them through a thicket of trees. The scent of pine mixed with the briny scent of the sea filled him, settling the uneasiness within his bones. Waves faintly echoed behind him as he journeyed onward to Finlaggan as he kept them to a steady pace. Grateful for the silence, he took the time to gather his wits and words before he'd meet with Rangvald.

Sunlight broke through the thick clouds, slashing light across the road and warming his body. He smiled. Determined to make this visit with his uncle brief, Steinar picked up the pace. Soon, the gray stone and wood fortress loomed before them. Finlaggan boasted two guard towers, and both appeared occupied.

One of the guards shouted his arrival, though he knew his uncle had been made aware of his arrival the moment ships were seen in the harbor. With the portcullis raised, Steinar charged his horse onward, galloping over the bridge.

Slowly, he brought the animal to a light trot around the main well that provided their source of water within the bailey. A young lad dashed out from the direction of the stables. Steinar swiftly dismounted, handing the reins to the eager lad.

"Hail, Steinar!" The lad greeted him with a tight hug before taking the reins.

Steinar returned the gesture before stepping back. "Tiernan, you have grown since my last visit."

"Put on a stone, as well." Tiernan pounded his chest. But as the others approached, the lad lifted his gaze to Inga and her horse. His mouth slacked open. "You are a beauty," he managed in apparent awe.

Confusion marred Inga's features.

Steinar placed a firm hand on the lad's shoulder. "The horse is a rare beauty, aye?"

Tiernan frowned in obvious confusion. "Who else would I be speaking of?"

Inga smiled. After dismounting, she stroked a hand along the horse's muzzle. "Her name is *Tove*."

Tiernan held out his hand, allowing the animal to become acquainted with his scent. "Her ears look like they've been dipped in goat's milk."

Inga laughed. The musical lilt of her voice surrounded Steinar. The sound reminded him of a place he'd visited but could not bring forth the memory.

Steinar removed the bundle of clothing from the back of his horse. "Why don't you take both horses to the stables, Tiernan."

The lad beamed proudly. "I'll order the others to come fetch these horses."

Arching a brow, Steinar asked, "Are you now the stable master?"

Tiernan puffed out his chest. "As good as one."

"Aye, you are," acknowledged Steinar softly, ruffling the lad's dark mop of hair.

"Do my eyes deceive me? Can it truly be Steinar MacDougall who has graced Finlaggan with his presence?" announced a young woman with a streaming mass of golden curls flowing down to her waist.

"Have I changed much since my last visit?" demanded Steinar in good humor.

Laughter bubbled forth from her. "A touch of gray at the temples and a few more lines crease your eyes. Aye, you have!"

Steinar fisted his hand over his heart. "You wound me, Sigrid."

She snorted, shaking her head. "The Pirate Wolf does not offend easily. But I cannot say the same for what tongue lashing my father will unleash. You have kept him waiting far too long this time."

He half-turned to the group behind him, explaining, "This is Rangvald's daughter, my cousin."

Sigrid embraced him warmly and then took a step back. She scanned those behind him. "You travel with strange companions."

"Business dealings with Leif Olafsson," explained Steinar, stealing a glance at his new acquaintances. Grateful for their silence, he added, "Arrangements I hope my uncle will welcome."

Her good humor faded. "The merciless deeds of the *Serpents* are known to many within Finlaggan."

"They wish to discuss trade with Rangvald, not bring down the fortress," he assured quietly.

"And the others?"

"Leif's brother, Jorik, sister, Inga, her woman,

58

Helka, and Snorri the Icelander."

Sigrid returned her attention to him, giving him a tentative smile. "Then let me show Inga to her chambers. I am certain the stream beckons you first before you greet your uncle." Glancing at the Icelander, Sigrid added, "We haven't had a skald at Finlaggan in many moons. We will welcome a tale or two at our meal."

Steinar dipped his head in favor. "My thanks. I shall not linger too long."

Sigrid laughed. "Shall I tell my father to expect you in an hour? Or two?"

"Or we can wait until after the evening meal," he chuckled, shifting his stance.

The woman glanced upward at the large arched window and pointed. "You do like to stir the ire of your uncle. He awaits you in his solar." Sigrid moved around him to greet Inga.

Steinar grimaced. No doubt Rangvald heard every word of their conversation. His time in the stream would have to be short. While gesturing to Haaken and the Olafssons, he halted, dropping his hand. Inhaling sharply, he sensed the power of another wolf nearby.

Curious, he halted the progress of his cousin with an outstretched hand. "Who is here from the Brotherhood?"

Sigrid's wry smile came slowly. "Aye, I forgot to mention, Gunnar MacKinnon has been here on the orders of King William to discuss trade relations with your uncle."

Shock swiftly turned to fury. "Then I reckon my uncle can wait an hour *or* two."

Not waiting for a response or for the others to follow him, Steinar stormed with intent toward the cooling waters of the stream. When Inga's gasp reached his hearing, he squashed the urge to turn and justify his harsh retort. He'd have to publicly explain that Gunnar was the last man who should be bartering a business proposition. Especially with the current Lord of the Isles. Clearly, Gunnar's position with the Brotherhood had changed.

Steinar clenched his fists, shoving aside tree limbs blocking his path. Fury and confusion seethed within. Why didn't his leader propose the plan to him? Or why not send Ivar?

But why did you choose Gunnar? Why, Magnar?

When the gurgling stream greeted Steinar, his steps slowed. The water lapped gently over the moss-covered rocks. Raking a hand through his hair, he chuckled softly.

Steinar fisted his hands on his hips. "There can only be one truth as to why you are on Islay. What are you planning to steal, Gunnar, *the Thief?*"

Chapter Six

While Sigrid spoke incessantly about the varied tapestries gracing the walls, and the history of Finlaggan, Inga did her best to commit to memory the woman's words, along with the details of the castle. When the conversation turned to past attempts to seize the fortress, the woman assured Inga that not one clan, king, or invader had ever succeeded to breach the walls.

She gave Sigrid a tight smile. *Your attempts to frighten me have not succeeded. Did you believe the Serpents desired to conquer your land? The sea is our home.*

Helka mumbled a curse behind Inga, obviously displeased with their host.

Ascending another set of circular stairs, Inga almost collided with the woman when she halted at the top step.

"How long have you and your brothers been at sea?" asked Sigrid, peering over her shoulder at her.

Inga stared at the length of the darkened corridor, lit with only one torch on the wall. "Long enough."

"Weeks, months?"

Snapping her gaze to the woman, she replied, "Why does this concern you?"

Sigrid shrugged. "'Tis a simple question, requiring a simple answer."

Silence hovered like an unwelcome storm cloud until Helka announced, "My lady wishes for a hot bath.

She can answer any further questions at the evening meal." The seer grasped Inga's hand. Her steely gaze lingered for a brief moment on her. "The long sea voyage has been a strain."

Inga bit her tongue to quell the laughter from bursting forth. Her, a great shieldmaiden, with the sea flowing in her veins. *'Tis a strain having to endure this torture of being treated like a weak lass.*

Sigrid inclined her head. "Aye, aye."

Leading them past other chambers, she came to the one at the end of the corridor. Opening the door wide, the woman motioned for them to enter. "I hope this will suffice for you and your woman."

Quickly inspecting the chamber, Inga surveyed the small bed. One wooden table and chair were placed near the arched window, a weathered trunk was shoved against the far wall, and a hearth barren of any heat. She kept her stance rigid. Helka would get the bed, and she'd have to find rest on the rough floor.

"I shall have two men bring the tub and light a fire. Do you require anything else?"

Inga clasped her hands together, determined to show her gratitude. "My thanks for your kindness."

Sigrid managed another tight smile before turning to leave the chamber.

When the door closed silently behind the woman, Helka smacked her fist into her palm. "Blood of the Gods! I thought she'd never shut her mouth. And look at the size of the bed. Not suitable for one person."

Holding up her hand, Inga hissed out, "Silence. Sigrid might be listening." She pointed to the floor by the hearth. "I shall sleep there," whispered Inga.

Helka blew out a curse. Going to the oak door, she

pressed her ear against the wood. Waiting for a couple heartbeats, she straightened and returned to Inga's side. "There is nae one there." The seer patted her back. "Let me work out the knots in your hair before you bathe."

Frustration and weariness crept into Inga as she wandered to the window. How she despised the appearance of being weak. A necessity each time they had to barter for goods, food, or horses. Until a bargain occurred, she had to maintain her false appearance as a woman who remained in the background while Leif managed the negotiations.

Her view of the trees bordering the castle protected any who were sailing nearby. Casting her gaze at the bed, she longed to seek the rest she had been denied while traveling on board a ship.

Helka approached, dragging the lone chair behind her. "Sit."

After discarding her cloak, Inga complied, letting out a long breath. While the woman took to unbraiding and untangling her hair, Inga rested her gaze outward. Was the stream Steinar spoke of out there beyond the trees? Was he a man to scrub only his face and arms? Or did he, too, strip fully and wade into the water? An image of Steinar without clothes came unbidden within her mind—one where he took long strokes through the stream, savoring the feel of the water over his skin.

Inga swallowed. Hard.

Heat swirled uncomfortably on her face. Fighting the urge to place her cool hands on her cheeks, she clenched them in her lap until her nails bit into her palms.

Why does this man stir emotions within me?

Closing her eyes, she concentrated on her training. She began to recite the guardians who watched over all warriors in the night sky during the summer months.

Revna, dark raven of the night, who guides over all warriors, be my compass. Alfarr, shifter of the beasts to aid us in our hour of conflict. Katla, mighty huntress, guard our steps while in the darkness of the enemy. Norna, whose wings of courage cloak all those—

"You must relax," urged Helka, tugging apart another piece of her knotted hair.

Inga winced. Snapping open her eyes, she blew out a curse. "'Tis difficult at the moment."

The woman rapped her on the head with her knuckles. "You have endured far worse. Surely you can manage this slight torture."

Wiping a hand over her nose, Inga snapped, "I would rather eat eels than have you yanking on my hair. Will I have any strands left after you are finished?"

Helka halted her progress. "Then eels you shall have."

Guilt plagued Inga. Twisting around in her chair, she grasped the woman's hand. "Forgive my harsh outburst. I have much on my mind. And my body is tired."

The woman's knowing smile held a deep understanding. She brushed a light finger over Inga's brow. "What troubles you, child?"

"'Tis many moons since you have called me thus, Helka." The endearment clutched at Inga's heart, aching to share her indecisions and feelings with the woman.

Helka cupped her chin within her warm, rough palm. "I might not have birthed you into this world, but I consider you a part of my kin."

"The Goddess blessed me with you on that cold, dark night," recalled Inga, giving the woman's hand a squeeze.

"Stormy, as well," added Helka, sighing.

A sudden knock on the door ceased their conversation.

"Blessed Freyja, let this be the tub," muttered Helka, quickly striding across the chamber. Opening the door wide, she stepped aside.

Two men carrying a large wooden tub managed to stumble their way into the chamber, finally placing it before the hearth. One of the men tasked himself to preparing a fire. Soon, the chamber blazed with warmth, banishing the chill and darkness.

A woman darted in with a bucket of steaming water, dumping the contents into the tub. Soon others followed, bringing more buckets.

Rising from the chair, Inga gave a nod of thanks to those who dared glance her way. Silently, she watched in fascination this preparation. In all her travels, she'd never been treated with respect and fear. *All because of my name. What would you say if you knew the truth?*

Sigrid entered, followed by a young girl. Making her way across the chamber, she placed a trencher of bread, cheese, apples, and two cups on the table. Taking the jug from the girl's arms, she set it near the food. "Given Steinar and Rangvald will be enclosed in his solar, the evening meal is hours away."

"Our thanks," stated Inga, shifting her stance.

Sigrid beckoned the girl out of the chamber. The woman paused, her hand resting on the door's latch. "Do you require a gown or fresh clothing?"

Inga swiftly gave a questioning look at Helka.

The seer clasped her hands together. A glint of mischief creased her features. "My lady shall be presentable at the meal as if she stood before a king."

Stunned into silence, Inga waited until Sigrid had closed the door behind her before she found her tongue. "Presentable for a *king*? All I stuffed inside my satchel is a blue woolen gown."

Helka dismissed her with a wave of her hand. "Smelled like dried herring. I tossed the garment aside while you were speaking to the MacDougall on the shore."

Glaring at the woman, Inga tapped her foot in annoyance. "Then what did you bring?"

"The gown in your trunk," she confessed, tucking aside a strand of gray hair behind her ear.

Inga's eyes widened in disbelief. "The ivory gown etched in gold and silver threads?"

Helka bobbed her head once. "Aye. A grand choice for the evening meal."

"*Nae!*" she managed to spit out.

Helka crossed the chamber to the tub. "'Tis best you get inside while the water is warm."

"I refuse to wear the gown," defied Inga, crossing her arms over her chest.

"'Tis lovely on you," argued Helka. "And your current garments need washing and drying. Did you think to wear trews at Rangvald's table?"

Inga's breathing became tight. She did not want to be presentable for anyone. She'd become defenseless— a woman—if she wore the gown.

"Do you fear the gown or is it the woman who hides beneath?"

Helka's question tore through her thoughts. Inga stared at her. Her tongue became trapped inside her mouth.

The woman tilted her head to the side. "Or is it the *MacDougall*?"

Once again, heat flared instantly to Inga's cheeks. Had the seer seen inside her soul? Refusing to share her concerns about Steinar, she turned away. She pinched the bridge of her nose. "Show me the runes of my destiny again."

"Odin and his hounds have cursed me since the day I shared my knowledge with you," snapped Helka.

Facing the woman's censure, Inga urged, "*Wisdom* you deemed important to me and my brothers. I need to view them again for any change."

Helka snorted. Reaching for the leather pouch of runes attached to a belt on her side, Helka dug inside with her hand to retrieve them. "For Inga the Ruthless—a destiny called, a destiny forged, a destiny unveiled." With an angry flick of her wrist, she set the rune bones flying across the wooden floor.

The seer laughed bitterly, while she walked between the path of littered runes. "They have not *changed* since the first time I cast them for you before we departed Dubh Linn."

She nudged one of the bones with her foot. "The turning wheel is your path on the sea. Until the sun rune brings the transition of light from darkness into awareness, from water to land." Pointing to another, her clipped tone spoke of impatience with Inga. "You have created a boundary from others with the thorn rune. You cannot gain wisdom until you remove the shield of protection."

While biting her lower lip, Inga bent on one knee. "What about the blank rune? Why does this continue to break into my quest?"

Stomping the floor with her foot, the seer chastised, "You are not ready to heed the advice from the runes, nor the Goddess. Your quest is undecided because you lunge forth instead of remaining patient. You persist in questioning all that the Goddess has shown you. Shall I continue?"

"Aye," assured Inga, standing.

Helka traveled around the runes, slowly, cautiously. "Their pattern remains the same—a journey for you. But you do not travel alone. Another shall enter at the forked road, bringing riches or destruction." She halted and closed her eyes. "For justice to rule, a life is given. The intruder will become foe or champion. To see the true path, both must relinquish what they value the most."

Inga clutched the sunstone beneath her tunic. Indecision over the seer's words left her unsteady. Did her mother not warn her of the same before she departed? Carefully, she removed the sunstone, letting it dangle between her fingers within the sunlight dusting the wooden floor. A rainbow of colors arched over the runes.

"The sunstone cannot illuminate your path or decision within the bones," expressed Helka, softly. "Perchance you are not meant to find the treasure for your clan."

Rising slowly, Inga regarded the woman. "My mother would disagree."

A flash of annoyance creased Helka's face. She poked her in the chest. "She did not make this voyage. Nor can your mother be the one to claim the treasure."

"As you ken, she is unable to journey with us," argued Inga, furious they had revisited this conversation from long ago.

The seer shook her head solemnly and bent down to

retrieve her runes. "Are you certain your mother did not follow your path?"

Inga's mouth gaped open, then she quickly snapped it shut. Crouching beside the woman, she pressed a firm hand on Helka's arm. "Explain," her voice barely a whisper. Inga swallowed, doing her best to infuse strength with her next question. "Did you see her *before* we landed here?"

The woman stiffened under Inga's hold. Meeting her scorn, Helka's lips thinned. "Nae. But again, I ask, can *you* be certain? The woman travels through the water as silently as you and your brothers."

Shaking her head, Inga stood and glanced down at the warm sunstone within her palm. Sadness engulfed her when she spoke. "My mother has nae desire to visit the isles. These lands brought her nothing but sorrow. She would not dare step onto the shore."

Helka approached her side. "Your mother made her decision a long time ago." Sighing, her weathered brow knitted. Grasping Inga's hand, she continued, "Now, your destiny awaits. Do not concern yourself with indecisions. Trust what you ken within your heart. You have lived a life among men. I view this has caused you to find your answers using logic."

Inga wavered, trying to comprehend what she was hearing. Crossing to the table, she rested the sunstone on the rough wood. "I do not have the luxury of finding wisdom within my heart, Helka. As leader of the Serpents, I must harden my heart against any weakness. My destiny has been the seas—aiding my brothers and those I lead to rule over any king—"

"Or God or Goddess?" interjected the woman.

She lifted her gaze to meet those of the seer's. Fear,

stark and vivid, glittered back at her.

Glancing over her shoulder at the trees and beyond, Inga affirmed, "Not to rule, but to live our lives without interference."

Helka gasped, the sound echoing off the walls in an eerie fashion. "You do not intend on keeping the treasure, do you?"

Going to the tub, Inga dipped her fingers in the tepid water. "Perchance I shall bargain the riches to the highest bidder."

"Your brothers will not be pleased with the sudden change in plans. For what purpose do you seek?" demanded Helka.

Inga straightened to her full height. "My *freedom*."

Chapter Seven

A lone guard inclined his head in greeting as Steinar made his way to his uncle's solar at the end of the corridor. He gripped the cold iron of the handle. Leaning his head back, he inhaled sharply. Steinar's lip curled, and he shoved open the door. After closing and bolting the door behind him, he entered the large chamber. He halted before the large oak table and clenched his hands behind him.

While waiting for an acknowledgement, Steinar regarded his uncle's rigid profile while the man maintained his attention riveted to the happenings in the bailey below. "Greetings, Uncle."

"I have heard mentioned that a man can tell the strength of their foe by the horses they keep," commented Rangvald, rolling his fingers in unhurried movements along the stone ledge. "What do you think, Nephew?"

Steinar preferred to keep silent. But his uncle required an answer and would not relent until he was satisfied. Rangvald's keen observation would also detect any lie. "I judge strength by skill with a weapon, or in the control, or when to hold back."

A log broke within the blazing hearth, the flames hissing onto the stones. Neither man made to move.

"I favor the woman's horse you have brought here."

The wolf prowled within him, restless. Steinar

clenched his jaw, fighting to control both—beast and man. "The woman and her brothers are not our foe."

Rangvald's hand stilled. "Their father killed our kin."

"*Kin* who made war with them on their land," reminded Steinar, as he shifted his sight to a darkened corner within the solar. His piercing glare dared the man to step forth.

"Depends on who is telling the tale." Rangvald's voice hardened ruthlessly. "Have you betrayed me—your kin—by traveling all these months with the Serpents? Is this why you have ignored my summons?" His uncle turned away from the window. "And do not insult me with lies on how battles and storms have kept you away."

Steinar returned his gaze to his uncle. "Certain duties have kept me from the isles. My loyalty is first to the Brotherhood *and* King William. You have always known this. Furthermore, I have only recently become acquainted with the Serpents. If you must ken, they saved me during a storm when I fell overboard. If not for them, I would have perished."

Rangvald nodded slowly, running his fingers through his beard. "Then I am grateful. But why bring them here? To my lands?"

The tension eased slightly across Steinar's shoulders. "They wish to discuss a trade."

His uncle's eyes widened in surprise. A great roar of laughter pealed forth from the man. After composing himself, Rangvald went to the table and reached for a jug. Pouring the mead into two cups, he presented one to Steinar, saying, "I am already negotiating trade with another. However, I shall hear what Leif the Bloody

Spear wishes to discuss. But be warned, there are many who will not take kindly seeing them here."

After taking the cup, Steinar turned slightly, resuming his attention to the corner of the solar. "Do you not think it wise to come forth from the shadows, *Gunnar*?"

The man chuckled low, rising from his chair. When he stepped into the light, Steinar observed wariness and a change within his friend. A man who often spoke of peace and the new religion now appeared haunted with strain and fatigue.

Rangvald beckoned Gunnar forward. "I advised him to stay hidden."

A snarl slipped from Steinar's lips. "My wolf alerted me to his presence before I entered the solar."

Gunnar held his cup out to Rangvald. "Did I not tell you the same?"

His uncle shrugged, then poured more mead into the man's cup. "Now that we are all gathered here, I judge we put aside the discussion about trade with the Serpents and attend to the negotiations of trade through the isles with the Brotherhood." He set the jug back on the table. "Of course, all with the approval of King William."

Steinar swirled the liquid within his cup. "For a man who did not have an inclination to discuss trade with the King of Scotland, I am curious to this sudden change."

Rangvald settled into his chair behind the desk. "The *king* has agreed to giving me lands in the north."

Quickly averting his gaze to his friend, Steinar arched a questioning brow.

Gunnar regarded him over the rim of his cup, then quickly drained the mead in one gulp. After wiping his mouth with the back of his hand, he nodded slowly.

"And what are you trading?" Steinar sipped his mead, uneasy with this latest information.

His uncle shoved aside the parchments strewn across his desk to remove a folded document with the king's broken seal dangling from the edge. "With a foothold in the north, I have agreed to allow him access for his ships in the harbor."

Steinar fought the argument he wanted to spew out. How many times had he heard his uncle mention he'd never permit King William along the shores of Islay. *Too many.* And his king argued constantly against giving his uncle any lands. *So why send Gunnar to bargain for lands when you have ignored my accounts?*

After quickly draining his cup, Steinar went to grab the nearest chair, dragging it to the desk. The mead did little to temper his growing fury as he took a seat across from his uncle. "Much has changed since my last visit."

"If you had taken my summons seriously—"

Steinar held his hand outward to halt his uncle's words. "As I stated, I had other business which kept me away."

Gunnar approached from the side and leaned against the desk. "And the king realized your mission was important. Otherwise, he would have waited for your return and not have sent me."

Unsure how to respond to his friend, Steinar kept his focus on his uncle. "Then if your business has concluded, surely you can meet with Olafsson. What they require are more horses and food."

Rangvald pinched the bridge of his nose. "I suppose they want lodgings for a couple of nights as well. And there still is the argument over which lands I seek to possess in the north." He glanced at Gunnar. "Let us resume this discussion in the morning."

Leaning forward, Steinar placed his cup on the table. "Both crews have been at sea for months. A few days rest is all we seek."

His uncle belched, fisting his hand to his chest. "So, your stay is merely temporary? Then you shall venture away to your seas and duty to the king?"

"I will see the Olafssons safely to Jura before returning for the remainder of the summer months."

Rangvald rose from his chair. "Good. There is much to discuss regarding your position here on Islay."

Steinar refrained from saying anything further. He had no desire to be chained to this island. If he complied with his uncle's demands, part of his duties would see him shackled to the land.

"Is your mission completed?" Gunnar nudged his shoulder.

Lifting his head, Steinar stared at the man. No doubt his friend would detect the lie. But he'd rather tell a falsehood than the truth in front of his uncle. His crew had lost a portion of their precious cargo of armor and coin obtained from a chieftain on one of the isles in the storm. The king deemed the mission a substantial risk, even though Steinar reassured him and his leader, Magnar, he could procure the items and information, returning safely to Scotland. "For now."

Scratching the side of his face, Gunnar smiled knowingly.

Bracing his hands on the desk, his uncle leaned forward. "I shall grant your request for the other crew. Extend an invitation..." Rangvald's brow creased. "Who else have you brought beside Leif?"

Steinar placed his cup on the table and stood. "His

brother, Jorik, sister, Inga, her traveling companion, and Snorri Sturluson."

His uncle's eyes widened. "The Icelander?"

Chuckling low, Steinar nodded. "Aye. I ken you would be pleased."

Moving around the desk, Rangvald clasped an arm around Steinar's shoulders, staring intently at him. "Have him seated near me. There is much I can glean from the man." He pointed a finger at Gunnar. "He has written of the giants who roamed the far North—farther than Norway. I would like to ken more about these men."

"An interesting discussion," acknowledged Gunnar.

A frown replaced Rangvald's good humor. "Though I must ask why the skald prefers to travel with the Serpents."

Gunnar shrugged. "I reckon there is a tale to be woven in every clan, even our enemies."

"They are not our enemies," argued Steinar, shaking his head. Though a small thread of doubt wove its way inside his mind.

Releasing his hold on him, Rangvald proceeded toward the door. While he made his way out of the solar, his uncle continued to loudly express his opinions along the corridor.

Steinar wiped a hand down the back of his neck. "I expected to be confined in this solar for most of the evening."

"He will enjoy the distraction with the Icelander. His recent mistress fled Islay with another lover."

On a groan, Steinar leaned back onto the desk, folding his arms over his chest. "Will the man ever take another wife? I must speak with Sigrid. Perchance she can find him a woman, so he can make male heirs and leave me alone. I have nae claim or wish to govern this isle. And my uncle has proclaimed nae daughter of his shall inherit the land."

"His attention is limited, and he will not listen to talks about marriage. In my brief time I have been here, Sigrid has presented a few women as possible wives. Your uncle shows nae interest." Changing his stance, Gunnar gazed at the flames snapping within the hearth. "In truth, there are other concerns."

Regarding his friend, he asked, "For the love of the Gods, why is the king granting lands to my uncle? And why did he send you?"

"*You* have been away at sea far too long." Gunnar's tone dripped with scorn. Striding to the door, he closed it quietly. Quickly returning to his side, he lowered his voice. "Your uncle is losing control of his grip within the isles. The king judged it wise to grant him lands—lands which shall be governed by one within the Brotherhood without your uncle's knowledge." His lips thinned. "With access to the harbors around here, we can maintain order, especially from those like the Serpents and others who pose a threat to the king and Scotland."

Steinar grimaced. When did the great bear of Islay fail in his firm hold? "How long have you been here?"

"Long enough to ken your uncle sees everyone as the enemy. With each passing week, he accuses his most trusted supporters of attempting to steal his lands." Gunnar tapped a finger against the side of his head. "'Tis as if the man's mind is addled."

A sliver of guilt plagued Steinar. Staying away might not have been the right decision. "I am here now. I shall speak with Sigrid."

Gunnar's lip curled in disgust. "The woman cares

not for what her father does. She seems to encourage his new behavior."

"Do I understand you have taken a dislike of Sigrid?"

Scrubbing a hand over his face, Gunnar replied, "She made it known on my arrival my God was not welcome here."

Steinar's mouth twitched with humor. He glanced away, not wanting to offend his friend. "Aye, aye, Sigrid does not tolerate those who seek the new path of the one God." Straightening from the desk, he wandered to the arched window. The late afternoon sunlight danced along the trees. Sea breezes floated on the wind, enticing him to return. He cast a glance over his shoulder. "So, King William did not send you here to procure—"

A glint of humor finally returned to Gunnar's features. "I have not stolen anything for many moons, even when I aided a traveler and his son on my journey here."

Steinar's eyes widened in surprise. "Truth?"

The man flicked a piece of lint off his tunic. "I cannot claim that food might have been taken to be given to the weary travelers. But in my defense, the table at the inn stayed laden with enough to feed many. I concluded a few loaves of bread, a thick slab of cheese, and several apples would not be missed." He stroked a hand over his chin in obvious thought. "Though I was sorely tempted to stuff a mutton leg in my satchel."

"Shameful you did not," chided Steinar, moving back to his friend.

Gunnar's good humor shifted to concern. "Are you not worried with the arrival of the Serpents? You do ken they bow to nae king. Theirs is to profit for themselves.

They are known for their thievery—take and ask questions later."

Steinar straightened his tunic and pointed a finger at his friend. "This from another thief?"

The man's brow furrowed. "You offend me. I steal and give to those in need."

"Aye, but let us not forget about the time you took a chalice from a certain lady—"

"That particular chalice had been previously stolen," corrected Gunnar, folding his arms over his chest.

"Or the scrolls from an abbey in the north."

His friend glowered at him. "The monks deemed to alter events by adding false accounts and chose not to share their knowledge with the local people."

Steinar nodded slowly. "And you sought to correct what they had done by stealing important scrolls and giving them in secret to travelers who were supposedly making their way to another abbey in Ireland."

Gunnar placed his hands on his hips. "Is there a reason you are listing my offenses? Do you—*the pirate*—now stand before me and pass judgement?"

"For the love of the Gods!" Steinar ran a hand through his hair.

The man grimaced. "Your Gods, not mine."

Clasping a firm hand on his friend's shoulder, Steinar spoke softly, "I have never judged you, my friend. There is only one in this chamber who continues to find fault with his actions. You."

Annoyance flickered in Gunnar's eyes. "Then why remind me of my sins?"

Releasing his hold, Steinar moved away from the man. "I do ken your meaning." Gesturing outward with his hand, he added, "If I recall, you continue to spout your *sins* at each meeting of the Brotherhood."

A frown creased Gunnar's brow as he clutched the wooden cross around his neck. "'Tis important I confess to those I trust. And most of the time, I repent along my travels."

The fading light of day brought weariness to Steinar. Arguing with his friend would serve no purpose. He believed in the old ways, and Gunnar followed a path he could not comprehend. His thoughts returned to his purpose here. Shoving aside the conflict within, he managed a small smile. "How long have you been away from the Brotherhood?"

Gunnar relaxed his stance. "Since late March. I had recently returned from Ireland and was making my way home when I received the news. A raven sent me a message from Magnar to attend to your uncle along with the news of the birth of his and Elspeth's son."

Steinar stilled. He recalled the distressing time when Magnar's twin brother had kidnapped Elspeth last year. He often pondered if the harsh treatment during her time with her captors had weakened the woman. Yet he swiftly banished the thought. Elspeth MacAlpin proved to all within the Brotherhood the strength she bore by her concern for those who came to her rescue, and her love for Magnar. He swallowed. "The bairn arrived early. All is well with both mother *and* son?"

Smiling, the man nodded. "Aye, indeed. They named him Thomas after Elspeth's brother."

"By the hounds! 'Tis good news." He strolled to the door, opening it wide. "Let us go grab a cup of mead to celebrate, and you can share what has happened to you along your travels."

Gunnar joined him. "And you, as well. I would like

to hear more about how the mighty pirate wolf landed in the seas. I reckon there is more to this account—a tale worthy for a *skald*."

Steinar struck his friend across the back while chuckling softly. The tension soon eased from him. No matter their different beliefs, they were brothers—forged in the same blood of magic. "I have missed you, *Thief*!"

Chapter Eight

Entering the great hall, Steinar slowed his progress. The heady aroma of food teased his senses. For months, his meals consisted of stale bread, hard cheeses, apples, seaweed, and dried fish. He inhaled sharply, detecting wild boar, venison, and his favorites—fresh salmon and cod in silken herb sauces. Steinar fought the urge to lick the scent off his lips.

Chuckling softly next to him, Gunnar nudged him forward. "Again, I say, you have been at sea far too long."

Lifting one shoulder, he replied, "I do not ken your meaning."

Gunnar coughed into his hand. "Liar. The sound your wolf is making tells me otherwise. And your gut is protesting in earnest."

One side of Steinar's mouth twitched.

His friend punched him in the arm. "Aye! I knew you were spouting a falsehood."

As Steinar made his way slowly inside the hall, he glanced sideways at the man. "Are you certain?"

Gunnar plucked a small bun off a trencher of a passing serving lass and handed him the offering. "One side of your mouth twitches when you tell a lie."

"Merely suppressing the laughter," he argued, stuffing the bun into his mouth.

"You never *laugh*, my friend."

Steinar barely had time to step out of the way of a lad carrying two jugs of ale. He swallowed. "Not true."

"Another falsehood," countered Gunnar. "You can smile, chuckle low, but rarely have I heard you belt out in laughter. At anything."

Stunned into silence, Steinar halted and gaped at the man, attempting to recall a moment when he actually laughed. The seas brought him joy and contentment. But once on land, his sullen behavior returned. His friend had to be incorrect in his account. Surely he'd laughed during their times at feasts or during any games? He narrowed his eyes in contemplation.

Before Steinar could offer any protest or proof, Gunnar announced, "Ah, I see your uncle is motioning us over to his table. Are those the Olafsson brothers?"

"Aye, *aye*," he mumbled, moving forward. "Snorri is seated next to Rangvald."

"Your uncle looks pleased."

"Let us hope the skald can manage to entertain him."

"He is serving ale over mead?" Steinar glanced around the hall.

"If I ken your uncle, he waits to see what Leif brings to the bargain table. He shall want to compare his mead here to theirs. Therefore, he will serve them ale until he is satisfied."

"He does enjoy his mead."

Gunnar slid into a chair farther down from Rangvald while Steinar settled on his uncle's right.

Rangvald shoved a jug of ale in front of Steinar. "Leif has been giving me his account of how he rescued you from the stormy sea water."

Although his body required the food before him, Steinar filled his cup to the brim with ale. "A debt I hope to repay."

Leif gave a quick nod in his direction, then lifted his cup. "Nae need. With your help, we managed to avoid the cauldron which surrounds the nearby isles."

Steinar arched a brow before draining his cup. *I ken my debt shall be fulfilled after I've assisted you in finding the treasure you seek.*

While keeping a partial ear to the conversation flowing around him, Steinar filled his trencher with wild boar, salmon, and cabbage mixed with wild garlic, mushrooms, and onions. When the first bite entered his mouth, he almost let out a groan. If anything, his uncle was known for the bountiful fare he set at his table for his guests. He resumed eating his meal, content to keep silent and listen.

Snorri shared how he came to travel with the Serpents when they visited his homeland many moons ago. He yearned for adventure in return for telling sagas during their long travels. Indeed, the man kept his uncle entertained with his tales. Even Gunnar grew curious and added his own questions about the skald's adventures.

After refilling his cup, Steinar wiped his mouth with the back of his hand and took a long draw of ale. When the din in the hall hushed, he lifted his gaze, and swallowed. Hard.

The vision gliding between the tables toward them stole the breath from his lungs. He blinked once. Twice. The light from all the candles appeared to surround her in its glow. With each step leading her closer, he became mesmerized. His gaze traveled over her ivory gown, hugging, caressing each curve—from the top of her full breasts to those round hips. Steinar's fingers itched to trace along the curve of her waist down to her long legs.

Legs he craved to have wrapped around him while he plundered the soft treasure between her thighs.

Inga. Gone was the warrior. In her place stood a Goddess with copper tresses flowing down her back with each sway of her hips.

Steinar downed the remaining ale and slammed the cup onto the table.

Their gazes locked. Curiosity stared back at him, and something else. She dipped her head in greeting, giving him a small smile. Steinar found himself spiraling into an unknown abyss within the depths of her eyes.

"Who is this beauty who graces Finlaggan?" demanded Rangvald.

His wolf padded closer in warning toward his uncle.

Standing abruptly, Steinar shoved his chair back.

He was not the only man to stand. Leif assumed a protective stance near his sister. "This is Inga, our sister."

His uncle slid a glance at Steinar. "Are you prepared to give your chair to this lovely lass? I have a desire to learn more from this Serpent."

"Surely you can speak with her from across the table," suggested Steinar, keeping his focus on Inga.

"You misunderstood my question. You will *allow* this beauty to sit beside me," argued his uncle.

Steinar clenched his jaw, doing his best to temper the man and beast.

Inga ignored the request from Rangvald. Instead, she gave the man a radiant smile. "I have nae wish to start an argument between kin. I shall enjoy sitting across from you *and* your nephew."

Settling into her chair next to Leif, she picked up a jug and sniffed. "Ale?" She glanced at her brother. "Where is the fine barrel of mead we brought for our host?"

Leif resumed his position in his chair. He grabbed a long blade on a trencher and sliced a portion of the boar. "We have not discussed our terms."

Inga leaned back, reaching around Leif, and tapped Jorik on the shoulder with her hand. "Go fetch the small barrel."

When her brother refused to do her bidding, she smacked Leif. "Give him permission."

Leif turned and gave Jorik a blunt nod to fetch the barrel, then continued to spear his meat as if he wanted to take the blade to his sister's tongue.

Rangvald's eyes widened in surprise at her. "You would give your mead freely, before I have spoken to your brother?"

Picking up a hazelnut from a small bowl, she rolled it between her fingers. "You have welcomed us into your home. 'Tis our thanks for supplying a chamber to rest after months at sea." She popped the nut into her mouth.

Steinar suppressed the groan lodged in his throat.

His uncle pointed a finger at Leif. "Your sister speaks wisely. Perchance I need to speak with her regarding trade."

"She speaks when she should remain silent," Leif scolded. He glared at Steinar. "And why do you continue to stand there gaping at my sister?"

"Aye, please sit," encouraged Inga. "I feel the strain on my neck while we speak."

Gathering his thoughts, Steinar ignored them both and gestured to another woman entering the hall. "Sigrid can sit next to you, Uncle."

Without waiting for an objection from Rangvald, he took his cup and went to the end of the table. If he did not distance himself from his uncle, Steinar feared his beast would dominate the man. For reasons he could not fathom, the wolf took a defensive position toward Inga. But then, so did Steinar. He craved to have the woman sit near him and no others.

Two young serving lads made their way around the table filling the empty cups with the Olafssons' mead. When one of the lads reached him, Steinar shook his head in regret. Drink would only add fuel to his fury, and the food he ate settled like knots in his gut. He had to regain control.

Gunnar glanced at him over the rim of his cup. After taking a sip, he leaned near him. "Is there something you would like to declare about the woman?"

Steinar drummed his fingers along the rough wood with his left hand. "What woman?"

"The one who has captivated your attention."

His hand stilled. "None of your concern." Though his loyalty remained steadfast to his friend and the Brotherhood, Steinar would keep his oath to Inga and her brothers. When the time presented itself, he would give an account to his friend to forward on to Magnar. The sooner they set a course to Jura and away from Finlaggan, the better for all concerned.

Gunnar drained his cup and then placed it on the table. He folded his arms over his chest. "Never have I seen the Pirate Wolf almost give reign to his beast over a woman."

Baffled by his words, Steinar's mind reeled with confusion. "I can assure you control never slipped from my hold."

"Your eyes stated otherwise."

"My wolf dislikes my uncle, as well you

understand." Tempted to ask for a cup of mead, Steinar balled his hand into a fist. He grew weary of Gunnar's probing questions and looks.

Inga laughed—rich and musical—at something his uncle said. He dared to steal a glance at the woman. Even with her womanly charms, the warrior flashed within her eyes, daring any man to challenge her.

Steinar shifted uncomfortably in his chair.

How wrong he was to believe she, Inga the Ruthless, unable to use her enchanting ways as a woman to learn and also weave her will around a table with powerful men.

Would you bring your enemy to their knees with a blade at their throat? Or with a kiss?

Steinar shook his head to rid the image of claiming those luscious lips. Suddenly, the hall became too warm, too confining. A fire blazed and snapped in the hearth. With each hiss of the flames, he found his mood darkening. He wiped a hand over his brow, willing his gaze to look elsewhere and not at the beauty who continued to wrap a charm over those gathered.

"Have you tried the mead? 'Tis better than what Ivar makes." Gunnar shoved a cup at him.

Steinar rose from his chair. "Nae. Make my amends to Rangvald. I must speak with Haaken."

Gunnar frowned. "He will not be pleased. You ken how he loves his drinking games."

"When is the man ever *pleased* with anything I do?"

Making long strides between the tables, he ignored his uncle's demands to return, hurrying out of the hall. By the time he reached the doors leading out of the castle, the tension coursing through his veins eased. When he stepped outside, he exhaled fully. The cool evening teased him with the salty brine of the sea breeze.

Crossing the bailey, he made his way toward the stables. Once inside, his eyes adjusted to the dim enclosure, leaving the wooden door partially open. Light from a lone lantern hung on an iron peg. Making soft clicking sounds with his tongue, Steinar waited for the usual greeting from his horse. A loud snort soon followed. His steps led him to the third stall on the right.

Halting before the stall, Steinar held out his hand and then took his fingers down the animal's dark mane. "I bring you nae gifts of food, Bran. I ken Tiernan fed you one too many apples."

"Only two," mumbled the lad in the corner of the stall.

Steinar chuckled softly. "Go seek your bed, Tiernan."

"'Tis warmer here," argued the lad, standing slowly. He plucked straw from his hair and then rubbed his eyes.

"Then go fetch food from the kitchens."

Tiernan yawned. "Haaken told me the same."

"Where is the man?" asked Steinar while unlatching the gate to let the lad out from the stall.

"He went to find food in the hall and seek rest."

Placing a comforting hand on the lad's shoulder, he stressed, "Food and rest for you as well. Go now, even if you find rest by the hearth in the kitchen. You are done tending to the horses today."

A blurry-eyed Tiernan muttered his thanks and slowly wandered out of the stables.

Bran nibbled on the back of Steinar's tunic. He glanced over at the animal. Dark beady eyes regarded him. "Aye, I do ken he is a good lad. He shall make a fine stable master one day."

Another soft whinny came from the stall farther down. White-tipped ears twitched as the horse stuck her head out of the stall.

Steinar dipped his head. "Greetings, Tove. Have you been served your share of apples?"

"'Tis not her favorite," interjected a familiar female voice, approaching by his side. "She favors soft berries mixed with her oats."

Steinar's breathing hitched. Keeping his attention on the animal, he asked, "Has my uncle grown tired of your company that you would leave his table?"

"He is enjoying a tale about the giants who ruled the far North. At present, Snorri has captured his attention. I left soon thereafter when he desired to sing a poem." Inga went to her horse. Unwrapping a small cloth, she held out the berries in the palm of her hand. "I did not forget about you, Tove."

Even with the scent of horses, dung, straw, and leather, Inga's scent invaded his body. The wildness of the sea hugged the woman, along with another scent— one of flowers. But which one, Steinar could not detect.

He glanced her way. "Why are you here, Inga?"

She rested her head against the forehead of the horse. "To reassure Tove. The sea journey remained long and grueling. Whenever we arrive on land, my duty is to make sure all our horses are adjusting." Brushing a soft kiss on Tove's muzzle, she gave one final pat along her mane and strolled back to him.

Steinar clasped his hands behind his back. Thank the Gods she had covered herself with a cloak. His fingers itched to trace a path along the threads woven into the material around the top of her breasts.

When she stood merely inches in front of him, she

lifted her gaze to meet his. "You left without sharing a cup of our mead. Why?"

Irritation seeped into his words. "Why do you care? Return to the hall and take the candle you brought with you."

Confusion shifted within those jeweled eyes and then they hardened. "Did I say I cared? Simply curious. And there is nae threat to the stables with a candle inside a lantern sitting by the entrance. Why is your mood so foul?"

Was it too much to ask to be left alone? To find solace without the intoxicating female clouding his mind and stirring the lustful beast? *Control. Harness. Bind the emotions.* He had to flee this moment before he did something he'd regret.

Steinar took a step back. "Enjoy your evening, Inga."

The woman grasped his arm. Her fingers dug into him. A great surge of heat speared throughout his body.

She looked behind him. "I have brought a jug of mead. Would you care to sample a taste?"

"Taste?" Steinar's mind reeled. *By Odin's blood!* What he craved was a taste of those lips.

He swiftly shoved aside the conflict. "Let me *sample* what you have, Inga."

Chapter Nine

Inga hesitated for several heartbeats, then released her hold on the man's arm. What possessed her to leave the safety of the feast? Rangvald had been smitten with her words and attraction during the meal. Though her brother glared and disapproved of her behavior with Rangvald, she had to secure a trade. The man proved easily manipulated, therefore aligning Leif in a formable bargaining position.

But the man standing before her? Inga's well-harnessed emotions slipped out of her like grains of sand sifting through her fingers. She slanted her gaze to the silver glittering on the wolf torc around his neck. The man's hair fell in ebony waves past his shoulders with a small section braided on the right.

Unbidden, an image came forth of the man standing on the shore with nothing on but his torc. Strong, magnificent, a God of the sea.

She blinked to get rid of the vision.

You're merely curious of another who has powers within them. Nothing more. Do not be swayed by Steinar. Do not be tempted to touch. Do not crave his arms around you. Dismiss him like you have all the other men who came before him.

Without a word, Inga went to the bench near the entrance of the stables. After composing herself, she returned with the jug of mead. "In my haste, I forgot to bring a cup."

"Were *you* eager to leave the feasting?" He took the jug, brushing his fingers over the back of her hand.

Inga suppressed the shiver. "Your uncle wanted to impress those with an ancient drinking poem while standing on the table. About a tale of a man joining with two women."

Steinar scowled and leaned against the wall. "Rangvald likes to entertain his guests with these certain poems. With much drink, his *singing* stories can be vulgar. Often, his manners are lacking with new guests. There have been many men who have challenged him over a certain tale. My uncle cares little about those he offends."

Anger rose within her. "Thank the Gods his daughter left before he began his bellowing."

"Agreed. But I have not known him to spout the tales in her presence *or* with women present."

She tapped a fist against her chest. "But I was there this time."

"Your brother should have halted the conversation and asked you to leave."

"My brother did urge me to leave," she confessed, shaking her head in disgust.

Steinar raised a brow in amused contempt with the beginnings of a smile tipping the corners of his lips.

"I find nae humor in this." She pointed a warning finger at the man. "Nor should you."

He raised the jug near his mouth. "For *Inga the Ruthless* who has maintained a life around men, I find your response…interesting." He then took a long draw of mead.

Stunned into silence, Inga gaped at him. Then her

eyes narrowed to shards of fury. Her fingers sought the brooch fastened at the top of her cloak and undid the clasp. Removing the cloak from her body, she tossed both brooch and cloak onto a nearby stool.

"How wrong you were in your earlier criticism of my skills as a woman. At Rangvald's table I was simply Inga, daughter of Olaf." She gestured to her gown. "Can you honestly tell me I look like a woman who is a leader of men on the seas?"

Steinar's expression stilled. He wiped the back of his hand leisurely across his mouth. "*Nae*," he rasped out.

There she witnessed the invitation in the smoldering depths of his eyes—dark with desire luring her forward.

Her heart hammered against her chest. Inga's mind ordered her to leave—escape the temptation to feel his arms around her. But her body betrayed and overrode all thought. Slowly, Inga removed the jug from his hand and pressed it against her lips. Tilting it back, she drank deeply of what remained. After tossing aside the jug onto the ground, she smiled fully. "Then I am correct."

Steinar pushed away from the wall. "You think to claim victory?"

Her breath rose heavily with each rise and fall. When did she become the prey and he the predator? "Always," she whispered, determined to grasp any shard of control or sanity.

In one swift move, Steinar clasped his hands around her waist and turned her around with her back against the wall. His body towered over her, trapping Inga. Escape not an option.

She gasped. Fight or surrender?

For the first time, Inga lessened the strings binding

her to an oath moons ago.

An oath to never let a man control her.

An oath to never let a man touch her.

Oaths be damned! She craved to have this man kiss her.

Candlelight flickered around them while his hands gripped her firmly. He lowered his head near her ear. "I see nae victory here."

Inga swallowed. Heat swelled within her body—traveling from her face down her breasts and to the place hidden between her thighs. "Do you challenge me?"

His hand traveled along the curve of her waist upward until his fingers traced a path along the neckline of her gown.

She trembled from his touch. "What are you doing?"

The smile he flashed her was as intimate as a kiss. A kiss she ached from the man. Would his lips be soft? Or firm as the muscles he hid under his clothing.

His lips brushed against hers as he spoke. "Tasting the *woman*." He then licked the soft skin below her ear, and Inga let out a moan.

Steinar drew back. "I think neither of us is the victor. I taste the woman *and* the warrior."

She threw caution out to the sea and wrapped her arms around the man's neck. "Are you certain you have sampled enough, *Pirate*?"

His low growl surrounded Inga. "You are a siren, Inga. A danger to any man. You should leave and bolt the door on your chamber."

"But I have surrendered to you," she confessed, eager to explore more.

Steinar crushed her against him. The first touch of his lips ignited a hunger within her, but when his mouth descended over hers, Inga reveled in the heady sensation—soft, full, demanding. The kiss sent her body aflame, sending her into a spiral of passion unlike any she'd experienced. She opened fully to the possession, letting the man take and plunder. When his tongue caressed the inside of her mouth, Inga replied by sliding hers across in invitation. Desire burned within her veins, *burned* in the most intimate places of her body. Shocked at her own eager response to the touch of his lips, she moved against him, feeling his hard length.

Breaking free, Steinar's lips trailed a path along the vein along her neck. "You dare to tempt me further?"

Inga closed her eyes, weak and confused after one kiss. The man tasted of mead and much more—the sea clung to his skin, to his mouth, to the breath sliding over her lips.

"Do you want more?" His question barely a whisper against her skin.

"*Aye*," she managed out between gasps of air.

When his hand cupped her breast, her eyes flew open.

He held her captivated with one dark look while his fingers pinched her hard nipple through the gown. Delightful sensations trickled down to her toes. "Sweet Goddess…this gown is too confining."

Steinar chuckled low. Bending his head, he dipped his tongue between the swell of her breasts. "You taste as if you've bathed in the ocean."

"As do you," she murmured, twining her fingers in his long hair. Her breasts tingled while he continued to lavish her with his tongue.

Inga tried to ignore the strange aching in her limbs. An ache only Steinar could ease. Indecision plagued her.

Stay? Leave? His kisses left her without any rational thought. Left her weak. However, the whispers of being with Steinar grew inside her, and she was only moments away from having him rip the lacings apart on the back of her gown.

On a groan, she whispered, "Kiss me again, *Pirate*, and then I shall take my leave."

Raising his head, he grabbed a fistful of her hair, gently bringing her closer. "Then *one* kiss I shall give you to take to your bed." His other hand then slid down to cup her bottom—bringing her fully against his hardened length.

"*Steinar—*"

His mouth covered hers hungrily, silencing her plea. The air left her lungs, but he filled her with his own breath. New spirals of ecstasy swirled through her, and Inga gave herself freely to the passion.

"Enough," he growled, tearing his lips from hers and moving away. After quickly retrieving her items from the stool, Steinar wrapped the cloak around her shoulders. His hands shook as he fastened the brooch.

Inga lifted her hand to the braided lock of hair over his eye. Gently, she shoved it aside.

He grasped her fingers, halting her progress. "My restraint is failing. If you touch me again, I fear I will take more than a kiss." He loosened his grip to allow her hand to fall free.

She studied him for a moment. Her gaze lowered to what lay hidden beneath his trews.

"Odin's blood, woman," he hissed out. "Leave, now!"

Inga gave him one more final glance before departing the stables.

Steinar remained rooted to the ground, unable to move. Inga's scent lingered everywhere. Licking his lips, he let out a groan. His body burned with fire for this woman. The moment she'd removed her cloak, he'd craved an opportunity to run his hands over her skin. To rid Inga from the gown that hid her treasures and take all she had to offer him.

By the hounds! What would the woman be like in his bed? Fiery? Passionate? A siren to tame? Or would she conquer him with her words, her hands, her kisses on his skin? Cursing himself for where his thoughts were leading, he shouted, "Nae!" He wiped a shaky hand over his brow in frustration. Why did he challenge her? Why did he kiss her?

Steinar clenched his hands. "Because you have thought of nothing else since she removed her helmet on the ship days ago."

The horses snorted uncomfortably around him. Bran stomped his foot in obvious annoyance to Steinar's outburst.

Lifting his gaze upward, Steinar placed his hands on his hips. His resolve hardened. "Inga is not for me. The sea is my mistress. Odin, strip this desire from my veins for the woman. Remove the temptation. Remind me of my duty to the Brotherhood. *Remind* me of my oath to never let a woman dull my senses, especially Inga the Ruthless. Her voice is one of a siren, and I fear the darkness she lures me into."

He lowered his head and took a deep breath in and out. The jug lay discarded on the ground. Curious, Steinar went to retrieve the empty vessel. Sniffing the contents, he pondered if Inga had woven a charm into the mead. Could she have done the same with others at his uncle's table? Or was this mead reserved for him? Was this the reason all control vanished from him when she stepped into his view? Or was it her scent? What seized him to discard duty? Risk everything for one kiss? Betray the Brotherhood by not sharing his knowledge with Gunnar?

Question after question hammered inside his mind, blurring him to any possible answer.

"Who are you, woman?" he bellowed. Steinar crushed the jug into splinters of wood, heedless of the damage he did to his hands.

"A *woman* who has twisted your guts and addled your mind after a few days," answered Gunnar, slipping inside. "Be careful the words you spout. Your uncle's men hide in secret in every nook within this castle."

Steinar flashed his friend a warning look and went to the barrel by one of the stalls. Plunging his hands in the icy water, he rid the last shards of wood from his palms. "You do not have to remind me. I have trained most of his men."

Gunnar shrugged, then closed the stable doors behind him. "But not Godred. In your absence, the man has replaced those who were close to your uncle with other men of his choosing."

Grateful for the shift in conversation, he said, "The man has an agenda, this I ken well. I will speak with my uncle regarding the change of his guards. 'Tis good I have returned."

"Agreed," mumbled his friend. "Though tread carefully when you mention Godred. He speaks well of the man and will not listen to anyone who complains about abuse from him."

Pinching the bridge of his nose, Steinar blew out a

frustrated breath. "My uncle understands well I have never trusted the man. An argument we have each time I visit." He pointed to what Gunnar held in his hand. "Why have you left the comfort of warmth, food, and good drink?"

Gunnar flashed him a smile and approached. "I thought to share the fine mead from the Olafssons. But I see you have already shared a cup or two with a certain lass?"

Grunting a curse, Steinar waved off the offering and went to his horse.

"What? The Pirate has forsaken mead?" Gunnar's brow knitted. "What happened in here?"

At a loss to find the words, Steinar stroked a gentle hand over the muzzle of his horse.

Gunnar drew by his side. "You realize I have always envied your freedom—to be gone for months with not a worry except the elements on the seas. Yet I sense a battle inside you."

Steinar gaped at his friend. "You have nae freedom because you're shackled between two paths—the Brotherhood and your new God." He leaned forward and peered inside the jug. "Perchance Inga is a witch who has caught me in a net with her siren's song."

Shock creased Gunnar's face. He quickly held the jug outward as if it contained vipers. "Then nae one is safe. Should we warn your uncle?"

Shrugging, Steinar resumed his attention toward his horse. Uncertainty clouded his judgement.

"Or are you conflicted on how you *feel* toward the woman?"

Steinar's voice grated harshly as he glared at the man. "I am not going to discuss my *feelings*. I have only known Inga for several days. If not for her, I would not be standing here."

Gunnar gave him a skeptical glance. "Was it not her brothers who rescued you? Or is there more to her than you are willing to share?"

Pushing away from the stall, Steinar looked beyond the man. The conversation had become dangerous. Steinar would confess all to his friend on his return. "As soon as Leif bargains a trade, I shall be leaving on the outgoing tide. Once I have seen them across the waters to Jura, I'll return. In truth, I reckon they will cross on over to Torvay."

"God's blood! 'Tis the woman who has dimmed your mind and actions! Who is this Inga that you would travel with her—"

"I travel with the Serpents. She is merely their kin."

Gunnar's smile held no humor. He slammed the mead onto the ledge of the stall. "And yet *she* appears to have slipped under your skin." Gunnar sniffed. "You even smell of her."

Outraged by his friend's remark, Steinar lifted the jug and dumped the mead over Gunnar's head. He shoved the vessel into the man's arms. "Now you *smell* like us both. Simply mead."

Gunnar's eyes turned to those of his wolf. "Never have I seen the Pirate lose control over a woman." With one hand, he swiped at the liquid trickling down his face. "*Ever*."

Steinar stepped aside and made for the entrance. His hand stilled on the bolt. Glancing over his shoulder, he warned, "You are my friend—my brother, so I will say this only once. Stay out of my affairs, Thief."

Gunnar flung the jug aside. "And if she is a witch?

Do I allow my friend to stray a dangerous path on the sea? Keep silent to the others within the Brotherhood?"

"*Aye*," affirmed Steinar. Shoving aside the bolt, he walked briskly out into the chilled spring evening.

Chapter Ten

Easily deflecting another blow with his shield, Jorik sneered. "Your focus is elsewhere, Inga. I have killed you twice now."

"You are wrong. I still breathe." Inga blinked once. Twice. She wiped away the sweat beading across her brow and trailing into her eyes.

Her brother spat on the ground. "By the Gods! You are in nae mood to train." Dismissing her with a wave of his hand, Jorik began his descent from the hill.

When the blade hissed past his ear, landing in the tree in front of him, he came to a halt. Glancing over his shoulder, he arched a brow in amused contempt. "You missed, *little* sister."

Inga fought the laughter threatening to spill forth. "Merely a warning, Jorik the Younger."

Tapping his blade against his shield, he corrected, "The Hawk, if you want to hear what I've learned, *and* the tallest of our kin."

Tossing her braid over her shoulder, Inga hid her smile while she made her way to the tree. Carefully, she pried the blade free. She placed her hand over the slash on the rough bark. "My apologies for any harm I did." She turned and faced her brother. "And my apologies to you, *Hawk*, for my foul temper."

Jorik went to a nearby log. Retrieving the aleskin from their belongings, he strolled back and handed it to her. "Can you explain?"

Sighing heavily, Inga took the offering and guzzled deeply. After giving her brother a nod of thanks, she returned the aleskin to him. Out of all her brothers, Jorik remained her trustworthy confidant. When she'd returned to her chamber the other evening, Inga kept silent, even as Helka probed her with questions about her disappearance after her meal. Emotions swirled and skidded inside her. And when dawn's light slipped into their room, Inga's mood had turned sullen. Why did she allow Steinar to kiss her? Why did she visit the stables? Was it simply to comfort her horse? Or did she secretly desire to see the man?

You continue to remain elusive, Steinar, and I must endure evening meals with your uncle attempting to lure me into his bed.

Inga ran a finger over the smooth blade, careful to avoid the edge. After giving a slight shrug, she sheathed her blade. "The Pirate confounds me."

Jorik's smile vanished, wiped away by astonishment. "Has he done something to make you question his loyalty? Has he spoken of the treasure with his uncle?" He slashed the air with his sword. "Was your decision to ask for his aid not a wise plan? We can toss him overboard once we are at sea."

"Nae, *nae*," she reassured, bending to pick up an acorn. Inga's gaze settled on a squirrel, scampering about in search of food. "Steinar is too valuable. In addition, I am certain the leader of the Wolves of Clan Sutherland would not favor us if we saved and then took Steinar's life." She laughed nervously and tossed the acorn outward to the animal.

"Then why does the man baffle you?"

"I do not ken," she answered truthfully. *Am I drawn to the power within him?* Heat slid through her, recalling his kisses.

"You should not be alone with him," stressed Jorik, coming to her side.

She touched his shoulder. "Let us share a meal, and you can give me your account of what you have learned."

Displeased by her shift in the conversation, Jorik's expression darkened, revealing the hardened warrior she had come to witness on their travels.

Crossing to the log, she opened the small satchel and removed an apple and wedge of cheese. Inga strayed to a nearby tree, dropped the satchel, and settled against the bark. "Are you not hungry, Hawk?"

His features softened. "You ken I am always hungry, little sister."

Relief coursed through her at his endearment. She inclined her head toward the satchel. "I smell bread mixed with honey and almonds. I shall let you take the first bite."

Jorik's smile broadened in approval. He hurried to her side. After dropping his sword onto the ground, he settled next to her and pulled out the small round loaf of bread.

They ate quietly, content to enjoy their meal. When Inga had her fill, she brushed aside the crumbs and tossed the apple core outward. She hugged her knees to her chest and leaned forward, taking in the beauty of their surroundings. "Even in the forest, the sea carries her scent to us, and the birds herald her song." She inhaled deeply. "'Tis peaceful here. I have enjoyed our mornings training up here."

"I can hear the sea calling. We should depart soon,"

said Jorik between mouthfuls of food.

Inga slid her brother a sideways glance. "You are eager to return to our ship?"

He licked the honey off his fingers. "I do not trust those on this isle."

She stiffened. "Continue."

Jorik leaned back on his hands. "I have heard whispers Rangvald's mind is addled. He stumbles over his words, is quick to anger for nae apparent reason, and cares only on gaining land on the mainland. Moreover, Godred controls many of the men at Finlaggan."

"Sweet Freyja," she whispered. "I ken Steinar does not favor the man by his reaction and words when we first arrived."

Jorik nodded slowly. "And Godred has spies everywhere. When one slips out, another takes his place."

She twisted her braid around her fingers and stewed for a moment. "I thought the man kept watch over our ships?"

Her brother snorted. "Nae. He returned soon after we arrived."

"Have you spoken with Leif?"

"A brief account. He urged me to bring this knowledge to you."

Inga stretched out her legs. "Did his meeting go well with Rangvald?"

Her brother yawned. "Aye, though displeased you did not return to the hall last evening. 'Tis wise we leave soon. The man might want to make an offer of marriage for you."

Inga grimaced. "Never. And I grew tired of forcing kind words with Rangvald."

Jorik nodded slowly. "I had thought to rest another day, but I sense a tempest brewing here."

Uneasiness settled inside her like choppy ocean waves during a storm. They had to leave now. This was not their battle. Lingering on Islay could prove dangerous to them and the treasure. Standing abruptly, she scanned the area. A lone hawk circled north, and she watched its pursuit. What if they were being watched? "Are you sure we were not followed when we left the castle?"

"Aye," he responded slowly, rising from the ground. He brushed off dirt and leaves from his trews. "I kept a watch each morning while you made your way on foot up the hill."

Uncertainty crept into her voice. "But what if someone followed you?"

"Because I took another path each morning."

Inga clenched her fist. "These people ken these hills. We do not. If what you said about Godred's spies—"

"Then I suggest we fulfill our trade and leave immediately," urged Jorik. "The sister of Leif the Bloody Spear sparring with a sword will raise questions."

She bit out a curse. "Aye. Return to the castle and inform Leif of our plans. 'Tis good we are leaving now. The full moon shall be upon us in three days. We must secure the area around the hidden isle and wait for the mists to part, even if we must maintain our position at sea."

Jorik bent to pick up his sword. Quickly sheathing the blade, he arched a brow. "If we depart within a few hours, we can arrive at Jura by tomorrow. What about the MacDougall?"

Making long strides, Inga retrieved her sword and

dirk. Returning to her brother, she handed him her weapons. "If I come upon anyone, I will appear less like a warrior. As you ken, I always carry two small blades hidden on me. As for Steinar, I will tell him of our new plans."

Wariness shone in her brother's eyes. "Do you trust him?"

I trust the wolf more than the man. But I am not going to confess this to you, Brother. "I trust nae one. Yet Steinar has given me his word not to speak of the treasure, therefore a part of me *trusts* him to remain silent," she admitted quietly.

He hesitated as if to say more but gave her a quick nod and took off through the trees.

"We should have never landed on Islay." Biting her lower lip, she scanned the area one more time. Picking up the satchel of food, Inga started her own descent back to the castle.

****

While Godred sharpened his blade on the stone, the woman huddled by the hearth regarded him with cold fear. "You are convinced you saw Inga and her brother training in the hills?"

The woman twisted the ends of her wrap around her body. "Aye," she mumbled weakly.

Godred lifted the dirk to the light streaming in through the entrance of the smithy. "I cannot hear you, Cora! Either you are unsure *or* spouting a lie!"

She swallowed and blinked. "Aye, I did witness them together in the hills."

He sneered at her. "Why does a woman need to train? Their sole purpose is to satisfy a man's needs, to cook, and to remain silent. From the moment Inga arrived with her brothers, she captured the attention of Rangvald. He is smitten with the woman like a rutting boar. Once he beds her, his interest will wane."

"I have heard the Serpents are fierce warriors. Possibly, they train their women as well," interjected Sigrid rising from a chair near the table. She grew disgusted with the man's increasingly crude ways.

Godred snapped his attention to her. The smile he gave her never reached his eyes. "I thought you disliked the woman?"

Sigrid lifted her chin and boldly met his gaze. "I do, but I also ken this clan. This is why I had my maid follow her."

"If this is all you have learned, you have wasted my time. Leave. Both of you." Turning his back on her, Godred resumed sharpening his blade.

"Do not dismiss us or you will not gain valuable information," warned Sigrid. "You forget who you are speaking to."

Instantly, the man stormed to her side. Leveling the dirk against her cheek, he traced a path on the other side of her face with his tongue. His rotten breath surrounded her, and Sigrid fought the bile threatening to heave from her stomach. "And you forget I can tell your father how you betrayed him. With me."

Sigrid stiffened at the threat. Though the man was correct, she would not succumb to his terror. A slave to his demands, aye, but one day she would gain her freedom. "Release me," she gritted out.

He drew back. Slowly, he dipped the blade across the tops of her breasts. "Remember, I have marked you, Sigrid, daughter of Rangvald the Bear. You are mine."

Never! She bit the inside of her mouth to squelch the

scream.

"There is more," interrupted Cora.

Godred released his hold and turned abruptly around. "Speak!"

Sigrid let out a sigh of relief. After nodding at the woman to disclose her information, she moved away from the man. Coming to stand alongside Cora, she placed a soothing hand on her shoulder. "Tell us what you heard."

The woman clasped her hands tightly in front of her. "She—*Inga* spoke of a treasure hidden in the mists and they had to make ready to leave."

His eyes were sharp and assessing. "*Treasure?*"

Cora bobbed her head once.

"Did she mention where?"

She swallowed. "Nae."

He tapped the blade against his palm. "Then my plans have changed."

Giving the woman a reassuring squeeze, Sigrid gestured toward the entrance. "You have done well. Go."

Sigrid started forward to leave when Godred's words made her pause.

"Are you certain your father is drinking the herbs you place in his cup at night? His eyes do not appear as clouded as before."

She lifted her chin. "Since his last mistress has fled, I join him in his solar each night, bringing him his warmed goat's milk."

He snarled in disgust. "Warmed goat's milk is for bairns. Your father has grown weak."

Sigrid's fingers itched to claw the man's eyes out. Godred continued to question everything she did, and this did not bode well. Had she not earned his trust?

Perchance she had chosen unwisely with the man.

Tempering her anger, she asked, "Now that you ken of the treasure what will we do?"

He gave her a skeptical glance. "Follow and see where this treasure is located. Obviously, Steinar did not mention this to your father. His disloyalty has nae bounds."

Sigrid almost burst out in laughter at his last remark. Godred maintained loyal to one. Himself. She dared to press the man further for more information. "And how will you explain your departure to my father?"

Godred gave an exasperated snort. "After I leave, mix a strong brew with the herbs and give it to your father." He angled his head to the side. "Take him for a walk along the cliffs. In his dulled condition, you can push him over the edge."

Her eyes widened in disbelief. "You want *me* to kill my father?"

"Either a slow, agonizing death by poison or quick and final. Are you unable to carry out the deed?" A silken thread of warning carried in the man's voice. "Do not look surprised, Sigrid. The herbs I have given you are already killing your father."

"Aye," she muttered hastily in agreement, trying to fathom what he wanted her to do.

"Good." Godred lowered his sword. "Can you trust Cora to keep silent?"

She drew her cloak more firmly around her, trying to calm the icy tendrils of fear slipping down her back. "Cora is as silent as the rats who scurry in this smithy."

Godred swiftly stomped his foot outward onto the ground. Bones crushed beneath his boot while blood oozed out, mixing with the dirt and stones within the smithy.

Sigrid jumped back. Placing a hand to her stomach, she fought the bile, once again. Fear and anger knotted inside her. The man was ruthless in the kill of the animal.

Godred's voice hardened ruthlessly while he tapped the ground with his sword. "I can *always* hear the rats."

Sigrid watched in stunned silence as the man lifted his foot to retrieve the dead body off his boot with his sword. He flung the carcass into the kiln. The flames hissed and snapped. Without another word, he abruptly turned away, disappearing out of the entrance.

With trembling steps, Sigrid managed to make her way out of the stench and smoke-filled smithy. Darting to the side of the building, she heaved the contents of her stomach into the corner onto the ground. Her breathing came out in short gasps as she wiped away the spittle on her mouth. Tears smarted her eyes, but she refused to let them spill.

Pressing a fist to her chest, she glanced upward. Would the Goddess hear her plea if she asked? Would Odin turn his back on her now that he knew the evil which controlled Finlaggan? Fear tangled like gnarled roots inside her for the first time since her agreement with Godred. Sigrid reasoned her actions were just at the time when she'd given herself to the wretched man. In return, he promised her power to possess what her father would not give her. She thought Godred would be the favored one and an alliance with him would see her reign over Islay.

An agreement which became horrifically wrong.

Sigrid turned and leaned against the stone wall for support. "Oh, Goddess, I have chained myself to one of Loki's beasts and doomed my fate in the jaws of fire."

Chapter Eleven

Shielding his eyes from the weak sunlight fighting the clouds overhead, Steinar stared at the yew tree. Powerful in its stance, the tree welcomed him home in the swaying of branches from the light breeze. Memories from long ago came unbidden to him—ones where harsh words spewed between him and his father, reminding Steinar why he chose to keep his visits brief. Rarely did he stay for long when his uncle demanded his presence. Pain resided here on the hilltop, hidden deep within the roots of the aging tree. Briefly, he closed his eyes, but his father's words and image rang forth inside his mind. He snapped open his eyes, yet the vison persisted, taunting him to relive the day all over again.

Unrest hounded him the moment he stepped forth onto Islay. What did he hope to gain returning to a place filled with anguish? Forgiveness from his father, unattainable. So why did he come to this spot where nothing could be resolved?

He kneaded the sides of his temple with his fingers to ease the torment and slowly closed his eyes again.

"I have entered the Brotherhood and will take my place at Steinn Castle to assist the king," announced Steinar, *keeping his hands clasped behind his back.*

"You would take your place there and not by my side at Finlaggan?" His father gestured out to the ocean. *"Can you not serve the king and your leader here, as I*

have done?"

His look of horror sobered Steinar. "You ken I was meant for the seas. I cannot stay on Islay."

"You might claim to be the Pirate, but this is your home!" his father snapped impatiently. "'Tis not the agreement I made with the seer when you were born on Orkneyjar! To give you freely to the Brotherhood in return for six moons of your time here." He kicked a stone out of his way. "An oath I made in blood!"

"You were not at my birth," corrected Steinar, struggling to keep his voice even.

His father snarled. "Your mother fled north before I could object." He leveled a cold stare at him. "Even her family kept me away."

"Do you blame them?"

"Do not place this shadow of guilt on me," warned his father.

The air grew thick with aggression.

Steinar unclasped his hands and pounded the yew with his fist. "We can stand here all day arguing over my birth, but the truth is, Father, I cannot stay here. You ken this!"

The man's fury rose. "I ken nothing! You come to me with news of departing and expect me to understand. Have I not trained you?" His father pointed out toward the water. "Taught you all you need to learn journeying the oceans? Put your small hand to a tool and showed you how to carve an ancient wolf symbol onto wood? Watched over you when you first shifted from man to beast?"

"For what reason should I stay?" Steinar challenged, anger burning each word that tumbled forth.

His father looked aghast. Holding his arms out

wide, he responded, "This is your home—to rule and remain by my side. 'Tis reason enough."

Steinar laughed bitterly, the sound strange to his hearing. "I am but another MacDougall bastard who shall never rule Finlaggan." He sneered at the man. "Find another son in the village who can rule by your side. My home is out on the water."

The man took a few stumbling steps back. "So you seek to rule the seas, instead of governing with me?" he observed in a hushed voice.

Steinar glanced away at the hurt reflected in his father's eyes. "Nae," he began, "but the truth is bitter to admit. When you die, I can nae longer remain here. As the pact made long ago by Somerled, only a true heir can be gifted Finlaggan." Resuming his gaze on his father, he added, "And you ken I am not the one."

Opening his eyes, he regarded the yew tree before him. Moving forward, Steinar placed his hand on the rough bark, witnessing the damage he'd done many moons ago. "Forgive me, ancient one, for the hurt I caused you." Raising his head, he continued in a voice raw with grief, "Forgive me, Father, for the pain and guilt I settled on you that day. Young, foolish, stubborn—I had much to learn and did so out on the sea." He placed his hand over his heart, trying to ease an ache that continued to haunt Steinar.

The scent of another drifted past him. Lowering his hand, he kept his gaze centered on the yew. Guilt of other actions slammed into him, but he had no regrets. Those of heady, lush kisses. "What do you want, Inga?"

"I did not mean to intrude on your time here, but I thought it best to speak to you right away."

Noting the concern in her tone, Steinar turned

around. "Is something wrong? Who told you where to find me?"

She wiped her hands down her blue overdress. "I followed you to the bottom of the hill. When you remained here for a while, I thought I should come speak with you here privately."

Wariness reflected back at him in those beautiful eyes. Did she regret that night in the stables? All he craved to do was to take her back in his arms. Soothe the conflict.

Nae! Do not be tempted again to take another kiss. Harness your emotions.

He swallowed and moved away from the tree. "Merely making amends from long ago, though I doubt they heard me."

"'Tis a quiet spot for solace," she observed. "Do you speak to those long gone from this world?"

Steinar's troubled mind sought to give her an answer. Would she be content with silence? He blew out a long breath. "Harsh words were spoken long ago between me and my father—here at this tree. I left never making my apologies. Remorse haunts me."

Inga directed her gaze to the tree. She bit her lip, studying the yew. "The tree has a perfect vantage of the sea. Smooth hills give way to jutting ridges and jagged peaks along the coast. This is a serene landscape."

Steering the conversation away from his past, he asked, "Are you here to speak your regrets for what happened in the stables? For I have none." He held his breath, fearing her reply.

"Goodness, no!" she answered in a rush. Heat blossomed like ripe berries on her cheeks.

Relief washed over him. He almost smiled at her

reaction, longing to trail his fingers over her soft skin. "Then explain," he encouraged softly.

Withdrawing a rolled animal skin from beneath the belt on her side, she cradled the item in her hands. "I need you to take a look at this map. We judged it best to leave today on the outgoing tide. With the full moon approaching, the magic will soon be upon us."

Steinar gestured to a patch of grass and wildflowers. "Show me."

Excitement flared over her features. Inga settled beside him on the ground and unfurled the map, weathered from time.

Steinar fingered the edges. "Ancient. Deerskin?"

"Aye," she confirmed. "Sacred and blessed by Odin."

Curious, he pressed, "Can you share how you came into possession of a valuable prize?"

A glint of humor sparked her eyes. "A gift from my mother."

Steinar arched a skeptical brow and drew his hand back. "Who is your mother that she should be granted a rare map of Odin's?"

"A woman you do not want to cross paths with, *ever*." She smoothed the map onto the grass.

Steinar leaned forward, making a note to inquire more about Inga's mother later. "I recognize the isles, except for this smaller one."

"As I explained before, Āsgarthr is a mirror here. Except for this smaller isle which cannot be reached unless you travel around the cauldron of water."

Tracing a finger between Islay and Jura, Steinar proposed, "Why not travel in this direction? We could be there within a day or two."

Inga tapped her finger to a point at the northern isles. "The jaws of a dragon protect the waters near the hidden isle. If we journeyed this way as you suggested, we would be trapped between the cauldron and the dragon."

Frowning in concentration, Steinar studied the map. "Many travel in this fashion, and I have heard nae trouble from anyone on the isles."

Inga swiped at a curl that escaped from her braids. "With the time drawing near, those who dare to cross through shall not succeed," she explained further. "The magic is awakening, and we must be there to claim the treasure, or it will be lost for another ten years." She blew out a breath in frustration. "This area can shift between the two worlds—one of ours and the Gods."

"And your suggestion?" A sliver of unease crept over his skin. To venture into an unknown land, especially one of magic, could prove dangerous to him and the Brotherhood. Each time she shared more, his keen senses detected uncertainty in her. There was more to this treasure than Inga professed.

"We leave Islay for Jura. 'Tis the best route."

He scratched the side of his face. "Nae. Why not cross to Torvay?"

A shadow of annoyance crossed her face. She flicked at a flower on the ground. "'Tis not possible."

Possible? Steinar stewed for a moment. "Torvay is your home, Inga, and directly across from this magical isle."

Quickly rolling up the map, she scooted away from him and stood. "Regardless, I have nae desire to land there."

Rising slowly, he started to grasp her hand but stilled the movement. He stared at her, baffled, trying to force his confused emotions in order. Was this the reason the Serpents spent most of their time in Ireland?

Inga slid him a hesitant glance. "Do not ask any questions."

"Too painful?" he shot back, stunned the words slipped free from him.

With trembling hands, Inga secured the deerskin back beneath her belt. She wiped a hand over her brow.

And Steinar stared at her in waiting silence while his wolf crept closer.

Keeping her sight fixed on the ocean, she began slowly, "On the day my father died, my mother came to counsel me. For you see, she did not live on Torvay. As you ken, my brothers and I are known as the Serpent bastards—though my brothers have the same mother, I have another. My father refused to be chained to any woman and wed neither of them."

"Something we have in common," interjected Steinar, dryly.

A nervous bubble of laughter slipped out of her. "Aye, *aye*. Though I do not hide a wolf within me."

This time, Steinar touched her hand. "Forgive my outburst. Do continue."

Tenderly, she gave him a squeeze and then slipped her fingers free. "Though the day was filled with sorrow when my father died, I thought she would remain with me on Torvay. But nae, a destiny had been forged elsewhere for her *and* for me." Inga withdrew the large stone wrapped around her neck. "Her parting gift of this rare sunstone is all I have left of my mother. On that day, the seas became my home, and Torvay lost to me—a place filled with shadows and sorrow. I have never spoken of the day, except to my brothers. You are the first."

Luminous light danced off the sunstone in an array of colors. He'd seen several in his lifetime, but never required the aid of one. His magic provided guidance on the seas. Yet something about this stone intrigued him. "This is how you navigate. Who now rules Torvay? Leif?"

"Aye to both, though he cannot fully claim the land since he was not made an heir by our father before he died," she acknowledged, sliding the sunstone between the valley of her breasts.

Steinar shifted his stance. "Your brothers accepted you as their leader without complaints?"

Her mouth twitched in amusement. "Not in the beginning. There were days and nights of loud arguments against this decision—mostly between my mother and Leif. My father remained silent." Inga shivered. "My mother can be convincing with her demands, and Leif relented."

More questions tumbled forth from Steinar. "What about the rest of your crew? They appear to take orders from you without resistance."

"They are men from my mother's home," she replied flatly. "They have sworn an oath to her to protect, serve, and honor my commands."

He stared at her in disbelief. *Gods, who is this woman who would doom her daughter to a life on the sea and leader of men, including her own brothers?*

"Did your parents live together?" she asked. When Inga turned toward Steinar, the deeply troubled expression in her eyes tugged at him, and he suppressed the urge to ask where her mother resided.

"Nae," he confessed. "My mother spent most of her

life near Steinn. During her last years, she returned to her home on *Orkneyjar*. In all my time spent with her, I never heard an unkind word about my father pass from her lips, though she heard many from me." He laughed bitterly. "Before her death, she made me vow to mend the rift with my father. Regrettably, I have failed her last request."

"It would seem our parents' actions have inflicted scars on our souls. We are similar, Steinar. Haunted by the past—by destinies we did not foresee or ask to take on. Do you not consider this to be true?"

He mused on her words while listening to the shrill sound of a nearby bird. "I have worn these scars of anger, hurt, and betrayal since I found out about my lineage." He placed two fingers over his heart. "I cannot undo what happened at my birth, but I can be grateful for the path that set me in the direction of the Brotherhood. In my early years, my father did attempt to train me in shifting from man to beast. Nevertheless, the Brotherhood is my home. My family."

Her voice rose in surprise. "Was your father part wolf?"

"Aye, but he served from the isles. His refusal to take his place at Steinn became a tense conflict between him and the king." His mouth pulled into a sour grin. "He never forgave me for leaving Islay and taking my place at Steinn. *Never.*"

She wrapped her arms around her as if she'd become chilled. "Do you believe in fate, Steinar?" Her question barely a whisper.

His gaze returned to the tree. "I make my own destiny. Odin has favored me thus far. But fate? Odin has saved me many times from a watery grave. I have witnessed the Fates weave their thread around others within the Brotherhood, but I do not *believe* they have destined a path for me." He pointed outward. "The sea will always be home. And one day, my entrance to Valhalla."

When she remained silent, Steinar dared to move closer. "Why now? Why me, Inga?"

"*Why?*" she asked softly, turning to face him.

"Why did you share with me about your parents?"

Tears shimmered in her pale eyes. "I grow weary of keeping secrets, nae matter whom I betray. And since you have shared yours, I judged it wise to let you know how my journey led me to become the leader of the Serpents. A destiny forged before I was born between my parents." She placed a protective hand over the map. "With this treasure, I seek to restore much more than wealth. Your aid shall ensure we get through to this mystical isle."

"You mean with my keen insight using magic. What is on this isle beside the treasure?"

A tear slipped down her cheek, and she swiftly wiped away the moisture with her hand. Her voice trembled when she spoke. "A treasure to change a life. A treasure to rule a world. And a treasure to remove the chains. Mine." She reached for his hand. "Please, I beg you, ask me nae more questions. I have put my life in your hands with this knowledge I have shared with you. Will landing on Torvay save us time?"

Steinar drew her hand to his chest. An overwhelming urge to protect Inga surged through him. "Aye."

Raw determination glittered back at him through her tears. "Then Torvay is our destination."

In that moment, Steinar witnessed the change from Inga the Ruthless to Inga the Sorrows and back to the warrior.

The woman was an ever-changing mystery.

One he yearned to solve.

One he vowed to save.

Chapter Twelve

Approaching the great hall, Steinar paused at the entrance. He smiled seeing his friend Gunnar enjoying a game of *hnefatafl* with a young lad. Quickly scanning the rest of the hall, he let out a sigh, grateful for the absence of his uncle. Earlier, he sought out Haaken to inform the crew of their altered plans. Now, he required one more task to complete. He made haste across the hall to the table to finalize his strategy.

Forgive me, Inga.

"Are those the game pieces Magnar carved?" Steinar touched one of the defenders while giving a smile to the lad.

Gunnar coughed to hide his mirth. "He had nae need for them while tending to his new son and wife."

"You *stole* them?" Steinar drew back, gaping at the man. "You do understand these are his favorite. He will not be pleased when he notices they have gone missing."

Padrig chuckled and moved a defender out of the way of Gunnar's king.

Steinar pointed a warning finger at the lad. "There is a lesson here for you."

"Aye," acknowledged Padrig. "Learn the strategy of your enemy by the shift in his eyes and then go for the kill."

"Loki's balls," muttered Steinar. "You are teaching battle tactics to a lad of what?"

"Ten summers," announced Padrig, puffing out his chest with obvious authority.

Gunnar bent his head in an attempt to contain his laughter but failed miserably. His face turned a shade similar to the sweet violets which carpeted the trees in the hills about Finlaggan.

Placing his hands on his hips, Steinar glanced upward. "Should I count to ten in Latin and recite one of your prayers until your humor has subsided?"

Gunnar quickly sobered. "You would mock my God?"

"Aye," he lied, reaching for a jug on the table. Sniffing the contents, he filled an empty cup to the brim.

Gunnar shifted in his chair. "Liar. Your mouth twitched. Though to hear you say a prayer might be—"

"Enough! You ken me too well, old friend." Steinar dragged a chair across the floor near the table and settled beside the man.

Touching one of the pieces on the board, Gunnar frowned in concentration. "You have become quite skilled, Padrig. Let us resume this game after my discussion with Steinar, and you have finished your lessons."

The lad beamed from the praise. "Aye." He jumped up from the table, snatched a bannock from a bowl, and darted away.

"Lessons?" echoed Steinar, taking a sip of ale, and giving a nod to two men leaving the hall.

Gunnar tapped the side of his head with his finger. "Most of the lads here require a sharp mind while in battle. Your uncle considered it wise to have them tutored, along with their daily training in the lists." He folded his arms over his chest and leaned back in the chair. "As I am knowledgeable—"

"Who will teach them after you have left?" Steinar glared at the man over the rim of his cup. When the question was met with silence, he shook his head solemnly. "There is none. The men here are trained in battle, but their minds were not taught like ours."

"Did you ken your uncle has also asked for another request from the king?"

Steinar took another sip of ale and then deposited the cup onto the table. "Beside land in the north? Again, much has transpired here in my absence."

"He has requested someone from the Brotherhood to oversee more training here." Unfolding his arms, Gunnar reached for his cup and swirled the contents. "I believe his first choice would be his nephew—"

Steinar grunted in disgust. "*Never*. My place is out at sea. And my uncle knows this well." He arched a brow. "Since you have done well here, I think *you* should remain."

Gunnar shot him a withering glance. "Finlaggan is not for me. I am assisting for a brief time until recalled back for another task. When you return from whatever quest you are on with the Serpents, I shall take my leave." He downed his ale in one gulp. After setting the cup down, he pushed back from the table.

Steinar held his hand outward to stay his friend's departure. "Let us put aside this conversation for another day. There is another matter I wish to discuss with you—one dealing with the Serpents."

His friend braced his forearms onto the table. "This has nothing to do with your current mission, aye?"

Glancing around the hall, Steinar noted only two other men engaged in a heated discussion over a drinking game. He twisted slightly in his chair and lowered his voice. "I need you to send an urgent message to Magnar."

Understanding his meaning, Gunnar wiped a finger over one of the game pieces. "Raven?"

"Aye, the fastest you can call to make the journey."

The man stretched his shoulders. "What is your message?"

"What is the connection with the Serpents and Odin, specifically, one they call Inga the Ruthless and the identity of her mother? I'm sensing royal blood with ties to a chieftain. Perchance one in Ireland."

Gunnar appeared to study the game board. He flicked away a piece of dried bread near one of the pieces. "Magic surrounds only her. Why is this her given name?"

Steinar gave a leisurely shrug. He had no intention of revealing Inga's leadership yet. "You sensed this within her? The magic?"

"From the moment she stepped into my view. Her weak disguise is a mask for others but not me. My wolf sensed the warrior within her."

"Interesting," observed Steinar, scratching the side of his face. "Took me longer."

Gunnar gave a snort of laughter. "Obviously, you saw other traits in the woman." In a more subdued tone, he added, "Are you troubled?"

Both turned toward the sound of footsteps approaching them.

"All is ready," murmured Haaken.

Steinar reached for the jug of ale. After pouring a small amount into a cup, he handed it to the man. "Make ready the horses. I shall meet you at the south gate. No guards are posted there."

"You could have given me more to drink," Haaken complained and then downed the ale.

Steinar lightly kicked the man's leg. "'Tis an appearance. I ken you've already shared a jug with one of my uncle's guards."

Haaken gave him a wink and placed the cup on the table. "You ken me well."

Steinar watched as the man left the hall. Returning his attention to Gunnar, he leaned forward. "To answer your question, I sense an uneasiness which I cannot explain."

"Where are you heading?" muttered Gunnar.

How he despised lying to his friend. Could he give a partial truth? "I am escorting them back to Torvay."

"And?" A thread of tension echoed from the one word.

Pressing his palms onto the rough wood, Steinar made to stand. He swore an oath to both—Inga and the Brotherhood. He clenched his jaw with the turmoil of indecision.

Yet the oath he swore to the wolf brothers was one given in blood. A vow he could no longer shove aside.

The gravity of what he was about to reveal left a bitter sting of betrayal. Rising fully, Steinar stared at his friend. "I am taking them to a certain *magical* cove—a cove where others have attempted to gain access but have been thwarted by the cauldron of water. As you are aware, my father spent numerous lives and ships searching for this land. I will share more with you on my return."

Gunnar gaped at him like a forlorn fish. He visibly swallowed. "Do you wish me to convey this additional knowledge to Magnar?"

"*Aye.*" Ignoring the knife-sharp coldness slicing through his skin, Steinar made his way quickly out of the great hall.

****

Even though she'd agreed to land on Torvay, regret plagued Inga over her decision. No amount of preparation could soothe the bitterness from long ago. She'd carry the scars until her dying breath.

Inga blew out a frustrated sigh while she shielded her eyes from the intense glare of sunlight dancing off the water. Sea animals glided effortlessly through the water near their ship, and she smiled at their joyful antics. She yearned to reach over the side of the ship and touch their minds with song. The sun's warmth invaded her body but not as much as the man standing next to her on the bow.

She stole a glance at Steinar. His demeanor changed the moment she saw him galloping on his horse onto the shore. After he quickly dismounted, he barely acknowledged her, preferring to give quiet orders to his men. They all agreed he would remain on board with her while Brant would stay on the other ship. With swiftness, they departed Islay, knowing their absence had been witnessed by a few of Rangvald's men.

Hours later at sea, his silence reigned between them like an unwanted companion.

Inga touched the sunstone—more for strength—and lifted her head to the sun. Did Steinar regret their conversation on the hilltop? She frowned, unaware of how she should respond. Never before did a man besiege her with conflict.

"If the Gods and Goddesses continue to favor us

with good weather, we will make Torvay tomorrow." Closing her eyes, she waited for the man to acknowledge her. She'd even welcome an argument over the weather.

When Inga heard him grunt an approval, she snapped open her eyes and glared at him. "Are you unwell or displeased with me?"

He turned around to look directly at her. "Neither."

She dropped her hand to her side. "Then explain your silence or guttural responses to my questions?"

Steinar scrubbed a hand vigorously over his face. "My thoughts are elsewhere."

"Are you worried about the journey we shall face?"

Ignoring her question, he moved his gaze beyond her. "Who is your mother? What clan is she from?"

A tremor of unease rippled over her skin, and she turned away. "Not important to our quest," she lied.

The man stepped into her view. "Then give me her name," he demanded softly.

Shaking her head, Inga chuckled and moved away from him. Settling against the smooth wood of the serpent's back, she tried to quiet her racing heart. What he sought, she could not consent to. Not now. Not ever.

When his shadow loomed near her, Inga fought the overwhelming urge to lay aside her own oaths, her own secrets, along with the one to protect her mother. Inga slid him a sideways glance. "Do not make demands on me, MacDougall."

Her reaction seemed to amuse him. "*MacDougall*?"

"Aye!" she snapped, resuming her gaze on the water.

"Why have I offended you with my request?" he teased, stepping nearer.

Inga arched a brow at the man. "If you come any

closer, Leif might be forced to take a blade to your back."

He smirked. "Surely, I would hear his footsteps. The man lumbers like a bear."

"For the love of the Goddess," she mumbled, trying to keep the smile from forming on her mouth. She could not find fault with Steinar's words and turned toward him.

"Which *Goddess*, Inga?" he whispered.

Inga froze in her actions. Beads of sweat broke out along her brow. His question left her uneasy. "There are many Goddesses in my reference."

"I merely asked for one."

His persistence irked Inga. He poked, prodded until he became content with a response. She grew weary of battling too many emotions. Silence became her chosen weapon against him.

The sail flapped in the strong breeze behind them. One of her brothers spoke of leaping from oar to oar when Torvay came into view, and the other men shouted their approval.

"Choose who shall go first, Inga!" shouted Leif. "'Tis an honor to return to our home after so many moons."

She spared a glance over her shoulder. Was her older brother mocking her? Did he not understand the battle raging inside her? Did he not realize her old wounds had surfaced? *Have you not heard on countless occasions my decision to avoid Torvay? Did I not fully explain my reasonings?*

Leif arched a brow in challenge.

Half-turning, Inga announced, "Jorik will go first. Let those who remained on Torvay witness how strong the youngest man has become."

"By your command." Leif saluted and slapped a hand across his younger's brother back while the other men gathered around them.

Inga detected a hint of disapproval in Leif's tone, but she gave no care. The man had become a legend on the seas, with his skill at trading and in battle. She had no doubt the residents of Torvay had heard many tales of Leif the Bloody Spear.

Steinar leaned his forearms on the edge of the ship's bow. "I have not thanked you for saving me."

Her tense stance relaxed a little. She resumed her position. "Did you not?"

A smile twitched at the corner of his mouth. A mouth she craved to taste again. The memory of their heated kisses burned within her dreams and haunted her in the daylight hours.

"Nae, *nae*. Nevertheless, I owe you a debt for saving me from the clutches of the sea. I ken my time will come—"

"You owe me *nothing*," she rushed out. "The sea is often without mercy, especially near the isles."

Steinar lifted his gaze to meet hers. "The siren's song lures many men in these waters and belongs to only one who controls them. You and your men were brave to fetch me from her icy claws."

Inga shrugged to hide her unease. "I understood what had to be done to save a life."

The man's gaze bore into her as if he could see everything she held locked away within her heart. Shoving away from the bow, Steinar stood directly in front of her. "The Goddess *Rán* will expect payment for a life not taken—one which I deem you already ken."

Inga realized the oaths she made long ago threatened

to shatter like shells against the rocks, and she turned away from him.

Chapter Thirteen

As was his custom, Steinar observed the last sentinel in the sky fade away, giving reign to the rose-tinged light on a new day. A habit he taught himself years ago—to rise with the first evening star and witness its descent come the morning. Though he found little rest on the voyage to Torvay, he uttered a silent prayer to Odin for their continued untroubled journey.

The conversation with Inga repeated throughout his mind during the quiet stillness of the night. After he mentioned the Sea Goddess, the woman quickly left his side and spent the remainder of her time with Helka. An emptiness filled him. Never did he yearn to have another woman with him on a sea voyage—to watch the sun give way to the moon and taste the sea saltiness from her lips. Nae, the women he sought were for pleasurable enjoyments, and brief.

But with Inga, he craved more, leaving him conflicted. Unfocused.

Steinar transferred his position on the cold deck and wiped a hand over his brow. *Why did you flee? Do you also fear the Goddess like me? I should have remained silent. I would have welcomed your company during the long night.*

"The only fear a traveler on the sea should have is uncharted waters," he uttered softly while scrubbing a hand over several days growth of beard.

Rising slowly, Steinar stretched his arms overhead and yawned. Stepping near a barrel of fresh water, he opened the lid and scooped a handful into his parched mouth. Repeating a couple more times, he ended by splashing his face with the freezing water to wake him fully. After closing the lid, he cast his sight on the others. Several men had risen from their slumber and others grumbled with the new dawn after keeping watch during the night. Soon, more would wake and assume their positions or break their fast with whatever food they had brought.

Scanning the deck, Steinar's gaze locked with Inga in the early morning light, bathing her in its glow. He dipped his head in greeting, hoping for an acknowledgement. But before he could witness anything from the woman, Snorri stepped in front of him, blocking his view.

"I sense another fine day," announced the skald.

"Aye," he managed, trying to keep his tone level. Steinar leaned to the side to get a glimpse of Inga who was now engaged in a conversation with one of her brothers. With the moment lost, he crossed to his satchel on the deck. After retrieving a packet of dried fish, he went to the front of the ship.

And Snorri followed.

"Would you care for mead?" offered the man, nudging Steinar with his hand. He presented the small jug outward.

Steinar popped a piece of the fish into his mouth. "Regrettably, I must decline."

Snorri eye's widened in shock. "You decline good mead?"

"I prefer to keep my mind sharp at sea. Nevertheless,

once we land, I shall request your kind offer of drink." Holding out the packet, Steinar urged, "Can I tempt you with dried fish to break your fast?"

"Gladly."

After eating in contented silence, Steinar leaned forward on the bow. His eyes searched the horizon, eager to see a glimpse of Torvay. The skald was correct. The Gods favored them with another day filled with sunlight and no threat of rain.

Smacking his lips in obvious satisfaction of the light fare, Snorri braced his arms on the side of the ship. "I have made a few brief notes about our journey to Islay with you guiding us there. You rode the serpent's back through the fury of the tempest. A true warrior. Not even the Olafssons have managed to stay secure on the back during a storm."

Steinar gave the man a sidelong glance. "We are all warriors on this voyage, regardless of our strengths."

The skald held up a finger. "Not all carry a wolf within them. On this particular journey, I am writing *your* tale."

"Aye," admitted Steinar reluctantly. "I had forgotten."

The man frowned in stern concentration. "If you oppose my—"

"Nae, nae," he reassured, returning his attention out to sea. "Is there anything you'd like to ask me?"

Snorri smacked his hand against the smooth wood. "You honor me. There are questions I have noted on my parchment, but I shall save them after the end of our journey. For now, I am content to observe."

Curious, Steinar half-turned toward the man. "Would it not be wise to write them down as they occur?

Or is your mind able to recall all the details?"

The skald laughed loudly. After quickly recovering, he explained, "Before dusk, I offer a prayer to Odin for another day I am allowed to remain here. Afterward, I write down what I have witnessed." He tapped a finger along the side of his head, and then to his heart. "The events are recorded in my mind, but I weave the tale from my heart."

"Will you permit me to read this saga?" asked Steinar, returning his attention to the water.

"When the time comes for us to part, I shall read the tale of my travels with the Pirate Wolf. If you find fault in my words, I will burn the account and scatter the ashes into the ocean."

Astonished by the skald's confession, Steinar looked at the man. "I have already heard the tales of the Icelander. You are honoring me with your account on this journey. I cannot find fault in a tale which is based on truth."

Snorri nodded slowly. He took a long draw of mead from the jug. After wiping his mouth on the sleeve of his tunic, he pointed outward. "Torvay beckons."

The southern tip of the isle jutted toward them in greeting. Shaped like a crescent moon, Torvay held a beauty unlike the other islands. Nestled deep in the green verdant hills, sprang forth a lush waterfall. Steinar recalled how his mother spoke of this place from a cousin who'd visited long ago.

Steinar inhaled fully and then exhaled. "Was Inga born on Torvay?"

"Unsure," responded Snorri, setting the jug on the bottom of the deck. "But I do ken she is not fond of returning. Even Helka advised her to stay on board and find another passage. Or to let her brothers search for the treasure without her."

"Inga would never abandon the hunt to her brothers," retorted Steinar, rubbing his hand down the back of his neck.

The skald belched into his fist. "You are correct in your observations of Inga."

"What else can you share with me about this warrior woman?"

Snorri sighed heavily. "A tale I am unable to recount. Your questions are for her."

Curious, Steinar pressed, "Are you not writing the tale of the Serpents?"

The man chewed on his bottom lip as if finding his words. "Aye, you are partially correct. I am writing about the Olafssons. Before we set sail, early on our travels, I made a bargain not to discuss Inga the Ruthless in my accounts. Her story is for another, so I was told."

Looking over his shoulder, Steinar let his gaze center on Inga. Her rigid profile told him everything. Even her features had turned pale. She didn't dislike returning to Torvay. Nae, the fear rolled off her in waves toward him. His hands clenched, fighting the urge to cross the distance and take her into his arms to banish the uncertainty.

Steinar contemplated if the shieldmaiden would permit his offer of comfort.

****

Inga pressed a fist against her racing heart. Torvay loomed before her, mocking her with its beauty—a beauty which held a secret. Tears smarted her eyes, so she settled them away from the land and on another. Steinar—solid, strong, a refuge to the memories threatening to slip through her mind when she'd step onto its shore.

The man smiled and held out his hand as if he understood her torment. Unable to wait a moment longer or struggle with what her brothers thought, Inga managed to cross the deck without stumbling over her steps.

Returning his smile, she clasped his warm hand and marveled at the strength of his grip. He gently tucked her hand in the crook of his arm. His warmth seeped into her skin, allowing some tension to ease from her shoulders.

He kept his gaze steady on the approaching shore. "Did you ken I always look at Islay the same when I return to the isle?"

Startled by his confession, she looked down at the waves lapping against the side of their ship, hoping to see her reflection in the water. Were her emotions splayed across her face for all to see? Or was it only Steinar who witnessed the uneasiness in her? As a trained warrior, she'd learned long ago to harness any display of unwelcome feelings. "Obviously, I am unable to contain my reaction to seeing Torvay." She tried and failed to keep the bitterness from her tone.

Steinar sighed. "'Tis not a sign of weakness to display your apprehension. Whatever caused you pain cannot be resolved by hardening the feelings. With any warrior, we battle conflicts. Some are manageable. Others haunt us to our dying breath."

Inga gave out a nervous laugh. "Are you sure you're not a seer or a druid?"

He turned toward her. A glint of wonder shown in his eyes. "My mother had a cousin who was a druid."

She squeezed his arm. "There you have it. Another

admirable quality within you."

Steinar drew away from her, chuckling softly. "You are mistaken."

"Are you saying you're not honorable or wise?"

His expression stilled and grew series. "Honor is the code that binds me to my wolf, and the Brotherhood. As for being wise? Ask me again in twenty years."

Inga's eyes widened in surprise. "So the Gods will favor you with so many more?"

The man shrugged. "I have not recently asked."

She gasped, dropping her hand from his arm. Inga stewed for a moment. "Do you mock them?"

"Never," he conceded quietly. "Though, I do speak with them each morning and at dusk."

"You are a good man, Pirate Wolf."

Steinar grimaced. "Many would disagree with you." In one swift move, the man removed his tunic. After rolling up the garment, he tucked it against her arms. "Return this to me once you are on the shore."

Inga drew in a sharp breath and grasped the tunic. "Where are you going?"

The corner of his mouth tipped upward. "For a swim to the shore. 'Tis not far and I need to cool my body." Leaning near her, he whispered, "If there was nae one here, I would ask you to join me." He gave her a wink before slipping over the edge of the ship with a resounding splash into the water.

Clutching the tunic against her chest, Inga studied the man with each stroke he made toward land. Steinar was all hard lines. Tall, broad-shouldered, and corded with lean muscle. A ripple of heat trembled through her, and she found herself unable to look away. The man belonged to the sea as surely as she did.

Bringing his tunic to her face, she dared to inhale the man's heady scent—primal, intoxicating—his own special blend of male.

Helka approached quietly by her side. "You now ken the man is the one, aye?"

Inga kept her sight on Steinar until he reached the shore. "Aye," she finally confessed.

"To destroy or save you?" asked the woman, leaning forward.

She gave the woman a tight smile. "I fear both, and there is nothing I can do to prevent the outcome. I have fought against the visions and all the signs. I can nae longer ignore them. I am prepared to meet my fate. He is the man destined for me."

Boisterous laughter resounded behind them. Inga glanced sideways. Three men, including Jorik, stripped and dove overboard. Her brothers appeared happy to have returned home. Pushing aside her distress, Inga presented a smile and waved at those who caught her gaze.

Helka rapped her knuckles against the wood. "Are you ready for the greeting from the people, especially the wise women who are loyal to the Goddess and also tend to her temple?"

After giving the woman a quick nod, Inga went to her satchel. She needed to steel her emotions. Removing her silver armbands, she carefully secured them on the upper part of both her arms. She traced a finger along the etched symbols. "For the people of Torvay. For you, Father. For you, Mother." She quickly stashed Steinar's tunic within and slung the satchel over her right arm.

When they reached the shore, Inga was the first to climb down the ladder. Her first step onto the land she'd left moons ago left her unsteady. She breathed in the salt-tinged air and turned to greet the crowd. Children rushed forward, kneeling at her feet with flowers pressed inside their tiny hands. Murmuring words of welcome, they stood and trailed the flowers in a circle around her. Choking back the tide of emotions, Inga touched each one lightly on the cheek in greeting. They swiftly scampered away.

The elder women beckoned her forward. Inga proceeded and pressed a fist over her heart while she made her way across the sand to them.

"Daughter of the sea, you have returned home," proclaimed one of the women. Her gray hair hung in soft braids down to her waist as she made her way to Inga. Lifting a necklace made of tiny seashells suspended from a leather cord from around her neck, she held it outward. "Time to reclaim what you left behind."

Unable to stop the swell of stinging tears in her eyes, Inga allowed them to slip down her cheeks. She dropped the satchel onto the sand. Placing a hand over the weathered and old fingers of the woman, she said, "Nae, Eira, I cannot claim what is not mine."

"You gave this to me on the day you left Torvay. Do you not recall our parting words?" challenged Eira. "Upon your return, I would place this necklace you granted me back in your hands."

"I can see the years have not dimmed the fire in you, Eira."

The woman snickered. "Not even my husband tells me what to do."

Inga smiled while brushing away the moisture on her cheeks. "If I recall, nae one makes demands of you."

Eira laughed, exposing a few missing teeth. Yet the

beauty of the woman shone like the stars on a clear night.

Clasping her hands in front of her, Inga shook her head. "My stay on Torvay is brief. Keep the shells as a way of remembering me."

The woman's good humor vanished. Sadness engulfed her features but only briefly. She lifted her chin. "One day you will stop running away, Inga, daughter of Olaf and—"

Inga gently placed a finger against the woman's lips. "Do not speak my mother's name, even in my presence." Removing the seashell necklace from Eira's hands, Inga placed it back over the woman's neck. "For now, this belongs to you."

"You have honored her but have forgotten where you belong," whispered Eira. Taking each of Inga's hands, the woman placed a kiss over her knuckles. "When you are ready, come visit us at our fires this evening and meet the other women who will be initiated as priestesses."

Before Inga had a chance to respond, the woman dropped her hands and rushed over to embrace Helka. Seeing this as her chance of escape, Inga retrieved her satchel and slipped away.

Leif approached, keeping steady strides with her. "They have missed you—us."

Shifting the satchel over her shoulder, she disagreed, "Returning to Torvay is difficult. Even six years cannot banish the bitterness of what happened to me."

He clucked his tongue in disapproval. "You were sixteen summers. Too young to accept learning about your heritage."

"I was a shieldmaiden."

"Not yet. Twelve months training with the warrior

women on Skye does not command all knowledge, Inga."

She snorted in disgust. "I should have been told sooner. Or not at all."

Her brother grabbed her arm, halting her progress. "How long will you carry this lodestone of fury."

Inga tried to shirk free from her brother's hold. "Release me," she gritted out.

"How *long*?" Leif's grasp tightened further.

"Until my bones are scattered in the sea," she snapped, more furious with herself. She'd tried to bury the angst of the past, but the emotions surged forth at unexpected times. All her training could not banish the anger and hurt simmering inside her, no matter the distance or time. She dropped her satchel by the base of a tree.

"You have not embraced who you are, Inga."

Inga gazed into her brother's eyes and swallowed. "Because nae choice was presented to me. I am a pawn between the Gods and Goddesses."

Releasing his hold, he smiled while placing his hands on her shoulders. "Then find a way to free the chains and take control of your journey." He looked beyond her. "You have already taken the first step."

She frowned, confused over his declaration. "I do not understand your meaning."

Leif turned her around to face a certain man standing with the others. "You defied everyone when you fetched the MacDougall from the sea. Make your choices for *your* destiny. We shall always support you."

She bit her lower lip. "What if they are wrong? What if my *choices* bring about my downfall? Or yours? I have read the runes *and* seen the visions."

He squeezed her shoulders. "A portent of one possibility. As you ken, I do not always favor, nor follow what the runes show me."

Smiling slowly, Inga murmured, "You are wise beyond your years, Brother."

Leif's brow knitted. "I ken we have guarded your secret all your life, but if your quest is with the MacDougall, then you are honor-bound to explain everything."

Inga snorted. "My mother will not be pleased."

Her brother dropped his hands. "Make your choice and stand firm, regardless of the outcome."

Chapter Fourteen

The skald hastily made his way through the crowd of people to Steinar while doing his best to give a few quick words of greeting to those he passed by. When the man's steps led him closer, Steinar relieved him of the jug of mead and proceeded to drink deeply. Though the heat from his wolf banished the chill from his bones, he welcomed the warmth of the liquid coursing a path of fire down his throat. After handing the jug back to the man, Steinar gave a quick nod of appreciation and watched the skald amble off to join the others.

As Steinar studied the people of Torvay—a varied mix of young and old with several children dashing around along the shore—he searched for their leader. Was this all who remained here? Who supplied strength and protection? The tiny island had managed to remain safe from the clutches of Norway, Scotland, and his grandfather—Somerled.

"A strange land," he whispered, folding his arms over his chest.

Glancing outward, he noted his own men had left the ship, eager to stretch their limbs. Ulrik waved in greeting while making long strides toward him.

Steinar stepped away from the group of people, crossing to a quieter spot.

Ulrik placed a hand on his hip, keeping his focus on the men. "Any orders?"

He chuckled softly. "I suppose the men could use a night of rest."

The man's eyes glinted with mischief. "*Rest*?"

"Do not seek women to comfort your bed. Not here," warned Steinar.

"And if they seek mine?"

Steinar looked beyond the man, catching the gaze of a certain woman. "Let us complete our mission and return to Islay. Your conquests can wait."

"Aye, aye. I shall tell the others." Ulrik wiped a hand across his nose. "Is there anything else? Do you sense danger here?"

Steinar smirked, returning his attention to the man. "There is *always* danger when we are wary of any quest. I am uncertain who leads this group of people."

"Even when Olaf controlled Torvay, nae one dared attempt to capture the island." Ulrik shifted his stance, allowing a small crab to make its way back to the water. "They say Torvay is cursed."

Steinar arched a questioning brow. "Cursed *or* feared? The Gods appear to favor this land. Have you learned anything in your time with Brant?"

Ulrik sighed heavily. "I'll be content when we are done with the Serpents. The man talks constantly, even when he slumbers."

"And here I assumed you made an ally with Brant. 'Tis always a good plan to listen to words spoken while your foe rests. Did you acquire any information?"

"Nae. Only that he enjoys his ale, women, a good battle, and asks too many questions about *you*. He and his brothers are suspicious of your wolf." He spat on the ground in obvious disgust. "But he challenged me to a drinking game after the feast tonight. If I bloody his mouth, he might be silent for the duration of our journey."

Narrowing his eyes, Steinar lowered his voice. "Those who have heard about the wolves are always cautious. 'Tis merely respect mixed with fear. Just remember, Brant has three more brothers, *and* a warrior sister."

"An even greater trial, though I'll leave you to challenge the *sister*."

"I do not understand your meaning," Steinar lied.

"You look at the woman as if you want to devour her in one bite."

Furious to have been watched so closely, Steinar snapped in cold sarcasm, "Your attention should be elsewhere and not on me."

Ulrik shrugged slightly. After giving Steinar a wink, he hastily made his way toward the other men from the ship.

Once again, Steinar resumed his gaze on Inga. A definite change occurred within her, especially when the women greeted her. Was she a part of the wise women who honor the Goddess of the sea here on Torvay? Shielding his eyes from the glare of the early afternoon sun, he whispered, "What leaves you so tormented, Inga?"

He pinched the bridge of his nose in frustration. "Soon we will be parted and nae longer my concern." Yet the words sounded hollow to him, and the reality of the truth blinded him.

Steinar yearned to learn everything about Inga.

Blowing out a soft curse, he departed the area where laughter and conversation flowed, making long strides toward the woman. A dog barked in greeting at him when he dashed around Steinar to join the others' merriment. Smiling, he continued up along a narrow path, littered with small stones and seashells until he reached his destination.

Inga's eyes widened when he halted merely inches before her.

"You were greeted warmly by the people here," he mentioned, clasping his hands behind him.

"Why would they not?" she shot back, shifting her stance, but did not move away from him.

"Simply an observation, considering your distress on wanting to land on Torvay."

Pursing her lips, she explained, "My *distress* is over my parents, not the people who dwell here."

"Your father is dead, and your mother nae longer lives on Torvay?" he asked quietly.

Inga nodded in acknowledgment.

"Who rules Torvay for Leif while you travel the seas?"

"Leif can never fully rule this island," she corrected hastily. "The elders have a set of edicts which were set in place by my father." She clenched her fist. "He should have made the leadership and his heir official by announcing Leif. Nevertheless, death took him before he made any declaration who would succeed him. I am certain the elders would appoint Leif if he desired to remain here and sought permission. But Leif refuses. 'Tis often an intense argument between us and our brothers." She tucked a strand of hair behind her ear. "Leif can be as stubborn as a boar's ass."

He grimaced in good humor. "I can understand your brother's dilemma. 'Tis one I share. You should not be so harsh with him."

Inga glowered at him. "At least you have an uncle who manages Islay! These people survive on their own with aid from others on nearby islands. Trade has always come easy here, and with the land rich for farming and fishing, Torvay survives. But as each year passes, the younger ones leave for the mainland or Norway."

"They seek adventures," he admitted softly, understanding why they would wish to seek lands beyond their homes.

Wiping a hand over her brow, she argued, "And leave the aging without help."

Steinar yearned to see a smile form on those lips, and to soothe away her frown with his fingers. Probing Inga with more questions about her kin would only stir her anger further. He wanted no more arguments between them. No more conversations about responsibilities not taken.

He coughed into his hand. "You have something of mine, or do you prefer to stare at my chest in front of everyone?"

Inga visibly swallowed, taken aback by his question. "I…I am *not* staring." She waved her hand outward over his shoulder. "There are other men without their tunics as well."

Always challenging my words, Inga. He bent his head near her ear. "Then what would you call your lingering gaze while I stood on the shore with the others? And trust me, your focus was on me."

Her cheeks turned red. "'Tis a strong chest, and I have a fascination with the markings on your back," she answered in a rush.

Steinar drew back and raised a brow in amusement. "The *markings* denote the wolf is protected. He is surrounded by the runes, which are symbols of water."

Inga nodded slowly in understanding. The warmth of her smile echoed in her voice. "You are a warrior for Odin. The runes protect the beast." Placing her hands on his shoulders, she added, "And the man. You are marked with the protection from the God, Odin."

The blood pounded in his veins from her slightest touch. No one ever understood their meaning. They simply assumed the runes were a part of his journey on the water. To keep him safe as he did his work for the Brotherhood and the king. He pointed behind her. "My tunic?"

Her smile faded a little. "Aye," she mumbled, turning around.

He noted her shaky movements while she fumbled inside her satchel. Steinar fought the urge to grasp her hands and return them to his shoulders. Silently waiting for her to retrieve his garment, he tried to cast his sight in another direction. Anywhere to cool the heat in his blood whenever she happened near him. No matter how hard he fought, the battle to harness his emotions started ebbing away.

"Here." Inga pressed the tunic against his chest, lingering for a moment. Her fingers seared a path over his skin, sending additional tremors of fire down his body.

For the love of the Gods! Hastily, he slipped the tunic over his head. "What is beyond the path hidden within the trees?"

Moving past him, Inga shoved aside several tree branches to give him a clearer view of the landscape. "Beyond the dip in the meadow and upward, are the standing stones dedicated to the Goddess of the sea.

Hundreds of years ago, the women of Torvay had the men place the stones in a crescent to face the water. The view from there is stunning on a clear night."

Steinar could barely see the top of the stones from where he stood. "Will you show me this place tonight?" The words tumbled free without thought.

Wariness reflected in her eyes, and she dropped her hand. "We should discuss our plans for the best route to the magical isle, aye? Tomorrow we set out for the Cove of Gríma."

Steinar hesitated, torn by conflicting emotions. She was correct. Study the best route, get the treasure, and leave. There can be nothing between them. "You are correct," he clipped out, irritation seeping into his response. "I would like to study the map again. I want to chart out a path around the dangerous waters. Furthermore, I have questions regarding the images on the map circling the cauldron."

Her brow knitted in concentration. "We thought them not important. Even Helka is unsure of their meaning. Possibly, they are scratches made by Odin to confuse any who seek the treasure?"

"I have seen those images before in the ancient texts at the Brotherhood. But I'll need to look at the map again to be certain. In all my studies, Odin doesn't resort to deception. That role is for Loki."

Her eyes widened. "Of course. Any wisdom you can offer would be welcomed."

Another thought occurred to him. "How many have viewed this map?"

Inga tipped her face to the sparse sunlight filtering through the branches overhead. "Only my brothers and Helka." She resumed her attention back to him. "Are you worried about the other men? As I have stated before, I can assure you all on my ship are loyal to me."

He gave her a slight smile. "A question requiring an answer. Nothing more."

As he turned to leave, Inga surprised him by reaching for his hand. Her fingers intertwined with his, strong and steady. "Do you really want to see the stones at night?"

He shrugged to hide his confusion. Did she battle with feelings like he did?

Inga tilted her head to the side. "Aye or nae?"

Uncertainty clawed at him. He ruled his life with his mind, not from feelings over a woman. To surrender meant losing control. Losing himself in emotions was foreign to him. *You can't even fathom what those feelings are.*

"I am just as conflicted as you," she admitted, squeezing his hand. "Or am I wrong?"

Steinar slammed the door on his uncertainty and tossed aside the struggle. With his decision now made, he drew her closer. Bringing their joined hands closer, he flipped her hand over. Slowly, he lowered his mouth and pressed a kiss along the vein in her wrist. Her indrawn gasp surrounded him. Lifting his head, he stared into her jeweled eyes. Lust shimmered back at him, mirroring his own desire.

"I desire you like nae other, Inga. Does this answer your question?" He stroked the vein with his thumb, and she trembled under his touch.

She licked her bottom lip. "I am unsure. You will have to convince me."

"By the hounds." On a low growl, Steinar pulled her through the trees. Aware they could still be seen, he wanted no witnesses to what he was about to do. Grateful for her silence and submission, he continued to follow the path through the dense trees. When he reasoned they were far from prying eyes, he grasped Inga around the waist and crushed her to his chest.

Her lips parted on a gasp, and he required no further invitation. He covered her mouth hungrily, devouring what she had to offer. Taking her moan deep into him, Steinar glorified in the sensation of her mouth—one filled with a honeyed sweetness mingled with the sea. When he attempted to break free, she returned his kiss with another in reckless abandonment.

Her kiss shattered Steinar's senses and tossed him into a stormy sea of pleasure. Unable to be gentle, his kiss became demanding—burning with need. He craved everything from Inga. His lips seared a course down her neck, to her throat, and then recaptured the velvet warmth of her mouth.

When she rocked against the hard length of his cock, Steinar let out a feral growl. With his restraint slipping, he tore his mouth away from hers.

"*Nae*," she protested.

Steinar gripped her chin, stroking her bottom lip with the pad of his thumb. His gaze roamed over her features, flushed from their heady kisses. "We must cease, or I shall strip what little clothing you have on and thrust deep into your soft flesh."

Inga bit down on his thumb, igniting his blood further. "Will it stop the aching need?"

"*Aye*," he rasped out. He pinned her arms to the sides of her body and backed her against a tree. Nudging apart her legs with his knee, Steinar settled his body between her thighs. She whimpered as he trailed a path with his tongue from the soft spot below her ear to along her neck. He pressed his lips to her throat and felt the wild beat of her pulse, and then bit down.

"What do you want from me?" he demanded against the warmth of her skin. "Is it to show me the stars *or* to lie with me beneath them?"

Inga moaned, tossing her head to the side. "Can I have both?"

Releasing his hold on her, Steinar's hands roamed intimately over her breasts. "Are you certain, Inga? Will you be content with one night under the stars?"

Pressing her palm to his cheek, she confessed softly, "I grow weary of wanting you—fighting this longing. I will give myself to you, Pirate Wolf. If all we have is one night, I shall not grieve our parting. For all we ken, our destiny might land us at the bottom of the ocean in our attempt to cross around the cauldron."

"*Inga.*" His tongue traced a path over her full lips before reclaiming her mouth.

Slowly, he raised his mouth from hers and took a step back. "When the moon starts her climb into the night sky, leave the feasting. I will follow shortly thereafter."

After giving him a seductive smile of promises yet to be fulfilled, she slipped back through the trees.

Steinar remained rooted to the ground, unable to think of anything but her. He desired her more than the treasure they sought. And this frightened him.

Raising his head to the cloudless sky, Steinar blew out a frustrated breath. "Oh, Gods, I fear one night with Inga will not be enough for me."

Chapter Fifteen

With each inhale, crisp air poured into Inga's body while she made her way steadily to the sounds of joyous celebration. The scent of woodsmoke brought a promise of a warm welcome and food, as her steps hastened over the leaf-filled path.

Food, drink, and Steinar.

Inga tugged on the sleeves of her gown. One of the younger women had gifted her with a stunning gown in pale green, woven with threads of silver and white from the waist and along the bottom of the garment, reminding her of sea foam.

Earlier, a hot bath had been prepared for her at one of the small stone and wood dwellings. At first, she'd refused the honor. Nevertheless, by the time the wooden tub had been filled, Inga eagerly stripped her clothing and basked in the warm water. A soap blended with crimson moss and wildflowers, along with a sea salt scrub were provided for her—a gift from the wise women. Helka had unbound her braids and brushed out her hair until it shone, leaving the copper mass to hang down below her waist. After adjusting her silver armbands, Inga proceeded to walk alone to the feasting.

Ancient trees shrouded the longhouse, shielding it from unwelcome visitors. As she passed the last tree, the Serpent's crest appeared like a beacon above the doors to the great longhouse. Inga paused in her observations.

Strange how she never gave any thought to the engravings carved into the wooden disk—one of a serpent, dragon, and a wolf.

Until this moment.

She leaned against one of the pine trees for support, recalling her father's words.

Inga ran her small fingers over the images engraved into the wood. "Why do you add the dragon and wolf, Father? They are not who we are?"

Her father's brow furrowed while he blew away bits of wood to reveal more of his handiwork. "They are the destiny surrounding us and Torvay."

"How?" she asked, looking around her. "Does a wolf or dragon come to eat us?"

Chuckling softly, he explained, "The serpent resides with us, with you. The dragon maintains order on Scotland for the Dragon Knights, and the wolf..." He dropped his small carving blade onto a tree stump. Kneeling down beside Inga, he took her hand and placed her palm against her chest. "The wolf guards the sea and land. One day, the wolf will guard you and Torvay."

Inga drew her hand away. "The serpents control the sea. Wolves are not welcomed on the water."

"According to the seer, a wolf will govern the seas as mightily as your mother and me."

Her eyes blazed with fury and anger heated her words. "Surely mother can banish the wolf to the deep ocean. He belongs on the land and not on our seas. Her magic is stronger than a seer's knowledge."

Rising slowly, her father fisted his hands on his hips and glared at Inga. "Never choose to align yourself with magic to solve a problem, Inga. Even a seer's vision can be more powerful than the Gods and Goddesses. And your mother understands this to be true."

Inga swallowed. "But mother teaches me every day to honor—"

"Nae! Do not be swayed by her words." He tapped his knuckles on top of her head. "Learn to think for yourself. Trust your wisdom. Do not follow what others have commanded you to do and think. Do you understand, Inga?"

She lowered her head and nodded solemnly.

"I did not hear you!"

Raising her head to meet her father's intense stare, she affirmed, "Aye!"

Inga blew out a long breath she'd been holding. "Where were you a year ago when I needed you, Father? You left this world far too soon."

Shoving away from the tree, Inga continued along the path. She paused at the entrance of the double oak doors, taking in the sights, sounds, and aromas teasing her senses. Tables, chairs, and benches had been positioned around the huge fire in the center of the room. Candles set in wrought iron holders hung suspended from the high wooden beams, bathing the area in a soft golden light. She smiled as several lads were playing a game with small stones and shells near the fire with Jorik—a game he'd mastered at his young age.

Brant had captured the attention of one of the women, assisting her with positioning jugs of ale and mead on the tables. Her smile grew, seeing his expression change from hardened warrior at sea to a light-hearted and relaxed man.

In a wry twist of fate, Inga had forgotten the joy she'd once experienced on Torvay. Forgotten the people who moved with the tides of the ocean. Forgotten the happiness she'd known growing up here. An island with people who were simple, fierce, and loyal, and who understood how precious each day meant to them.

The sea's salty brine had seeped into Inga and her brothers' skin, crusting their emotions, and sealing off any who sought to invade their hearts.

Heavy footsteps pounded the ground behind her. Though tempted to sneak a glance over her shoulder, she clasped her hands in front of her.

"Are you waiting for an invitation?" Leif took his place on her left. His eyes danced with mirth.

"Admiring the scene before me," she confessed softly with a smile.

"By the Gods," exclaimed Balder coming to stand on her other side. "You look beautiful."

She snapped her mouth shut, stunned by her brother's bluntness.

"This is a first," teased Leif, leaning forward to look at his brother. "You have shocked our little sister into silence."

Balder smirked, brushing a hand through his light beard. "Don't you mean, *our leader*?"

Regaining her composure, Inga held up her hand. "Enough." She bowed slightly to Balder. "I thank you for the praise."

"Let us join the others," suggested Leif.

Inga motioned for them to proceed. "Give me a few moments."

Her brothers smiled in unison and strolled inside.

Inga stepped aside to allow others to enter. Her gaze traveled throughout the longhouse—to those speaking quietly in corners, and others sharing food at the tables, and along the second floor. Even with so many inside,

Inga searched to find the one man she sought. While the sun slipped below the horizon, the shadows of dusk fell around her.

Even though you are a maiden, stop acting like one. Steinar will appear when he is ready.

Before she took her first step, a prickle of another teased her senses from behind. Slowly, she glanced over her shoulder. The last glimmer of light engulfed the man. Inga stared wordlessly at him, her heart pounding. She could scarcely breathe from wanting him so much.

Steinar approached at a leisurely pace. Reaching for her hand, he placed a kiss inside her palm, and then released his hold. "I am pleased to see you have unbound your hair."

Her mouth dropped open, and then she quickly snapped it shut. "My hair?"

"Have my words offended you?" he asked, studying her.

Composing herself, she responded, "Not at all. I am not accustomed to all this praise for my appearance. First, my brother, then you."

Steinar placed a firm hand on her lower back. "You are a vision, Inga. A woman whose beauty rivals even the Goddesses."

She choked on her laughter. "There are a few Goddesses who would disagree with you."

His eyes danced with mischief. "Let them challenge me."

Inga lightly pressed a finger against his lips. "Do not tease them. You could stir their wrath."

Steinar's good humor vanished. "For tonight, let us put aside our fears. I have nae desire to argue over offending a God *or* Goddess."

She mused over his words, uncertain how he'd feel when he discovered the truth. "Nae fears," Inga whispered.

Allowing Steinar to guide her inside, she went to the table positioned at the far end of the hall. Leif was engaged in a lively discussion with Ulrik and two other men. She drew comfort in the ease of those gathered.

Inga sat in the chair Steinar offered. She inclined her head to a woman passing by with a trencher filled with breads and reached for a jug of mead. Glancing around the table, she looked for an empty cup or two.

Steinar settled himself next to her. "Should we drink from the jug?" he teased.

"The mead is excellent. I have never seen such a welcome, even from your uncle," interrupted Haaken from across the table.

"Nor I," affirmed Steinar, and reached for Haaken's half-finished cup of mead and downed the remainder. "You are correct!" He licked the moisture from his lips.

Haaken roared with delight. Rising from the table, he looked in all directions. "Let me fetch you a cup."

"'Tis good to see your men enjoying themselves," remarked Inga, reaching for a couple berries from a bowl. She popped them into her mouth, savoring their sweetness.

Steinar nodded slowly. "The people here have welcomed them—*me* warmly. Truthfully, 'tis good to see you relaxed and smiling."

"There is a fierce pride and loyalty on Torvay," she began, "which binds these people."

"Tell me," he encouraged, softly.

"Not yet." Inga grasped his hand under the table. "Let us enjoy this moment, this night."

Placing her hand on his thigh, his thumb caressed her skin. "Trust me, I shall enjoy tasting you, *my kærr*."

Heat speared a path from her face to between her thighs. Steinar's words of endearment pierced through Inga's shields, straight to her heart. Before she had a chance to respond, Haaken came darting through the crowd shouting to those to step clear from his path, while he carried two oxhorns, each filled to the brim with mead.

When he stood before them, he graciously handed her the first one. "For Inga the Ruthless."

"My thanks," she acknowledged, taking the oxhorn. She sipped slowly, enjoying the warmth of the liquid and the man seated next to her.

Steinar accepted his drink with a nod of appreciation. He leaned near her. "I must confess, the men make a fine mead here. We should take a jug with us tonight."

Inga sputtered on the liquid causing her to cough loudly.

"Did Inga get a bad cup of mead?" shouted one of the men at another table.

The crowd roared for someone to find her another oxhorn and refill it with more.

A young lad quickly accepted the task. Yet Inga dismissed him with a wave of her hand when he neared the table and directed the lad to give the oxhorn to someone else.

"I can tell by your response you are in agreement about tonight?" His breath was warm against her neck.

She fought the urge to place her hand against her cheek to cool the fire within.

After several moments, Inga dared to slide a glance

at Steinar. His heated gaze bore into hers. "Stop looking like you want to devour me," she whispered, and then quickly averted her attention to the oxhorn in her grasp. "And I'd advise you to give your praise to the women, specifically the priestesses. They are the ones responsible for the delicious mead you are enjoying."

"Truth?"

Inga smiled. "Aye." She took a sip while looking at him over the rim of her oxhorn.

"They must share their secret with me," Steinar urged with a glint of wonder in his eyes.

"Never. Even I do not ken all the special ingredients or the precise method they use."

He arched a brow in amusement. After finishing all of his drink, Steinar placed the oxhorn onto the table. "I can be *verra* persuasive."

"Nae matter your charms, they will not work on these women." Tempted to lick the droplets from his lower lip, she clenched the oxhorn tighter.

Steinar's hand came to rest on her thigh. "Until you have experienced my charms, do not be so quick to judge."

Sweet Goddess! The heat from his touch seared straight to her core, leaving Inga without a retort. She pondered if Steinar should be given another name besides pirate. The man slipped beneath her skin, shattering every defense she'd built over the years.

In one long gulp, Inga drained the rest of her mead.

****

With each sway of the ship, Godred's lips curled in disgust. Though the hour late, he managed to make out the distant land markings of Torvay. He clenched his fists into balls of fury, eager to strike out at any man who crossed his path on the deck. As the hours bled into the next, his impatience grew. The spy he'd sent to gather information had yet to return, and he strained to see any sign of the man.

However, his anger remained directed at one man. Steinar MacDougall.

Have you acquired an allegiance to the Serpents? What do you seek to gain? War against your uncle? Interesting...

Unclenching his hands, he placed them on the rough wooden edge of the bow, determined to fathom this new alliance. A chill breeze drifted over him, but this did little to sway him from his thoughts.

Why not remain on Islay and take what your uncle has spoken to you about? Islay is yours for the asking.

Godred dug his nails into the wood.

"Why?" he bellowed, turning away.

One of his men dared to scurry forth. "Do you require something?"

Without thought, Godred backhanded him. The man staggered from the blow, clutching his jaw. "Did I not warn you to stay clear of my wrath? I am charting a direction and require silence!"

The man placed his hand over the hilt of his sword.

"Are you challenging me, Declan?"

"Nae." He pointed outward. "Michael returns."

Godred swept his attention to the small boat bobbing with the waves toward them. "Thank the Gods," he muttered. Cracking his knuckles, he moved away from the bow to greet his trusted friend.

"Lower the ladder," Godred ordered, making steady strides to the middle of the ship. Waiting for his order to be concluded, he let out a yawn. Relief coursed through him, hoping the man had gained valuable information.

Once Michael slipped on board, the other men secured the small vessel to the side of their ship and raised the ladder.

"Fetch some ale," commanded Godred.

The man dismissed the offer with a slash of his hand. "I've had my fill of good mead this evening."

Godred quirked his eyebrow questioningly. "You drank with the men? Or did you resort to thieving?" He peered over the side of the ship. "Did you bring back any?"

Michael raked a hand through his hair. "None in the small boat. They all thought me to be one of the MacDougall's men."

"Dangerous," complained Godred, shaking his head. "Even Steinar knows your face."

"I did not go into the longhouse where a great feast is taking place. I remained outside with some of the other men. A simple task when there are many enjoying the company of drink and food. I managed to obtain a bit of knowledge, but the people of Torvay knew nothing about the arrival of the MacDougall."

"Explain." Godred gestured for the man to follow him away from the others. When they got to the bow, he crossed his arms over his chest.

Michael leaned against the side of the ship. "Their interest is with the woman who arrived with her brothers. Most—"

"Inga?" interrupted Godred in confusion.

"*Aye*. Apparently, she holds sway over the isle. They regard Leif as her warrior of protection, along with her other brothers. The people were surprised to witness her return to Torvay. I've gathered from the conversation she has lived elsewhere most of her life."

Godred's eyes narrowed. "'Tis her home. Any brother should guard a woman like her. Although, I have heard she trains with them."

Michael lifted one shoulder. "Then she is not who she presented while on Islay during her time with Rangvald."

Blowing out a soft curse, Godred shifted his stance. "Was there any mention of a treasure?"

The man slid him a sideways glance. "You should have given me clearer instructions, Godred. If a *treasure* is what they seek, I would have remained to find out more."

Godred nodded slowly in understanding. Stepping near the man, he placed his forearms onto the edge of the ship. "This treasure I speak of is between you and me. Not one word to the men until I ken all the details. Either the woman is Torvay's treasure with possible connections to the King of Norway, or there is a highly valuable one the Serpents and Steinar are after." His muscles tensed. "With Steinar informing his uncle he would return soon, I can surmise this treasure is nearby—possibly on Torvay."

Michael scratched the side of his face and then let out a yawn. "What are your plans for Rangvald?"

"His daughter has been given her final instructions."

The man gave a low whistle. "Your trust in the woman surprises me. You should have left the deed to me."

"Nae," snapped Godred, shaking his head. "'Tis better to have Rangvald's blood on her hands than one of us. By the time we return, the great Bear shall be dead. The people of Islay will ken her actions and pass judgement on her."

"And here I assumed you wanted Sigrid as your woman." Michael's mouth twisted into a sour grin.

"Loki's balls, nae! She'd chained me to her bed with demands I could have nae other women. She'll hold nae power on Islay once her father is dead."

"When you control the isle, send her away."

Godred smirked. "Or dispose of her and toss her body into the sea along with her father's."

Glancing outward, Michael asked, "Should I return and spend the night on Torvay?"

"Aye," he whispered, and added, "I shall instruct the men to land on the southwest side of the island away from the harbor. Meet us there at dawn."

Michael spat into the water. "Done."

Chapter Sixteen

Anticipation drummed into Steinar's skin with each steady stride he made to the standing stones. The stars hung heavy in the night sky, luring him forward to his destination. He quickened his pace as he chased after something he desperately craved—Inga. Steinar tried to harness the quaking desire, but his body shook with a need to conquer and claim.

"Claim?" His steps faltered. Slowing his progress through the trees, he clenched his jaw. "Nae, nae, *nae,*" he uttered into the stillness of his surroundings and leaned against a pine tree. Steinar's annoyance increased when he found that his hands were shaking. He felt adrift and unable to harness his desire—his feelings for Inga. They surged forth like the swell of an ocean's wave.

His wolf howled in frustration.

I cannot claim her. Ever!

But his wolf would not be swayed, continuing with his persistent howling.

Steinar swallowed, refusing to admit the truth he'd already known—a truth he was determined to keep locked away within his heart. But with each battle, his shields had begun to crack, leaving splinters of hardened steel around him. Like a storm, Inga had already swept into his heart. And there rooted in the center existed his love. A love he thought he'd never attain.

"I might have professed one night with you, but I

cannot deny wanting more. Will you want both? Man and beast?"

He laughed at the absurdity of his uneasiness, and with great effort, soothed the beast within. *I shall convince her she's mine. Ours.*

An owl hooted in greeting as Steinar left the safety of the trees. He paused to take in its flight as it went in search of food or rest. The roar of the ocean waves drowned out the last of the revelry down below, and Steinar inhaled sharply, sensing no others behind him.

His steps hastened, making long strides toward the ancient white guardians. Their starkness glimmered in the moonlight as if embracing him in greeting. As Steinar approached, the air grew warm, with no breeze to cool his skin. He lightly touched the first stone in passing, igniting a spark of curiosity. Raising his head, he studied the rune markings on the tallest of the stones set in the middle of the crescent. Most of the runes were dedicated to the Goddess of the sea. Others denoted the seasonal shifts of the tides and stars.

Removing his cloak and dirk, Steinar slipped behind the stones, settling against an aging oak tree. After taking off his boots, he stretched out his limbs and folded his arms over his chest. Nocturnal animals came and went unaware of his presence. When an hour had drifted by, his restlessness increased. He braced his arms over his bent knees, searching for any sound or scent of the woman.

Steinar's heightened senses detected nothing. Picking up a stone next to him, he tossed it outward in frustration. On a heavy sigh, he stood. "Is this a sign or are the stars not aligned for us, Inga?"

Taking a step forward, he froze. A familiar tremor

of awareness slammed into him. Steinar's heart pounded against his chest while he waited within the shadows. Though her footsteps led her closer to him, he refused to come forward. His mind willed her toward him.

Inga let out a soft curse and dropped what looked like a small bag onto the ground.

Steinar's smile came slowly.

"Did you leave or were you never here?" she complained in irritation. Inga placed her hands on her hips.

With careful steps, Steinar emerged forth. "I thought *you* had reconsidered coming here tonight."

She spun around. A small smile of enchantment touched her lips. "Merely late." Inga took a tentative step closer to him. "I had to meet with the women who are becoming priestesses and are residing in the temple. I should have told you. Forgive me?"

"There is nothing to forgive."

Her smile broadened. Inga removed her cloak and tossed the garment aside. "Then why does your mouth quirk on one side. I judge otherwise."

With powerful strides, Steinar bridged the distance between them. He grabbed a handful of her stunning locks and gently tugged. "What do you ken about *me*?"

Inga bit her lower lip, teasing him further. "I overheard one of your men speak of a certain habit you have when you lie."

Steinar became fixated on her mouth. His steely control ebbing away. "You must not trust everything my men say about me. Some may spout falsehoods to sprinkle doubt among my foes."

She arched a brow in skepticism. "Am I now the enemy, once again?"

"Uncertain," he whispered truthfully. With one look, Inga had disarmed all his shields, making him exposed and defenseless. He felt lost with no clear path in front of him.

Her smile faded. She grasped his hand. Placing a kiss inside his palm, Inga blew the words across his skin while keeping her gaze on his. "I could never be your enemy, *Pirate*."

A low growl burst forth from within Steinar. His mouth swooped down to capture hers, drinking in the sweetness of her lips. Her tongue teased along the edges of his, and he groaned. He deepened the kiss, inhaling her seductive scent and filling him.

Inga returned the kiss with reckless abandon and wrapped her arms around his neck.

Steinar drew her against his chest. Letting loose the passion he'd held back, he took possession of her and kissed her with hot, desperate kisses. Reveling in the heady sensations, his hand roamed over her body, caressing her curves until his fingers sought her full breast. When he encountered the pert bud, he gently squeezed. Her moan filled him, and Steinar's kiss became urgent, demanding more from the woman. His other hand slid back down to her bottom and drew her against his hardened length.

Steinar's desire became ravenous for Inga—to take and conquer. A hunger which he could no longer deny.

Her gasps turned to panting, and she released her hold around him to pull on his trews. "*Steinar*."

His name on her tongue spurred him wildly. Steinar's mouth moved from her lips to the soft spot below her ear. He trailed kisses down the side of her neck to the pulse that beat wildly. "What do you want, Inga?"

Steinar's question sounded hoarse even to his ears.

Inga tugged harder and his cock swelled more.

Grasping her hands, he halted her movements.

Raising her head to look at him, she protested, "Too many clothes. You are tormenting me."

Steinar rubbed his cheek against hers. "You speak of *torment*, but mine burns for you Inga. 'Tis an ache I cannot quench until I sink into you."

"Then what are you waiting for, *my Pirate*."

"If I am your first—"

A flash of fury replaced the lust in her eyes. "There have been nae others."

Regardless of her anger, Steinar's heart leapt at the knowledge he would be her first.

Gently, he cupped her face with his hands. Words he thought never to confess to another poured forth from Steinar. "When I take your body, I shall claim you, *my kærr*."

Her lips trembled when she spoke. "You *claimed* me the moment I saved you from the sea. I have denied my own feelings until this moment."

Stunned by her declaration, Steinar could not utter a word in response. Did she truly understand what he'd meant? Did she fathom the love he bore her? That once he claimed her, there would never be another? He sought to say the ancient words—either aloud or silently. Once he did, Inga would be joined to him for all eternity. Body and soul.

Inga took a hesitant step back. "I shall be first."

He watched in a blinding haze of desire as she slowly undid the lacings on the sides of her gown with trembling fingers. Then, Inga quickly removed her shoes and tossed them aside. She swallowed visibly, and then the siren tugged the gown from her body until the material pooled at the bottom of her feet. Hesitating briefly, Inga then quickly rid herself of her chemise.

She stood before him as both warrior and woman, leaving him without breath or any thought. There would be no loving Inga the Woman without Inga the Ruthless. He loved and craved them both.

Steinar's breathing became labored. Moonlight dusted her ivory skin. "You are a vision beyond any, *kærr*, and I shall taste all of you by the time the first light of dawn streaks the sky."

A rosy stain crept up her neck and to her cheeks. She gestured to his clothing. "Your turn."

Steinar's restraint deserted him, and desire took reign. With shaky hands, he removed his trews. His cock sprang free, thick and rigid with need. Her hungry gaze traveled the length of him, and he fought the urge to stroke himself in front of her.

"Give me pleasure this night—"

"And always," he vowed, dragging her against him.

The touch of her warm skin against his ignited the firestorm. Gently, his hand outlined the circle of her breast before cupping the heavy warmth in his palm. He watched as the color of her eyes changed to brilliant shades of blue, reminding Steinar of all the colors of the sea.

"*More*," she demanded, placing her hands on his shoulders.

Grasping her firmly around the waist with one hand, he recaptured her lips—demanding and forceful. His tongue sought entry, and Steinar took all she offered. When he drew breath, he bent and lowered his mouth over the lush softness of her breast. He suckled, ravished, and teased the taut nipple with his lips and teeth.

Inga's gasp surrounded him.

Steinar trailed kisses in the valley between her breasts and then took his time feasting on the other one. Her fingers dug into his scalp, urging him onward. Lost in the abyss of her scent, Steinar let out a growl and swiftly lifted Inga into his arms. Making long, steady strides, he carried her beyond the ancient oak tree behind the stones to an area filled with more trees. Moonlight gleamed through the heavy branches as he placed her gently on a soft patch of wildflowers in the center.

After he settled himself alongside her, he trailed his thumb over her bottom lip, swollen from his kisses. "You are a beauty, *my kærr*."

Inga pulled on his braid. "My pirate. Mine."

Slowly, he brushed his hand down over her body. Inga watched his movements. The first touch of his fingers on her soft thigh had her breath coming out in gasps. But when his hand encountered her silken curls, he was the one to let out a moan. Dipping one finger between her soft folds, Steinar stroked inside. Removing his finger, he licked the wetness from his finger. "Your sweetness fills me, beauty."

"Touch me there again," she pleaded, reaching for his cock, and squeezed.

He let out a guttural groan, nearly spilling his seed into her hand. "*Nae.*"

Grasping both her hands, he held them above her head with one hand. Raw, blinding possession and desire raged through him. Steinar found her center and stroked his thumb over the sensitive core, watching the flame of her desire build further within the depths of her eyes. With each flick of his thumb, her body quivered two-fold from his touch. He pressed firmly against the nub, and she jerked in response. Inga arched wildly against him. Her tormented groan that followed was a heady invitation for more and he complied by slipping one finger inside her.

"You are a feast I shall enjoy savoring, *beloved.*"

"Sweet Goddess," she uttered on a hoarse whisper.

Desire roared inside Steinar's blood, pounded within his mind, and blinded him to all thought. Conflict ripped through him to be gentle—to go slow with her.

As if she read his thoughts, Inga pleaded in a voice raw with need, "Do not be gentle with me. I ken there will be pain, but I want you inside me now."

Steinar rubbed his cheek against the side of her neck. "Sweet Goddess, what have you done to me?" Nudging her legs farther apart with his knee, he guided his swollen cock to her entrance. Relentlessly, he caressed her sensitive nub, stoking her passion. Her moans became forceful, and she begged him for more.

The tight knot within him begged for release, but not yet.

Onward, he continued to pleasure her with each steady stroke of his cock. When Steinar knew her to be near her release, his lustful beast drove fully inside her.

"Oh!" Inga's cry halted his progress.

Her slick heat engulfed him, and he released her hands. He brushed his hand over her nipple.

"Nae, nae, *nae,*" she ordered. "Do not stop."

Steinar's mouth descended over her lips, giving her all he had to offer in the kiss.

Sliding his hand to her hip, Steinar withdrew slowly and sank deeper inside her. With each thrust, the storm within him grew. While her passion crested, his increased. Slipping one hand under her thigh, he pressed farther inside her wet heat. He continued his loving assault on her body until Inga arched wildly screaming his name as the tide of desire swept through her.

Unable to hold back, the liquid fire exploded forth from Steinar. On a guttural roar, he emptied his passion into the woman he claimed and loved. The ground rumbled beneath them, and thunder rolled in the far distance. Yet his love poured into the woman in his arms.

While cradling her quaking body, Steinar rolled over, bringing her with him. She snuggled against his side and placed her leg along his thigh. He trailed a shaky hand down her back while whispering the ancient words to claim his beloved to him forever. With his final word, he placed a kiss on top of her head.

Inga tried to calm her breathing. The pulse continued to thrum between her legs and flow inside her body. His words opened the barriers she'd hardened against any man. Sensations she'd never experienced before infused her. Contentment washed over her, filling her soul. Her eyes welled up with unshed tears. As she lifted her gaze to the man who held her still shaking body, her heart leaped at the knowledge she bore for him.

Love.

Love for her pirate.

Love for his wolf.

Inga placed her hand on his chest. *I love you, Steinar. Until the ocean becomes a barren wasteland, my love is yours. Always.*

His hand skimmed over her back. "You mentioned I had claimed you when you drew me from the water. How did you ken?"

Her breath caught in her throat. Inga realized what

she had to reveal to Steinar might sever the bond between them. Her stomach quivered. Shoving aside the turmoil, she gave him a tentative smile. "Do not despise me for what I'm about to share."

His brow knitted in confusion, but he continued to stroke his fingers leisurely over her skin. "Tell me everything, *my kærr*."

"Your wolf."

Steinar halted his movements. "How can you speak with my wolf?"

Warning spasms of alarm erupted inside her. Regardless, the truth had to be spoken. "Not only can I speak with those who dwell in the sea, but also with the animals on the land, though constrained. I connected with your wolf, first. The *völva* spoke of a prophecy about a wolf who could either be my destiny *or* destruction."

Steinar gave a bitter laugh. After removing his arm, he rolled away from her. Rising slowly, he raked a hand through his hair and lifted his gaze to the sky.

Her misgivings increased with each second he remained silent.

"I have always known magic surrounded you, Inga." He regarded her over his shoulder. "I cannot find fault with my beast. And I will not hear words about destruction. Never did I follow the wisdom of any *völva* or seer."

A shiver ran through her. "Are you not curious to my magic?"

Humor softened his features. "If you follow the path of the Goddess of the sea—"

"'Tis more than following," she corrected. Inga stood and went to retrieve her thin chemise. Slipping it over her head, she then went to his side. With one hand on his forearm, she swept her other out toward the sea, and confessed, "I do not *follow* but walk beside the Goddess Rán. I am her *daughter*."

Steinar jerked as if he had been burned. Inga noted the emotions battling within his eyes. Confusion. Betrayal. Hurt. Did she actually hear him curse inside her mind?

"Loki's blood!" He moved away from her and began to pace while continuing to spew forth curses.

She winced and clasped her hands in front of her, fighting the urge to reach out and touch him.

After scrubbing a hand over his face, Steinar halted. "I thought you belonged to the wise women who honored the Goddess! By the Gods and Goddesses, what have we done?"

Inga spoke with quiet, but desperate firmness. "Though there are wise women among the priestesses, there are none who possess the gift to speak to those who dwell in the sea and land. Forgive me for my deception if that is what you feel."

Silence became an unwelcome companion between them. A warm breeze settled against her chilled skin, and Inga wrapped her arms around her body. "This night should never have happened," she uttered softly, biting her lower lip to stifle the sob threatening to break free.

Steinar was at her side in two strides. He grasped her around the waist with one hand and lowered his head against her ear. When he spoke, his voice was tender, almost a murmur. "Hear me now, *beloved*, I have nae regrets for tonight. Aye, I am stunned by your declaration, but this changes nothing." He leaned back and stared at her with such intensity it stole the breath from her lungs.

She placed her hand over his heart. "Nor I, my *Pirate Wolf.*"

He leaned his forehead against hers. "Is there more you need to confess?"

Inga laughed nervously, and then kissed his lips tenderly. "Regardless of the prophecy of a wolf who would either be my destiny or destruction, my purpose is two-fold with the treasure we seek."

"Continue," he encouraged, stroking her face with the back of his hand.

She nodded slowly. "A year ago, my mother came to me on Torvay—"

"The Goddess walks on land?" Steinar asked in a hushed voice.

"Aye. She is permitted to leave her home in the sea for the duration of one cycle of the moon, but nae more."

"Interesting," he mused.

"She sought to soothe my turmoil with a quest. As much as the sea is a part of me, I harbored angst over her decision to place me as leader of the Serpents. I was given nae voice to speak my fears. I've always judged Leif should have been given the honor. When she came to me, she told me about the magical treasure Odin bestowed on the Northmen. Only one item did she request for herself. The Shell of Wisdom. She called it her golden pearl of the sea. Odin had stolen this shell from her a thousand years ago."

Inga looked beyond Steinar, recalling her mother's tempting words. "In a heated argument with the God, he removed the shell from her possessions. Without this knowledge, those who dwelled with her were unable to study the seas of *all* realms in the ancient sea library. As the years passed, her resentment grew toward Odin, and she forbade him from entering her world beneath the water." Inga returned her attention to Steinar. "I often wonder if my mother conceived me to stir the wrath of Odin—to punish him for what he did to her."

Steinar cradled her in his arms. "You are a daughter of a Goddess, making you a pawn in any battle or argument between the Gods and Goddesses."

Her eyes filled with tears, and she sighed heavily. "I grow weary of being a pawn. Until you crossed my path, my heart hardened to one of a warrior, especially with my training on Skye. There stood nae place as a woman and warrior—not in my world or my mother's. Now..."

"*Now?*" echoed Steinar, tipping her chin up with his finger.

Inga blinked and refocused her attention. She drew strength from the man in her arms. The man who held her heart. The man she loved. "Now *I* will be the one to make the decisions—to control my fate. In return for the Shell of Wisdom, my mother must grant me my freedom from the Serpents and hand over control to Leif."

Smiling slowly, Steinar lowered his head near her mouth. "A wise plan, but dangerous. Regardless of what will happen, you are mine, Inga. Forever. I have claimed you. Vowed to protect you with my body, shield, and axe. I defy any God or Goddess to take you away from me. I *love* you." His last words were smothered on her lips.

Inga opened fully to the kiss, needing more of the man. On a groan, she bit his lower lip. "Make love to me, Steinar."

"I have yet to taste all of you." He breathed the words against her neck. With deft skill, he removed her chemise over her head. Gently, Steinar maneuvered her back toward the patch of wildflowers while keeping his gaze on hers. "From my heart to yours, we are one."

She cupped his face. "A love I give freely. A love so powerful even the Gods and Goddesses cannot destroy. Born from the sea and bonded with the wolf—we are one. My vow to you."

In her quiet reflection, Inga trembled with the revelation that she had become an enemy to both—her mother and Odin.

Chapter Seventeen

The sound of horses' hooves across the slope of the hills got Steinar to his feet. He shielded his eyes from the early morning light and yawned. Hastily retrieving his tunic and trews, he got dressed and searched for his cloak, dirk, and boots. As he made steady strides to where he had left them, his thoughts returned to his beloved who had departed only an hour ago. Her scent surrounded him, invading his skin and reminding him of all the pleasures they enjoyed under the stars. Her eagerness to learn brought Steinar to new heights of desire.

Tripping over a tree root, Steinar blew out a soft curse. After grabbing his boots, he shoved them on and smiled. True to his word, he had feasted on most of her skin and desire slammed back into him.

Was this what Magnar and Rorik meant? Only when you give your heart to a woman, then you shall know true passion.

He chuckled softly. "I was not ready to listen."

Leaving the standing stones, he waved to Ulrik and Haaken as they galloped toward him.

"Did you bring any food or drink?" Steinar asked in good humor, running to greet them.

Both men glanced at the other before returning their attention to him.

"Nae," replied Ulrik. "We came in search of you

since not one person could recall seeing you after the feasting. Inga is already with her men on the ship and is asking for you."

"I chose to rest under the stars near the guardians of Torvay." He stretched out his arms wide. "A grand view." *Especially with Inga in my arms.*

Haaken snorted in obvious disapproval. He removed Steinar's axe and sheath from the side of his horse and tossed it onto the ground.

"And the rest of our men?" Steinar asked, dropping his cloak. With quick movements, he fastened and secured his weapon across the back of his body.

Ulrik leaned forward on the pommel, studying him. "Some have returned to the ship to keep watch on the harbor, and the others will stay on the shore." The man looked beyond him as if searching for someone. "Why do I think you did not sleep alone? And why are you so cheerful?"

"I can think of one reason," suggested Haaken, rubbing a hand over the side of his nose.

Ignoring both men, Steinar retrieved his cloak and gave a pat to one of the horses while he ambled along the path through the trees. "I require food and drink before we depart."

Steinar fought the urge to glance over his shoulder. Most likely his friends were glaring at him.

When he reached the longhouse, a few of the older men were waking and others were content to keep on with their snoring. Reaching for a jug, Steinar sniffed. Mead was not what he wanted. Grabbing a block of cheese, an apple, and a small loaf of bread, he wrapped them in a cloth. While he wandered through the hall in search of any water, he came upon a young lass holding a bunch of wildflowers and humming a soft tune.

Bending down on one knee, he tugged gently on her braid. "Can you direct me to the well? I am thirsty."

Her green eyes widened in alarm. "Do you not like our ale or mead?"

Steinar gave the lass a broad smile. "'Tis one of the best I have sampled. But I require water this morning."

Gently, she pressed her tiny hand against his face. "You are the one they call the Pirate Wolf?"

"Aye," he acknowledged quietly.

"I do not fear your wolf," she admitted with a smile reflecting the absence of two front teeth.

Smiling, Steinar placed a kiss over her knuckles. "My wolf favors and protects the young."

Her brow furrowed. "Because we cannot defend ourselves. War has not come to Torvay." She lowered her hand to his chest. "But a storm is coming to another isle. Be wary of the one who remains hidden."

"You are wise for one so small." Steinar rose to standing, regarding her steadily. Why did her words of warning cause his wolf to pace?

Her smile returned in earnest. "I shall one day lead the wise women who guard the temple to the Goddess."

"A seer." He shook his head in good humor.

"I am called Alvilda." She pressed the flowers against his knee. "Give these to Inga."

"And the well?"

"The south side of the longhouse."

After Steinar accepted the flowers, he dipped his head toward her. "I thank you for your words of wisdom."

"Then heed them when the wolf howls three times."

Before he had a chance to respond, Alvilda

scampered away.

Shoving aside the lass' words of warning, Steinar made haste out of the longhouse and toward the well. After quickly filling and cleaning his body with the cool water, he hastily walked toward the harbor.

He greeted his men with a slight wave, and then proceeded to the ship of the Serpents. Leif's orders bellowed in the warm breeze while Steinar climbed the ladder. Once on board, he nodded to Jorik in passing. Inga's brother regarded him in a sharp and assessing matter. For a brief moment, Steinar pondered if the one they called the Hawk had observed the feelings he and Inga had for each other, especially if the man had noticed the flowers he had tucked within his belt beneath his cloak. Dismissing the thought, he strode with intent to the woman standing at the bow.

Inga's hand stroked the back of the serpent's scales, reminding Steinar how those long fingers caressed his balls during their lovemaking. Desire slammed into his body, and he quickly squashed the yearning.

They were about to embark on a dangerous, uncharted journey. Steinar's focus had to remain fixed on finding the treasure and securing Inga's freedom. He clenched his fist. *Nae one shall stand between us, my kærr.*

"You are late, Pirate Wolf," she protested while maintaining her sight on the water.

Removing the flowers, he held them outward in front of her. "These are from Alvilda."

Inga turned around. She granted him a small smile while a flicker of desire flashed through her eyes. Her fingers brushed against the back of his hand as she accepted the offering. "You saw the lass?"

"Aye," he acknowledged. Removing his cloak, he tossed it onto a bench. "I was on a quest for water, and she happened to be in the hall of the longhouse."

"Interesting," mused Inga. She plucked a petal free. "Rarely does Alvilda wander away from the temple. She lives nearby with her mother."

Steinar scratched the side of his face in recollection. "The lass informed me she will become the leader of these women who guard the temple."

Inga's mouth gaped open briefly and then snapped close. She returned her attention to the water. "Alvilda must have had a message for you. I cannot fathom any other reason. Even I seldom see her entering near the shore or main longhouse."

"Aye, she did have a message regarding my wolf," he expressed quietly.

Inga frowned and leaned over the side of the ship. "Heed her words, Steinar."

He watched as she tossed the wildflowers into the water. "Yet you discard her offering to you?"

His beloved burst out in laughter. She tilted her head and stared at him. "Those were not for me. They were for my mother."

Steinar fisted his hands on hips and shook his head. "I do not understand why the lass didn't do the deed herself."

Inga's features sobered, and she nudged him slightly with her elbow. "Because Alvilda understands we're venturing on a quest for the Goddess. The flowers are a symbol of protection from the land to the water. And my mother loves the wildflowers of Torvay."

Fighting the urge to touch her, Steinar clasped his hands behind his back. "Show me the map. I'd like to look at those markings."

Inga removed the map from beneath her belt. Motioning him to a nearby barrel, she unfurled the aging deerskin. Her lips pursed in concentration.

He leaned over, committing to memory each position—from the outer isles to the magical one and the entrance to the cove. Steinar pointed to the markings north of Torvay. "As I thought. They are similar to the ones I've seen in other texts. I now recognize how we can manage through the waters. The Fates' Cauldron poses nae danger to us. We shall guide our ships through these waters, instead of avoiding them."

"Nae! Death will devour us," she scoffed, leveling her fist over the markings.

Furious at her lack of trust, Steinar arched a brow. Slowly, he removed her fist. "This is a map infused with magic. Each symbol is the opposite of its true meaning. I studied the same on an ancient map at the Brotherhood years ago. If you look at the directions, they are not where they should be. For the north, Odin has drawn the dragon representing the south. 'Tis the same with the others."

Inga crossed her arms over her breasts. "You must be wrong in your observations. I will not risk our—"

Steinar's wolf gnashed his teeth, and Inga's eyes widened in alarm.

She lowered her arms. "Did I just hear your beast inside my mind?"

"Aye!" he snapped. "Because you do not trust my wisdom."

"My uncertainties are warranted," she argued, adding, "How can I hear him?"

Steinar found his anger growing. He pinched the

bridge of his nose. "You can hear the beast because I have *claimed* you. And Inga, if you cannot *trust* my counsel, then I am of nae use to you."

Her indrawn breath surrounded him. "You would leave me?"

Pausing to take a deep breath in, Steinar released it slowly, allowing part of the rage to subside. All he wanted to do was wrap his arms around her. But her lack of trust bothered him. "Nae, Inga, I shall never leave you. But you did ask for my advice on the map." Steinar's fingers slipped over hers, reassuringly. "Odin did not intend to make this a simple quest. If he did, any who had the map in their possession would have been able to secure the treasure many years ago. Did your mother give you the map?"

Biting her lower lip, Inga nodded slowly. "A year ago, when she presented the quest to me." A frown creased her brow. "We are so close, Steinar."

"You're letting the fear of this journey question each move you make, especially when another is telling you what you should do."

Inga's features brightened. "Aye, you're correct. But patience is not a quality I possess."

Squeezing her fingers, he urged, "Trust me, *kærr*, to keep you safe and those of our crew. You're going to have to convince your brothers and your men, so I require your complete trust. Furthermore, I disagree with you. I have seen the disciplined warrior in you. Your impatience is because the prize is highly valuable to you—to us."

"I so want to kiss you," declared Inga, her eyes alight with desire.

Her words disarmed the last remnants of Steinar's

anger to ashes. Stunned into silence, he allowed the love he bore Inga to shine forth in his eyes. When footsteps sounded behind them, he slipped her hand free. Stepping aside, he made room for Leif to consult with his sister and went to lean against the serpent's scales.

"Are we ready to depart?" asked Inga, rolling up the map.

Leif gave a swift nod. "Though Helka is remaining."

"I spoke with her this morning. She judged it wise to stay with the women. Her bones are weary from traveling at sea."

"And Snorri?" inquired Steinar, folding his arms over his chest.

"Quietly making notes on a sheaf of parchment," replied Leif, pointing to the far end of the ship. "Either he drank too much or is concentrating on his current saga of the wolf. Your men seem to be giving him an account of one of their adventures with you."

Steinar noted the edge in the man's voice and peered beyond Leif. The skald remained tucked between two barrels on the side of the ship, with Ulrik and Haaken standing over him. "Depends on whose version they are telling the man. Often, my men argue who has witnessed what event."

Gazing upward, Inga smiled. "Sounds similar to my brothers."

Leif blew out a curse but quickly laughed to cover his annoyance.

She patted the map and rested her gaze on her brother. "I'm going to go speak with Jorik. Then give the order to leave."

After Inga walked away, Steinar shifted his stance. Turning around, he braced his forearms on the edge of the ship. Seabirds drifted by him, and he watched their flight. "Are you prepared for the voyage?"

Leif approached by his side. "'Tis a dangerous journey you have taken, MacDougall."

Keeping his focus steady on the bird's path, he argued, "I asked if *you* are prepared."

"And I am not speaking about the magical isle," warned Leif in a hushed tone.

Steinar regarded the man. "I do not ken your meaning."

Leif darted a glance at Inga, and then returned his stormy gaze to him. "Our sister is not a quest to conquer, MacDougall."

Steinar's wolf disagreed. His low growl rumbled against his chest. "Your sister is now under my protection."

The man's eyes flashed in outrage. Placing a hand over the hilt of his sword, he warned, "Then heed my words well, MacDougall, if any harm comes to our sister, I'll take my blade to your heart and that of your beast."

Allowing the strength of the wolf to come forth within Steinar's eyes, he nodded solemnly. "On this we are in agreement."

Confusion replaced his anger, and Leif lowered his hand to his side. "You love Inga?"

Hesitating on his response, Steinar pushed away from the side of the ship. Resting his gaze beyond the man, he uttered with conviction, "With all my heart."

"By the Gods, do you ken who she is?" Leif raked a hand through his hair.

Sweeping his sight out toward the water, Steinar acknowledged, "Inga is the daughter of Rán."

"The Goddess of the sea will not favor this union,"

expressed the man, blowing out a long whistle. "Especially to a man whose magic was created by Odin."

Steinar let out a nervous chuckle. "Regardless, Inga is mine. When this journey is completed, I shall speak with Inga's mother."

Leif snorted and punched Steinar's shoulder. "Remind me when you plan on speaking with the *Goddess*, and I'll warn the other men to remain on land."

"Quick to anger?" asked Steinar, compelled to find out more.

"A tempest. She'll most likely slay you with the tail of a sea serpent, followed by slow torture tangled in the tomb of warriors who are trapped in the seaweed depths far below."

"You speak as if she has threatened you."

The man scowled uncomfortably. "Once. I argued over her decision to make me second in command of the Serpents. Without warning, she snapped her fingers and sent me to the watery prison. Though I remained there for a brief moment, I took that as a warning never to quarrel against her."

Steinar would not be swayed with threats or even death. His love for Inga remained steadfast. "If I have learned any wisdom during my travels on the sea, 'tis a respect for those who dwell beneath the water, and Odin who has always shined his light in the darkest of storms. All mothers are protective, even those who wield powerful magic."

Sighing heavily, Leif repeated, "'Tis a dangerous journey, MacDougall."

Lifting his gaze toward his beloved, Steinar willed her to look his way, repeating her name silently inside his mind. When she stopped speaking with her brother, she glanced over her shoulder.

Her smile warmed Steinar from across the ship. "Aye, but worth the risk," he admitted to the man.

Chapter Eighteen

Sigrid kept a firm hold on the arm of her father. Fierce winds made it difficult to manage the path, but she would not be swayed from her plan. "I am happy you considered taking a walk with me. We have not done so in years. In truth, I cannot recall the last time we strolled up here."

"'Tis a foul day," muttered Rangvald, stumbling over a mound of dirt.

"Simply a brisk breeze," she chastised, patting his arm with her other hand while doing her best to keep her footing secure.

Her father slurred his response, and she smiled inwardly.

The heavy brew she had made him drink made his steps unsteady. Grateful he did not request a guard to escort them, Sigrid rushed him from the castle, encouraging him with each step he took toward their destination.

"Do you not enjoy the view of the ocean?" She moved him onward away from the worn path.

"A storm is brewing." He coughed and spat onto the ground.

"Are you chilled, Father?" Sigrid's voice stayed calm, her gaze steady.

Rangvald wiped away the spittle from his mouth with the back of his hand. "Even Odin's hounds wouldn't venture out here."

A flash of lightning splintered the sky in the far distance.

Sigrid laughed nervously. Quickly glancing upward, she half-expected the God to make an appearance to thwart her plan.

Her father squinted and leaned his head back. "See, even Odin reckons we should leave and return to the great hall."

Straightening, she pressed them farther through the thick grasses. She would not be discouraged by an approaching storm, or her father's harsh words. "When did Rangvald the Bear fear the wind or a storm brewing on the sea? Has my father grown old and weak?"

Once again, Rangvald stumbled. He tried to jerk free from her hold. Due to his weakened condition, he failed in his attempt.

Sigrid considered another tactic. Halting her stride, she released her hold on him. "Perchance you are correct. Your old limbs are betraying you. Return to the comforts of your chair and fire." Her jaw tightened as she stepped around her father.

"I did not teach you to speak to me in this manner. These bones are not old."

She bit the inside of her cheek to keep the smile from forming on her mouth. Keeping her back to him, she reasoned, "What would you have me think when all I wanted was to spend time near the cliffs? I have fond memories here. We would wait for the ships to leave and then return to the shore to collect shells."

"You had nae interest in the ships," he corrected. "And I am not so feeble to forget those days."

She sighed and lowered her head, hoping her father

would sense her anguish. "Aye, aye. This was not a wise idea."

"Let us continue to the edge of the cliffs, then we can return to the comforts of a good fire," suggested Rangvald.

With victory in her grasp, Sigrid's smile unfurled. She had achieved her purpose. Turning around, she held out her hand to her father.

Together, they trekked through the wildflowers dotted between the tall grasses. The wind slashed against them, bringing the bite of the sea to their faces. Onward, Sigrid pushed them until she neared the edge. Releasing her grasp, she bent on one knee, searching for a sizeable rock. After finding one, she stood and stepped several paces behind her father.

"Remember the game we used to play long ago? We can compete to see who can toss the rock the farthest out into the ocean," advised Sigrid, holding fast to the cold rock inside her fist. "Even though I was small, you'd praise my strength."

Her father grumbled a curse. "The fog shrouds the view."

His slurred words encouraged Sigrid further. "Then I shall confess at the evening meal how the daughter of the Bear bested him with my skills of strength."

"Then you find me a rock."

You are a stubborn bear, even in your stupor. Crouching down, she managed to secure a rock for her father.

Rising, she held it outward. "Here."

Rangvald never turned around. He lifted his palm upward.

Mumbling a curse, she dropped the rock into his

hand. Tension coiled within her, knowing the time had come to finish this farce. She had plotted out every detail. The storm merely added to the tale she'd tell the others. Upon her return to the castle, her distress and screams would fill the hall with the news of Rangvald's death. In an effort to save his loving daughter, the Bear had slipped and crashed to the rocks below, where the sea had claimed his body.

Moisture dotted her forehead, and she clutched the rock tighter. Lifting her arm, she poised to strike his head, followed by a shove over the side.

"Shall I step aside for you?"

His question startled her causing her to stay her movements. "Nae need," she managed to grit out. Sigrid propelled her arm forward.

"I disagree," snapped Rangvald, swiftly turning and deflecting her blow with his arm.

She cried out as pain shot up her arm to her shoulder. The stone tumbled from her hand to the ground while her father held her arm in an iron grip. A grip too firm she judged for a man in his dazed condition. Her father's fury and strength surrounded Sigrid. Gone was the man who only moments before appeared weak and confused. Now, Rangvald the Bear stood towering over her.

Sigrid shuddered. *Gods! He knows what I have done!*

Rangvald's grip tightened. "*Why?*" His question thundered inside her ears.

With her heart hammering wildly, Sigrid attempted to think of an answer. She clenched her jaw. *He will ken any lie you spout.* Trying not to tremble beneath his terrifying gaze, she maintained her sight on the frothing water below.

Sigrid swallowed. Her fate now resigned. "For what you would never give to me. Power. You neglect my counsel—"

"*Power*?" bellowed Rangvald, spittle flying against her face.

She would not cower. Her father was simply another man who sought to control her. Sigrid lifted her chin in defiance and stared at him. "Aye," she returned.

He shoved her back. Curses flew from his mouth when he flung his rock outward into the water. Fisting his hands on his hips, he raked his disapproving gaze over her. "I have given you the freedom *and* power to run Finlaggan. You have been my eyes and ears when betrayal loomed within the isles. When jarls and earls sought marriage contracts, did I not present them to you first?"

She flinched and retreated a step. Her mind was congested with doubts and fears, mostly from one man. Godred. And then an idea blossomed. Sigrid clasped her trembling hands in front of her. "Aye, Father, on this we are in agreement, but recently, you had reconsidered."

"Loki's balls! Nae! And yet, this was enough for you to plot my *death*?" Rangvald's eyes narrowed to shards of fury. "Do you think I am a fool? There is another who has planted these falsehoods to turn you against me."

Aye! I shall blame this all on Godred. Sigrid chose her words carefully. "I can nae longer keep silent on the treatment of one of your guards. He…he has abused his power. Forced me to do things against you. *Forced* me into his bed. He has shamed me, Father." Raising her hand outward, she pleaded, "If I did not submit to his demands, he threatened to slash my throat and yours."

Rangvald folded his arms over his chest. His expression bordered on mockery. "Let us be clear in your account. Was it fear *or* power that drove you on this quest to kill me?"

The distrust in his eyes chilled her to the bones. "Both," confessed Sigrid.

"On that we can agree, *Daughter*." After unfolding his arms, he shook his head solemnly. "Your betrayal has cut deep, Sigrid. You and any husband you'd have chosen would have ruled the isles. Since Steinar refused to become my heir, documents had been drawn up for him to relinquish any claim, therefore transferring control to you upon my death. Though he is a bastard, his father negotiated with other jarls to leave Steinar in charge. I had hoped to share this knowledge with him but regardless, he will not want to rule over the isles."

"Steinar does not realize this knowledge," she whispered, shocked by her father's revelation. Clutching her hands to her chest, she asked, "Then there was nae need—"

"Nae need for your betrayal." He dismissed her with a curt wave. "But my nephew continues to make the seas and the Brotherhood his true home. Now, he shall have nae choice. He must accept his duty here. Obviously, I cannot have my traitorous daughter lead my people, or those disloyal to me to remain at Finlaggan."

Warning spasms flared inside her. "Godred forced me," she blurted out, hoping to appease her father's good nature.

Rangvald's faint smile held a touch of sadness. "As you have already admitted. I have known of his treason and yours for many moons, Sigrid. All I needed was to hear you utter his name."

"Godred has taken a ship, possibly with the intention of killing Steinar," she hastily offered.

"Aye, I am aware of the man's actions."

A frown creased her brow. "You have always known?"

He stepped forward and gripped her elbow moving her away from the edge. "After the first time you gave me a brew with herbs that made me ill. I gave the cup to the seer the following morning to confirm my suspicions. I suspected Godred's withdrawal of loyalty long ago."

"You should have confronted me then." Sigrid shook with uncertainty, realizing an apology now would serve no purpose.

Her father's laugh became bitter as he released his hold. "I had to see how far you would venture with this plan. If Godred had truly forced you, did you not think of another solution?"

She regarded him warily, then shrugged.

"By coming to me in the beginning about the man's true intentions, you would have secured your loyalty to me. Obviously, your hatred of me is greater. Betrayal of my kin cannot go unpunished, even from my daughter."

Sigrid hesitated, measuring him for a moment. Would her agony linger? Or be swift? She balled her hands into fists by her sides. "Will my death be by blade, axe, or drowning?"

He arched a brow in disgust. "Even though others shall want your death, I am not ready to take my daughter's blood in vengeance. You will serve another purpose. The freedom you previously enjoyed has now ended." Placing two fingers in his mouth, he blew out a whistle. Three guards appeared from the trees, making their way toward them.

"What are you going to do to me?" Her question barely a whisper.

Rangvald gripped her chin. "Your belongings have been packed, and a ship is waiting to take you to Norway. From there, you will travel farther north to a small island called Kiru. There's an aging jarl who doesn't care if you go to his bed chaste. As long as you provide him with sons, you will live. If not, he shall decide your fate— death *or* slavery to another man." He dropped his hand.

Sigrid's stomach roiled. Tears burned her eyes. "I'd have preferred death," she mumbled.

Gesturing to one of the guards, he lowered his voice, "An option you can take yourself, Sigrid. Or consider making a new life elsewhere."

A small glimmer of hope rose inside her. She'd put her blade through this jarl before he laid a hand on her. Could this be her chance to gain control on another isle? Would the people accept her? She'd fight for her freedom.

Reluctantly, Sigrid let the guard lead her away while the others followed behind her. Yet her father's words made her pause, and she glanced over her shoulder one last time at the man she had underestimated.

"You are now a threat and an enemy to all who reside on Islay and the other isles. Your betrayal will be announced in the great hall this evening. Do not think about returning, Sigrid. Your name shall be stricken from all accounts, except the one of your betrayal." He pointed a warning finger at her. "Do not make enemies on Kiru either. This jarl is known by Sven the Deadly Hand. He drinks the blood and eats the flesh of those who even smell of treachery. Let this be my final warning."

Sigrid swallowed the bile threatening to heave onto

the ground. A great sob caught in her throat. For a brief moment, she considered freeing herself from the guard's grip and throwing herself over the cliff.

When lightning flashed beyond her father, Sigrid shivered. And her hatred for Godred grew mightily. Squaring her shoulders, she regarded her father. "I have one final request before I take my leave."

Rangvald shifted his stance, giving her a curt nod to continue.

"Use the blade you gave me on my twentieth summer to end the life of Godred. Justice in my name with *my* weapon?"

"Done!" His clipped tone sent a chill down her spine.

Turning away from her father's scorn, she uttered quietly, "May the Gods favor you a safe journey, Rangvald the Bear, until you strike the heart of Godred."

Chapter Nineteen

Inga's nails dug into the wood on the side of the ship. While the warm breeze pushed them along the water, she feared the approaching swirling tempest. Staring at the frothing waves surrounding the cauldron, she maintained her position, unable to look away or to protect herself from falling overboard. Inga dared to sweep a glance to her right. Her brothers had formed a line along the edge of the ship, waiting, watching while Steinar directed them onward.

Trust. The one word she urged her brothers to accept with Steinar. They gaped at her with uncertainty when she told them of Steinar's interpretation of the map. If not for Leif, she doubted the others would have given their consent to allow the Pirate Wolf total control. Steinar's men would follow their leader to the end of the world, but these men had doubts, considering a few of them were warriors for the Goddess Rán.

She balled one hand into a fist. *This is not only for my freedom, but also for my brothers, especially Leif. My time to lead has come to an end. His journey begins.*

Returning her attention to the turbulent waters, Inga tried to calm her breathing.

"Keep moving forward!" Steinar's bellow surrounded her.

Snapping her head in his direction, she marveled at the man standing on the scales of the serpent. Power, control, and confidence poured off him. He commanded the seas as much as she did. Perchance more. Her love for the man eased the tension coursing through her. Though death might await them, she prayed the Gods and Goddesses would protect them on this quest.

Without warning, storm clouds descended over Fates' Cauldron. Inga slipped free from the side and went to stand below Steinar. "Odin knows we are here."

Steinar slid down the side, landing near her. Placing his arm around her waist, he reassured, "Together, we are powerful. This is not the time to hesitate."

Inga laughed nervously. "A wolf and the daughter of a Goddess. Odin might see us as a new threat."

Placing a finger over her lips, Steinar soothed, "We will show him our love. All Father created the wolf within me. I have not betrayed the God."

Grasping his hand, Inga added, "Nae matter their love for us, they do fear a time when we become more powerful."

Lightning flashed beyond them, and a great roar filled the skies as if Odin's hounds had descended. They both glanced in the direction. Darkness consumed the swirling mass of water. She swallowed and squeezed his hand. "I trust you, Pirate Wolf. But I'll be glad when we venture out of this tempest."

When another lightning bolt grazed the side of the ship, Steinar secured Inga more firmly to his side. "I have nae desire to be more powerful than a God or Goddess."

Inga noted a trace of laughter in his voice and placed her hand on his chest. "Nor I. Get us out of here."

Quickly releasing his hold, Steinar returned to the back of the serpent. He shouted over his shoulder, "Steer north along the edge of the water until we pass beyond the cauldron! Keep your focus beyond the darkness. If you look inside, fear will dim your judgement. Even the slightest hesitation can pitch us into an abyss. Pass this knowledge to the other ship as well!"

Wrapping her arm around and through one of the ropes attached to the ship, Inga refused to worry about those behind her. Their repeated grumblings and curses filled her ears each time the ship dipped and swayed near the frothing water.

She bit her lower lip to stifle the cry when the ship listed to the left. It took all her strength to keep a firm grasp onto the rope. More men shouted their disapproval. Leif slipped and slammed against her legs. Inga sucked in a breath, fighting against the pain. Blistering winds replaced the gentle breeze, making the path to navigate more difficult. Her brother managed to straighten, giving her a look that would singe the hair from any warrior. Yet he barked out an additional order to maintain their position as he moved away from her.

Time moved in slow torturous minutes along with their ship. To rush through the waters might hasten them to their death. She'd even considered pleading with her mother but believed the Goddess might be unable to assist. If she did interfere, the wrath of Odin would surely descend.

And I have nae wish to speak with you until I put the Golden Shell of Knowledge and Wisdom into your hands, Mother.

When the ship slipped past the dangerous edge, a shaft of sunlight pierced the sky beyond them. Inga raised a fist in triumph with the sounds of cheering from the men surrounding her. Steinar continued to remain steady in his position until the last wave from the cauldron smacked against the side of the ship in passing.

"A farewell warning," announced Steinar, descending onto the deck.

Inga fought the temptation to wrap her arms around the man's neck and kiss him thoroughly. Instead, she turned and gave a warm smile to the men behind her. "Once on the other side, we shall anchor until the sun sets and wait for the rising moon. Tonight, the island will become visible."

A resounding cheer echoed from some of the men, including the voices of her brothers and those on Steinar's ship.

"The first test of courage is behind us, *my kærr*," murmured Steinar, placing a hand against her lower back.

The touch of his breath along her cheek sent tremors down her body. Inga stole a glance sideways at the man. "You have gained the trust of my men."

He arched a brow questioningly. "Even Leif?"

"My brother trusts nae one," she offered, lowering her gaze.

The shrill cry of a sea bird caught her attention. Crossing to the side of the ship, Inga gripped the sides, watching the bird's flight. "We are definitely in the right direction. The bird is too small to be heading away from land. He senses the island ahead."

Steinar followed. He pointed outward. "We'll continue there and wait."

"Hungry?" she asked, tipping her head up to the sun's warmth.

His low rumble skimmed over her. "Aye, but 'tis not food I crave."

Heat crept up from her neck onto her face, recalling

images of the pleasure he had brought her. His body appeared chiseled by the Gods. "You encourage trouble from my brothers."

"Not once have your brothers questioned my slight touch or grip around your body," he uttered quietly, adding, "They have accepted the fact I have claimed you."

"Sweet Freyja," she hissed out, moving away from the man. "I require some ale or mead."

"To cool the heat from your face and quiet the fire in your body? Your rosy glow makes me think you *crave* me, as well."

Inga turned to face her pirate.

Steinar folded his arms over his broad chest.

By the Goddesses, she burned for the man. Without considering the consequences, Inga clasped his head with her hands and kissed the smirk off his lips.

****

"Where did he go?" shouted Godred, slamming his fist onto a barrel. "One moment he is nearing the edge of the circling waters, and the next, he vanishes. Both ships gone!"

Michael squinted in the gray light of the approaching storm. "Unsure."

"Were they swallowed up in the abyss of water?" demanded Godred. "Could this be our victory?"

"Nae. I did not see them pitch into the water. They were traveling at a slow speed. No sign of danger as they maneuvered to the edge of the tempest with their ships. Then a shaft of light appeared, and they vanished."

"Impossible! Why would they travel closer to the center of the cauldron? And my sun compass indicates we are heading in a southern direction. 'Tis not correct!

I can see by the fading light we are going north." He tapped the compass with his finger. "Now, I'm forced to disregard the direction of the shadow and sunlight. Madness!"

Moving away from the bow, Michael turned around. "We are in an area of uncharted waters. This place holds magic. Can you not sense the shift in the wind? I say we follow in the same direction as the other ships."

Godred studied the man. "You are certain this treasure is one Odin placed on a magical island hundreds of years ago? To press forward without a clear direction is dangerous."

His friend snarled. "While casting my net for fish, I overheard one of the MacDougall's men talking about the elusive treasure his father sought. Years ago, many considered it unwise for his father to waste men and good coin. However, I sense the Pirate has found the location. His men seem convinced."

Grateful for the man's keen ability to blend in anywhere and not be noticed, Godred considered the information his friend had acquired. Many judged Michael to be one of those who lived on Torvay, therefore, speaking freely.

"Aye, aye, I have heard the tales numerous times at Rangvald's table. His brother spent far too much time traveling the seas in search of this treasure." Smiling slowly, Godred wiped a hand over his chin in satisfaction. "And now the Bear is dead."

Michael reached for a small aleskin off a bench. His eyes lit with excitement. "Shall we drink to his death *or* to your new claim on Islay?"

Giving out an exasperated snort, Godred took the offered drink. "The man went to his death without his sword clutched in his hand, so nae I cannot drink to his death. Nor do I care. Loki's giants intend to eat on his flesh in the Underworld. When I return to Islay, all will be revealed to the people. For now, we must consider following in the same direction Steinar traveled."

"And not be seen," added Michael, removing his dirk from its sheath at his waist.

Godred gave his friend a skeptical glance. "Another offering for the Goddess of the sea?" He watched as the man carefully sliced another small portion of his braid, and then tossed the hair into the water with a whispered prayer.

Michael's expression remained a mask of stone. "She will guide us through these waters and keep us safe."

"Do you fear her song? Or those from her sirens?"

The man grimaced. "Do you not?"

Godred shifted his stance and placed a hand over the hilt of his sword. He had little time to worry about who dwelled within the waters. Especially a female Goddess. "With you giving pieces of yourself, I think we are safe. Unless you'd like to give her some of your blood?"

"One can never be confident if she seeks to guide us safe passage or doom us to her monsters below. My blood will not appease her appetite but yours might."

After taking a long draw of ale, Godred wiped his mouth with his hand. "Because I lead these men?"

Returning the dirk to his side, Michael answered calmly, "Your doubts carry to her ears from her sea creatures."

"Loki's balls—"

"She despises the deceitful God."

"Why do I even consider you a friend?" snapped

Godred, losing his patience over this discussion.

"Loyalty," supplied Michael, reaching for the aleskin from Godred's hand. "Ever since you killed my father, I owe you my life." After taking a sip, he tossed the skin aside.

Looking beyond the man, Godred tempered his anger and mused. "The deed was long overdue. His cruelty left its mark on your back and mine."

Michael shrugged dismissively. "He saw you as a threat and me his slave. Eventually, I would have taken an axe or blade to his head."

"You were close to death after his last beating," Godred reminded.

His friend gave a slow nod of understanding. "With his death, you saved my life."

"Necessary," he admitted, glancing outward.

Michael stretched his arms outward and cracked his knuckles. He then removed his sword from its sheath. "Let us follow onward through these waters. A victory is our only option. To return to the safety of an island is not wise. If death awaits us on the other side, I would be honored to enter Valhalla with you by my side."

A hiss of steel rent the air when Godred retrieved his weapon from the sheath attached to his back. His lips twisted in a cruel smile. They were both warriors, not weak men. The frail and unsteady bloodline of the MacDougall was almost at an end.

Godred pointed his sword out toward the cauldron of water. "Then let us hope my blade will taste the blood of my enemy before I depart from this world!"

Chapter Twenty

With the fading sunlight slipping away, Steinar cast his gaze outward. Both ships bobbed gently side by side within the waters. A hushed stillness descended around them as they eagerly awaited the rising of the moon. Earlier, a bet on who would view the first sighting of the moon's light lessened the tension between the men. After passing around the edge of the cauldron, their directions turned to confusion when they emerged on the other side. There were no birds, the sun continually shifted in all directions, and even the use of Inga's sunstone proved unable to give an accurate position.

Magic enclosed them in a sphere, and most of the men expected Odin to appear and hurl them to the Underworld. Ulrik voiced his concerns stating this was a deception by Loki.

Steinar ignored them all, relying on his wolf to sense any threat of danger.

"Smooth water and fair winds, Gods," whispered Steinar, leaning against the side of the ship.

"Eat," urged Inga, striding across the deck and pressing a small bundle against his chest. "I ken all you've had is water since we've left."

He smiled, tempted to ask for another kiss. Instead, he took the offering of food and went to a small bench. Gesturing for her to join him, Steinar waited.

Inga settled comfortably beside him. She closed her

eyes and let out a sigh. "There's a peacefulness here. Can you sense it?"

"Aye, but my wolf is restless," admitted Steinar while opening the bundle of bread, hard cheese, and dried meat.

She stifled a muffled yawn. "The unknown?"

"As we both honor Odin, we do not ken what to expect or encounter on this island. This might be a test or one of honor," answered Steinar between mouthfuls of food.

She snapped open her eyes. "Does your wolf sense danger?"

"Nae," he reassured, tucking a stray strand of hair behind her ear. "Merely uncertainty. His respect and fear for the God is great."

When her eyes widened in alarm, Steinar took her hand into his and squeezed. "Do not mistake my meaning. My loyalty is to Odin, but the wolf inside me understands the magic of the God more than me. He fears what we might confront on this quest. To face Odin as a man might cause the beast to fight for control inside me."

Removing her hand from his, Inga placed her palm over his heart. "And if the wolf faces Odin?"

His wolf pressed against him and gave a low growl.

Inga gasped but held her hand firmly against him. "He would protect you until death took you both."

Steinar's hand stilled. He swallowed and stared intently at her. "We've never had to face a situation like this *or* a fight with a God."

A frown marred her features. Inga glanced down. "Can you be certain?"

"Aye," he affirmed. "I have fought evil but not against a God or Goddess."

"Hmm…"

Steinar cupped her chin, forcing her to meet his gaze. "Is there something you want to declare?"

"Nae." She pointed out toward the water. "I cannot sense my mother here. Though I ken she is waiting. Since the seas do not belong to Odin, I wonder who is able to cast this magic around us."

After dropping the bundle of food to his left, Steinar brought her to standing. Moving her to the bow, he set his sight over the side of the ship. "Perchance 'tis Odin. Do you sense any of the sea animals?"

She shook her head.

"If I went for a swim, we'd find the answer."

A look of horror passed over her face. "Nae!"

Chuckling softly, he wrapped an arm around her waist. "Possibly, the magic surrounds the air and touches only the surface of the water." Her scent filled him, and Steinar fought against nuzzling the soft spot below her ear or licking a path across the vein in her neck.

Inga trembled beneath his hold. Leaning her head against his shoulder, she confessed, "As soon as we have secured the shell and whatever treasure the men want, let us leave soon thereafter."

"Have you spoken to Leif about turning over leadership to him?" he asked quietly.

Biting her lower lip, she blew out her response. "Not yet. I want to wait until after my business with my mother has concluded."

"Do you believe this to be a wise decision?"

Inga snorted and moved away from him. "Once I have the shell in my possession, my mother will sense the transfer and appear. There is nae doubt of her arrival, nae matter whose magic controls the area. Truthfully, I half-expect her to wait until we return to Torvay."

"The moon is rising!" Jorik shouted, making long strides to the other side of the ship. He came to a halt near Steinar and Inga.

They turned as one to glance where Jorik pointed. The moon slowly rose in a luminous glow. As her light spread like a cloak across the water, the island appeared before them—majestic and inviting. There in the middle they witnessed the Cove of Gríma.

Steinar lifted his gaze to the skies where there appeared no threat of a storm or lightning. The stars emerged one by one against an ebony evening sky. Without waiting for Inga to give the order, he yelled, "Move onward to the cove!"

Anticipation beat along his skin, the closer they approached. When the ships settled near the shore, Steinar hesitated before jumping overboard. He turned around.

Leif, Jorik, Balder, and Brant stood behind Inga—a strength of unity for their leader.

Steinar held out his hand to her. "Your quest. Your journey. Lead the way and I shall protect you."

The smile she gave him pierced straight to his heart. Trust. Trust and love for him and his wolf.

Returning her smile with one of his own, he seized her hand. Bringing her fingers to his lips, he kissed them. "The second test of courage awaits in the cove. Seek your freedom, *my kærr*."

Another one of their men secured the ladder over the edge of the ship, and Steinar assisted her to the side. Watching as she swiftly descended into the water, he quickly followed. When they reached the shore, Steinar knelt on one knee and offered a prayer of thanks to Odin.

After rising, he removed his axe from its sheath attached to his back and crossed to where Inga stood.

Ulrik, Haaken, and Inga's brothers took up positions on either side of them. The rest of the men remained on the ship, including Snorri. The skald would listen to the account from all when they returned to the ship.

Steinar wiped away the water from his eyes. The full moon's light shimmered near the entrance of a cave. A faint glow emanated from within, dancing along the inner rocks.

"Odd that there is light inside," mentioned Leif, shifting his stance.

Inga placed a hand over the hilt of her sword. "Nae doubt, Odin has provided the light." She looked at Steinar for confirmation.

He shrugged to hide his confusion. Even his wolf remained silent. "Let us proceed."

They trekked forward across the shore, littered with multi-colored shells and small pebbles. Once inside the cave, they all came to a sudden halt. Water trickled down the back of the cave and into a small pool of water. Light bounced off the walls from a number of torches as a gentle breeze drifted past them. The sound of the ocean barely a whisper inside, as if they had entered another realm.

In the center of the cave on a large polished amber slab was set Odin's treasure. A silver trunk encrusted with pearls and emeralds along the smooth edges lay open, its wares spilling over the top in a variety of gems, gold and silver goblets, coin, and vast supply of weapons.

A treasure surpassing any Steinar had seen in his travels.

"By the Gods," muttered Leif. He tapped his sword on the sandy ground. "Why do I not feel this is meant for us. There is a hum of restlessness inside this cave."

"Aye," agreed Ulrik and Haaken in unison.

Inga walked forward. Her focus appeared beyond the treasure. "Take what you'd like, or not. I am here to claim what was stolen long ago."

Leif reached out and snatched her arm. "Explain."

Steinar's wolf gave a low rumble of warning. The man gave him a reproachful glance but removed his hand.

"You might have claimed her, but she is still my sister *and* leader," warned Leif. Returning his attention to Inga, he demanded, "Why are we here? The truth."

Choosing to remain silent, Steinar gave a nod to his beloved.

She straightened fully and looked at all her brothers. "Let me show you."

Her steps were determined as she walked past the treasure to a small wooden box at the back of the cave. Its dark, weathered look blended in with the sheen of the rocks. Without hesitation, Inga lifted the box into her arms and made her way back to them.

A muscle twitched in her jaw. Slowly, she undid the clasp to reveal what lay hidden. Upon opening the lid, the sheer transparency of the shell radiated a golden hue as it set nestled against the black velvet.

Inga's eyes brimmed with unshed tears filled with determination when she looked at Steinar and then to her brothers. "A year ago, my mother sent me on a quest, not only for the treasure, but for what was stolen from her by Odin. The Golden *Skel of Fræði and Speki*—shell of knowledge and wisdom—belongs to her and the people in her kingdom. When he took the shell, he mocked her with its location in the cave." When Leif started to interrupt, she held up a hand to stay his words. "But I have my own demands. In return for *her* treasure, she must release me as leader of the Serpents."

Inga swallowed, looking directly at Leif. "The time to lead is now yours, *Brother*."

"By the Gods!" barked out Leif, raking a hand through his hair. "You should have told us sooner!"

Her brothers began to shout in earnest—each adding their own opinions and questions.

Ulrik and Haaken both looked at Steinar with confused expressions. He winced and rubbed a hand down the back of his neck. "Her mother is the Goddess of the sea."

Ulrik shook his head. "Gods' blood! A battle over power between a God and Goddess, and we are trapped in the middle. 'Tis not a good plan, Steinar."

"Aye," whispered Haaken in a shocked tone. "The treasure might be cursed as well."

As the argument became more vocal between Inga and her brothers, Steinar motioned his men to another part of the cave. If he knew anything about the Olafsson brothers, their shouts would merely increase until they got all their answers. Lending his voice in this instance would incite more wrath, and Steinar did not want to put more strain on his beloved.

Steinar wiped a hand over his forehead, uncertain about the wealth they witnessed. "I am in agreement about this treasure belonging to Odin. He might have created these riches after he took the shell from the Goddess."

Ulrik poked him in the chest. "And you are in

dangerous waters by claiming her daughter."

Shifting slightly, Steinar's expression stilled and grew serious. "Regardless of her lineage, I will fight any God *or* Goddess who opposes my love for Inga."

"Then let us pray the Goddess of the sea allows this union between her daughter and a wolf of Odin," responded Ulrik quietly.

Clamping a hand on the man's shoulder, Steinar ordered, "Speak with the others on both ships. Give them an account of what has occurred. If any desires to take a portion of this treasure, they must retrieve what they can carry."

Both nodded slowly and then retreated from the cave.

While the intense argument had simmered to a much lower tone, Steinar studied his beloved's features. She continued to give clipped responses but listened fully to each of her brothers.

I love you, Inga.

She lifted her head and smiled fully at him. Holding out her hand, she beckoned him to her.

Complying with her request, he went to her side. He tucked her hand in the crook of his arm, and then regarded those before her. "I have spoken with my men. They have decided to not take any of Odin's treasure. But I've instructed them to pass along to those who want a portion but must do so themselves. Each man must make his own decision."

Leif stiffened. "You are certain this is what you want, MacDougall?"

Steinar's resolve hardened as he looked at Inga. "I have already claimed a treasure more bountiful than what Odin can give to me. Your sister has given me a gift, filled a void I judged not worthy of having. Her love."

Inga traced a path over his heart with her fingers. "You *are* worthy, Pirate Wolf."

He winked at her. "Let us finish this quest."

"Aye!" echoed her brothers in unison.

Steinar's wolf howled three times. Alvilda's words of warning made him pause. He discarded them believing they had made the right decision to leave the treasure.

As they silently made their way out of the cave, Jorik paused and glanced over his shoulder. "Do you think I could take one gem?"

Shrugging, Inga replied, "If you so desire."

Her brother scratched the side of his face as if in deep thought. Finally, he laughed. "Nae! I don't want Odin to come seeking his goods. I'd rather we resume our trading."

Leif wrapped an arm around Jorik's shoulders. "The Hawk has made a wise decision. Let the God keep his wealth. I firmly trust this started with a feud between Odin and Rán."

Approaching the entrance, Steinar's warrior instinct detected the sounds of a battle. In seconds, he retrieved his axe from the sheath on his back and assumed a protective stance in front of Inga. Too late to deflect the blow, the hiss of an arrow pierced into his left shoulder with a sickening thud. His wolf howled in fury, demanding to be set free to taste the blood of Steinar's enemy. The beast slammed against his body causing Steinar to stumble over the rocks. It took all his control to temper the beast and fight the fiery pain slicing into him. He grimaced as he realized this was what the young seer had meant. *A hidden enemy!*

"Godred and his men are attacking both ships!" shouted Leif, charging around them and into the ongoing clash on the shore.

Inga's cry of alarm filled Steinar's ears as he dropped to his knees onto the ground. While Jorik took up a defensive position with his shield in front of him, Inga crouched down beside Steinar. More arrows shot past them, and Jorik cursed.

After giving a quick glance over Steinar's shoulder, she placed her hand on the side of his face. "The arrow did not go through to the other side. Tell me what to do." With great haste, she shoved the wooden box behind a boulder just inside the cave.

Gritting his teeth, he met her worried gaze. "Pull the bloody thing out of me."

Inga drew in a shaky breath. "Sweet Goddess, give me a steady hand."

He placed his hand over hers. "I trust you, *beloved*."

Inga pursed her lips in concentration. Placing one hand on his right shoulder for support, she yanked the arrow free. "What in the God's name were you thinking?" she hissed out, tossing the offensive weapon aside. "You did not need to step in front of me. I can defend myself."

Blood gushed out of Steinar's wound, and he winced. "Simply to protect the woman I love, even giving my life to save hers."

"*Men*," scolded Inga, though a small smile curved her lips. "You should be grateful I'm also a healer as well as a warrior." Retrieving her dirk from beneath her belt, she sliced a part of her tunic from the bottom. "Before we depart, let me apply a patch of sea moss to the wound. There are great healing qualities from the sea moss."

Steinar shook his head. "Nae time. Since the arrow is out, my wolf can tend to my healing. We have to assist the others."

Inga scooted away, digging apart the moss attached to a group of stones. She quickly returned to his side. "Do not argue with me, Steinar."

He chuckled softly, the effort inflicting further pain. "Am I nae longer your *Pirate Wolf*?"

Ignoring his question, she took her dirk and made a small cut in her palm. After squeezing a couple drops of her blood onto the moss, she then pressed it against the open wound along with part of the torn tunic. "Combined, the blood and moss shall aid in your healing."

Watching her face set with determination, Steinar asked, "Your healing comes from your mother?"

She gave a slight nod while wrapping the shredded material around his arm and shoulder. "Jorik, what is happening?" demanded Inga, securing a knot in the bandage.

Her brother kept his focus trained on the skirmish in front of him, while he blocked several incoming arrows aimed at them. "Godred is intent on slaying any man who gets in his way. He keeps shouting your name, MacDougall."

Steinar sneered and gripped his axe. "I'll kill the man. Should have done so many moons ago." Rising slowly, he flexed his arm. Noting the fear in his beloved's eyes, he reassured, "I require one blow with *one* hand to strike the man and end this madness. Then, we have to return to Islay. My concern is for the people if Godred has killed my uncle."

"But have you considered it might be your uncle

who sent him to kill you *and* gain the treasure?" Wariness filled her question as she made to stand.

"Nae, *nae*." Steinar set his sight on the man striding across the shore, slashing at any who dared to stop him. "I have had my suspicions regarding Godred but nae proof to present to my uncle. Now I fear the man has killed Rangvald for power and seeks to destroy me." Turning to her brother he said, "I thank you for your protection, Jorik, but move aside. Go help our men. Godred is *mine*."

Inga withdrew her sword. "You have my ship and men. We will go with you after we vanquish this enemy. And my *Pirate*, let your wolf assist you."

Steinar bent and kissed the frown between her brows. "Do not fear, beloved, I would *never* keep my beast hidden in a battle. Especially when the enemy has already struck once." His mouth covered hers hungrily, committing to memory every taste and scent that was Inga's.

When he broke free from her lips, Steinar gave a brief nod to her brother. With one last parting glance at Inga, he ordered, "I ken you are a warrior, but I cannot stop the fear coursing through my blood. If anything should happen to you, my beast will slaughter all those in his path to slay his enemy. And, beloved, I shall give him full control to do the deed."

Inga's eyes widened. Placing her forehead against his, she avowed, "Then I'll do my utmost to stay alive."

After Jorik tossed his shield to Inga, they both charged forth to join the others. Steinar squashed the anxiety of seeing his beloved entering into the battle. On a silent prayer, he asked for protection over them and a strong arm to take down their enemy.

Allowing the wolf to emerge forth within his eyes, Steinar leveled his axe outward. "Your blood shall be mine, Godred!"

Chapter Twenty-One

"Did you send your dog to do your bidding?" Steinar blocked another blow from his foe while Godred stood to the side, laughing and taunting him. Regardless of the burning pain lancing across his shoulder, he used both hands to strike and defend.

Godred kicked the sand in their direction. "Did you hear what he called you, Michael?"

"Aye, I head the wolf pup."

Steinar's wolf howled in fury, gnashing his teeth, and craving to sink his teeth into the man.

The battle between them continued with their steps leading them away from the main source of conflict. Thunder roared overhead, adding to the deafening sounds of the violent battle. Steinar landed another blow with the end of his axe to the man's head.

Michael staggered. Sweat mixed with blood trickled down his brow. When lightning seared the sky, the man blinked in an attempt to focus.

Taking advantage of Michael's momentary lapse of concentration, Steinar stepped to the side and swung with all his might. The blow severed the man's head from his body.

"Traitor!" bellowed a familiar voice among the clash of weapons and shouting.

Steinar shifted his stance and turned his attention elsewhere. Storm clouds had gathered, blocking the moonlight, and making it difficult for Steinar to set his sight on the man he'd heard and the enemy. "Where are you Godred?"

"Not yours to slay, Steinar! The evil swine's life belongs to me!" The man roared with a fierceness coming from only one Steinar recognized.

Stepping over a dead body, Steinar shouted in disbelief, "Uncle?"

Blocking a blow aimed at his head, Steinar promptly removed the enemy's arm with his axe. He glanced outward, slashing at another man intent on ending his life and came face to face with Godred. Lightning sliced through the air, landing near both men.

Steinar raised his axe, bringing forth the beast for the strength to kill his foe.

Yet Godred's horrified expression halted Steinar in his steps. Fear, stark and vivid glittered in the man's eyes as he lowered his gaze. The blade had found its mark—struck clean through Godred's chest while he stood several feet away from Steinar.

The man coughed once, twice—blood splattering a gruesome trail over his mouth and chin. Godred choked in an attempt to draw in a breath and clawed at his face with his hand. When he slumped to the ground, Rangvald the Bear towered from behind him and swiftly removed his sword from the man's body. With a final kick to the back from his uncle, Godred fell forward, dead.

Rangvald coughed and spit on the man. Removing the sword from Godred's hand, he flung it to the side. "You are not worthy to sit at Odin's table with the other warriors. You are nothing but a traitor."

Stunned by the appearance of his uncle, Steinar cleared his throat and lowered his arm. "You are here.

How?"

"I have known about his betrayal for some time," his uncle answered quickly before taking down another man with his sword. "I had a smaller ship follow him when he left right after you did."

Steinar glanced beyond his uncle, noting the battle had turned in their favor with the appearance of his uncle's men. He lowered his axe and approached the man. "But how did you manage to travel past the cauldron and find the island?"

Rangvald rumbled with laughter. Pointing his sword to the night sky, he declared, "As soon as we met with the smaller ship, we were blown off our course. The fierce winds carried us here to you. Or should I say, *All Father* guided our ship to this island to assist you."

Scrubbing a hand over his face, Steinar exhaled fully. "Indeed, all praise to Odin."

Rangvald embraced him, then drew back. "So, have you found the treasure?"

He gestured behind him. "In the cave. But the decision of both crews is to leave it behind. Its beauty and riches are tempting, but we agreed this was a test, possibly of honor or courage. I cannot fathom."

"Then 'tis wise not to venture inside. I might be tempted, although I'm convinced your father would have done otherwise."

Steinar looked past his uncle, searching for the woman who held his heart. "There is another treasure more valuable to me."

Rangvald smiled knowingly. "Aye. The *woman* has beauty and wields a sword mightily."

The wolf within Steinar paced with uncertainty. *Where are you, my kærr?*

As he started to move forward, he paused. Inga came running toward him, leaping over dead bodies and boulders. Once, she tripped, but quickly righted herself. He found himself unable to hold back the smile and dropped his axe to pull her against him.

"Victory is ours!" she exclaimed, kissing him passionately.

Steinar growled, savoring the taste of his beloved. Concern overtook his desire, and he broke the contact. "Are you injured? Is this your blood?" His fingers traced the slight swelling on her cheek and let out a hiss.

Humor softened her features. "When one of my braids came unbound, someone tried to hack it off. But nae." She darted Rangvald a questioning look. "I thank you for your assistance, but how did you manage to find us?"

"Odin!" exclaimed Steinar and his uncle in unison.

Inga clucked her tongue. "Not only the God, but I also reckon Rán lent her support."

His uncle scowled. "Why would the Goddess of the sea—"

"I am her daughter," announced Inga, stepping out of Steinar's hold, and made long strides toward the cave. "And I've come to retrieve what was stolen from her."

Rangvald the Bear blanched, the first time Steinar witnessed his uncle show any fear. He nudged the man. "There is much I need to share with you."

"Obviously," mumbled his uncle, watching Inga part from them. He blinked and resumed his attention to Steinar. "And I, too. Many thought me to be addled in the mind but all a deception to find the traitor. Are you returning to Torvay?"

"Aye, then returning to Islay. You do realize King

William grew concerned."

"Then my plan succeeded. Good. Since I am without a successor, I require a discussion about the isles when you return."

Steinar grunted a curse. He wasn't ready to return to their previous conversations about ruling Islay and the surrounding islands. Bending down, he retrieved his axe. His brow furrowed. "Without a successor?"

As if sensing his frustration, Rangvald explained, "Godred had another traitor working with him. *Sigrid*. I have banished my daughter to a jarl in the far north. Furthermore, this leaves me without an heir. Grant me an hour to present my plan?"

"Sigrid," echoed Steinar. "By the Gods, I never thought she'd betray you."

"She *betrayed* everyone on Islay and beyond," he amended. "I will give you the full account when you return. For now, let us gather on the shore, build a fire, and drink to our victory!"

****

When the first light of dawn creased the azure sky, Inga opened her eyes and stretched her arms overhead. Digging her toes into the sand, she savored the sensation. Though eager to finish her task and hand over the shell to her mother, she longed to remain for a while longer. Steinar rested next to her with one arm draped over his forehead. Earlier, he had stripped his tunic and dove into the sea to rid himself of the battle's grime and blood. Her body heated in wonderful places while she watched him. Unable to join him, she had to be content with viewing him from the shore while she cleaned her face and hands.

She nudged her pirate's leg with her foot. "Your uncle has already departed?"

227

Steinar yawned but made no move to sit. "Apparently, all compasses are now pointing in the correct positions, and he wanted to make haste back to Islay."

"Does he have concerns?"

"He worries another shall take Godred's place," he affirmed quietly.

Leif barked out an order they were ready to depart.

Steinar drew himself up and stood. Holding out his hand, Inga grasped it firmly. When she stood before him, he raked his gaze over her body.

She shivered. "What?"

"When did you change and where did you get this gown?" His fingers played along the sculpted edges near the top of her breasts. "You are beautiful beyond words."

Chuckling softly, she answered, "When you slept. I went to the cave and changed. This is a gown my mother gave me long ago. I brought it with me, expecting to greet her here *or* back on Torvay. I go to her as her daughter and warrior, but never as a woman who has battled men. She would not approve."

Steinar glanced at her sword belted at her side, then snapped his concerned gaze to her. "Are you expecting trouble?"

"With my mother? Always."

He bent and placed a kiss on the soft spot below her ear. "Then I will stand beside you."

Inga started to object, but he silenced her with a searing kiss. She melted into his embrace until Leif's loud protests became demanding, along with threats of leaving without them. Inga let out a sigh, pressing a hand to her pirate's chest and pushed away from him.

Collecting the wooden box next to her, she wrapped

her other arm through Steinar's. "Are you certain you want to have Leif guide us back to Torvay?"

"Our journey is over. 'Tis his right to lead. Or yours?"

Pausing at the edge of the water, she glanced at both ships. Uncertainty with this new direction made Inga realize they had not discussed what would happen next with their lives. Would they travel the seas together? Or would he return to the Brotherhood? Would he even expect her to join him in future tasks for the king?

"What are you thinking about?" asked Steinar, swiping at a lone curl over her cheek.

Smiling, she shrugged. "More plans."

In one swift move, Steinar lifted her into his arms. "Tell me after you return the shell."

Inga gasped and slapped his arm. "What are you doing? I am not a weak lass because I'm wearing a gown."

"Do you not wish to be acceptable when you greet your mother? And did you just hit my injured shoulder?"

She rested her head against him. "You are fully healed, my Pirate Wolf. I saw the wound when you took a swim in the water. 'Tis barely a scratch. Did I not tell you the moss and my blood would aid faster with the power from your wolf?"

"Observing my body, again. If you only knew my thoughts about yours, beloved."

Inga squirmed in his arms. "Show me later," she whispered into his ear.

His growl surrounded her, even as he lifted her onto the ladder of the ship. Jorik climbed partially down and retrieved the box from her arms until she managed the rest of the way on board.

Soon, they were heading away from the Cove of Gríma. Inga kept her gaze on the island until the mists shrouded their view. She dipped her head in farewell, uttering a silent prayer to Odin for his protection and safe passage.

Settling against the stern, Inga remained content to watch the steady rise and fall of the waves as they made a steady course to Torvay. Her pirate was giving another full account of the battle to Snorri. The skald judged it wise to have Steinar keep talking about the details. And the man gladly complied.

Hours slipped by and once, she spotted a sea animal. Inga called out a greeting by tapping her hand over the side of the ship. The animal leaped into the air in a graceful arc before descending with a splash into the water.

You will give me what I want, Mother. 'Tis time. With a new sense of purpose, Inga smiled broadly.

Steinar approached, slipping an arm around her shoulders. "Snorri is impressed not one man sought to take any of the treasure."

Nervous laughter bubbled forth from her. "In truth, I cannot fathom why Odin did not try and halt me from retrieving the shell. With all the lightning, thunder, and the ground rumbling beneath me while I slashed away at our enemies, not once did I come to harm."

He shrugged and narrowed his eyes. "Perchance he yearns for peace between him and your mother."

On a sigh, Inga turned toward him. "There'll always be disagreements between the Gods and Goddesses." She tugged on his unfinished braid. "Allow me?"

"Aye, *my kærr*. Finish the task."

His voice, deep and sensual, sent a ripple of longing

through Inga's body. Doing her best to keep her focus on braiding and fastening the one braid on the side of his face, she tried not to think of those full lips that made hers burn.

"Do you think we can spend the night at the stones?" Steinar asked, his breath warm against her cheek.

Inga snapped her gaze to meet his. Desire shone within those sapphire depths, stilling her movements. She yearned for more than a night. Would her pirate be content to remain with her on Torvay? Or did he seek to return to the seas? "How many nights?" she blurted out, fearing his reply.

His smile disarmed every other thought or worry. "For now, let us think of tonight. We can discuss our future plans later. *After* I have feasted on your body—"

"And I yours," she interrupted in a throaty whisper, tracing a finger over his silver torc.

"Tell me what you shall do," he urged.

"I'd love to trail my tongue down—"

"Torvay!" bellowed Leif near the bow of the ship.

Steinar pressed his cheek against hers. "You can show me tonight."

A renewed sense of purpose filled Inga with this return to her home. A year-long quest ending. Eager to view Torvay, she darted to the front. Gripping the side of the ship with one hand, she waved to those gathered along the shore.

Steinar roared with laughter.

Stunned by his outburst, Inga whipped around and stared at him, along with her brothers. Yet Steinar's men stood in shocked silence liked they'd witnessed Odin himself.

Steinar held his hands upward. "What?"

She tilted her head to the side. "In all our time together, I've never heard you laugh."

"Nor us," mentioned Ulrik, rubbing a hand through his beard.

"And we've never seen our sister become so excited and wave in greeting like a young lass," declared Leif, crossing his arms over his chest.

Inga reached out and poked her brother in the chest. "There's always a first time."

Her pirate bridged the distance between them in long strides. She reached out her hand to him.

Grasping it firmly, he tucked her hand in the crook of his arm. "Definitely a first. And you make me laugh, *kærr*."

Turning him toward the welcoming crowd, Inga whispered words meant for him, "Forget about waiting until tonight. As soon as the shell is in my mother's hands, we shall take our leave and have our feast alone."

Steinar's eyes darkened with emotion. "Agreed."

Chapter Twenty-Two

Clasping his hands behind his back, Steinar quieted the beast within as they waited for the appearance of the Goddess Rán. His wolf grew impatient, while Steinar sought to quell his own irritation. He set his sight beyond the horizon, grateful only Inga's brothers had remained.

The people of Torvay departed soon after the greetings were exchanged. Even his men sought refuge, deciding drink and a good meal in the longhouse appealed more than confronting the Goddess of the sea.

But the Olafsson brothers refused to leave and sat nearby beneath a grove of small trees. When Steinar asked what to expect from the Goddess, they all shared the same account. Rán obeyed the laws of the sea—her edicts. Those who opposed or broke them were banished to the dark watery abyss. Though they all deemed she loved her daughter, she also possessed a fierce temper. On more than one occasion, Inga retreated from their intense arguments, bending to her mother's will.

Steinar returned his attention to Inga, leaning against a tree.

His beloved stood on the edge of the shore with the water lapping against her bare feet. Her hair glimmered in the late afternoon sunlight. In her arms, she cradled the wooden box.

I desire to see those braids down, and the strands brushing over my skin. 'Tis so soft, and I ache to twist a lock around my hand.

Are you speaking to me inside my mind again?

He smiled. *Aye.*

Stop. I need to concentrate on calling forth my mother.

Steinar grunted, unclasping his hands. "We have been waiting on her arrival for an hour! Can she not hear your summons?"

Inga shot him a haughty glare. "One does not summon a Goddess. You *request* an audience." She resumed her gaze outward.

One of Inga's brothers laughed. Steinar glared at them all.

"Steinar?"

"Aye, beloved?"

"Please quiet your wolf. His growls are filling my mind, and I find I cannot concentrate."

Though her back faced him, Steinar dipped a bow. "By your command."

Inga's shoulders shook with quiet laughter.

Drawing in a huge breath, Steinar filled his body with the sea air, striving to settle the beast. On the exhale, he closed his eyes, allowing the rhythm of the ocean waves to soothe both man and wolf.

"The Goddess is coming forth," Inga announced.

He opened his eyes but remained firm in his position. Until Inga called him forth, he'd be content to watch from a distance.

Inga placed the wooden box containing the shell onto the shore. Removing her dirk from her side, she rested the weapon next to the box. Glancing over her shoulder, she ordered, "Do not approach until she speaks to you."

Steinar inclined his head in acceptance.

A brilliant flash of colored lights drew his attention beyond Inga. The Goddess Rán emerged forth from the water in a shimmering haze of beauty. Her hair hung down in silvery waves below her waist, brushing against a gown of blue and green covered in pearls that wrapped around her form. Though her skin radiated a pale sheen, it was the Goddess's eyes which spoke of the power within the woman. As if all the colors of the sea were formed into one brilliant color. With each step she took, the Goddess appeared to be gliding over the water to her daughter.

Steinar exhaled slowly. His wolf padded closer, and the Olafsson brothers stood.

When her bare feet touched the shore, the Goddess halted and held out her arms.

Inga slipped into her mother's embrace. "Welcome back to Torvay."

"The quest is completed?" Rán drew back.

His beloved gestured toward the box. "Done." Bending, Inga lifted the wooden box into her arms. Unclasping the latch, she opened to reveal the Shell of Wisdom and Knowledge.

The Goddess let out a sigh. "The ancient librarians shall be grateful to you, Daughter, as am I." She lifted her hand to touch the shell.

Inga closed the lid. "Before I return the stolen relic, I have requests."

Her hand stilled, then slowly lowered. "Requests *or* demands?" A hint of censure reflected in her mother's tone.

"I nae longer desire to be the leader of the Serpents. Now is the time for Leif to step into the responsibility.

Think of this as a bargain, Mother. You've obtained a valuable treasure to the sea kingdom, and I get what I want. My freedom."

Silence reigned between mother and daughter. A white bird circled around them, before heading out to sea.

"Come forward, Leif, son of Olaf!" ordered the Goddess while keeping her attention fixed on Inga.

The man strode with easy strides to the edge of the shore. Leif bowed his head in greeting. "Goddess Rán."

"Kneel." A deep azure crystal wand appeared in her hand. The crystal's light fractured all around her.

After Leif complied, the Goddess tapped the wand once on each shoulder. "I hereby transfer leadership from my daughter to the eldest son of Olaf. You shall rule and be guided by those within the sea kingdom. With this new position, you are also required to receive counsel from the God Njörd. Without his approval and acceptance, his power over certain parts of the seas and winds could prove fatal to you and your men." Pressing the crystal against his chest, she asked, "Do you accept this responsibility, Leif, son of Olaf?"

Leif lifted his head. "Aye, I accept."

The Goddess snapped her fingers and the wand vanished. "Even though I have sensed your impatience, I am honored by your dedication, and those of your brothers to stand united with my daughter." She motioned for him to rise. "You may leave us."

Leif remained silent as he made his way back to his brothers. He gave Steinar a quick nod in passing.

Rán ran the back of her finger over her daughter's cheek. "You appear…changed."

"I have found love on this journey, Mother."

The Goddess looked beyond and straight at Steinar. Her lips puckered with annoyance. "*Wolf*!"

Irked by the Goddess' cold censure, Steinar did not wait to be granted permission to speak. "I love Inga and have claimed her."

Her eyes flashed with outrage. "*Claimed*? A beast of Odin shall *never* have my daughter. And you both have chosen unwisely."

"Nae, Mother!" Inga held out her hand to Steinar. "Do not be angry with us. How can you deny the love we have for each other?"

Steinar did not hesitate to join his beloved. Choosing not to take her hand, he wrapped a possessive arm around her waist. Regardless of the Goddess who stood before them, his love for Inga far outweighed any power.

"Never! I forbid this union!" snapped Rán, the waves crashing around her, matching her wrath.

"This *beast* aided your daughter in the capture of the Shell of Wisdom and Knowledge, regardless of the God who stole it. Odin could have easily ended mine and my wolf's life for betraying him," explained Steinar in a firm voice.

Rán's laughter sent a chill down Steinar's back. He hugged Inga tighter to his side.

"Please, Mother—"

The Goddess slashed her hand in dismissal. "You have forgotten the edict of the sea, Daughter. You have forgotten the siren's song. And you have *forgotten* what you promised when I saved this wolf's life. A life for a life!"

Steinar's mind reeled with confusion. The shock of discovery hit him with full force. Slowly, he turned toward Inga. "*Yours* was the voice I heard arguing when

I became trapped in the water."

Inga swallowed. She trembled within his grasp. "Aye," she finally managed on a whisper. Then sweeping a glance at her mother. "Surely, you can forgive this in exchange for the shell."

Rán's expression turned to one of horrified disbelief. "Even I cannot undo this ancient edict. A proclamation sworn in blood by those before me. Those in the sea kingdom will demand payment or cause havoc on land until a warrior is brought forth to the abyss. By law, I cannot stop them."

Steinar battled his inner turmoil, fighting for a solution. But none presented, save one. Give up his life for the woman he loved. Releasing his hold on his beloved, he cupped her chin. "How cruel the Fates are to give us love and then demand it back."

Rán took a step forward and lifted her hand. The power surged forth from her fingertips, circling around Steinar. "A life for a life. If you are unable to comply with the law, then I assert the power to take this man."

Sadness engulfed Steinar. He'd forfeit his life for the sake of his beloved. His decision made, he turned to the Goddess. "I give my—"

"Nae, nae, nae!" yelled Inga, shoving her mother backward into the water, and reaching for her dirk on the shore. She twisted around and aimed the weapon at her. "He is mine!"

Outraged by her daughter's actions, the Goddess leveled a blow of power against her, lifting Inga into the air. With a flick of her wrist, she sent her daughter sailing across the shore where she slammed against a tree.

A great roar filled Steinar as he rushed to Inga's bent form on the ground. Falling to his knees, he gently placed his palm over her heart, ignoring the blood trickling from her mouth. After enduring several long minutes, he finally detected the faint beat of her heart. "I am here, beloved. Can you not open your eyes?" He tried to stir her but to no avail. His beloved remained motionless.

Inga's brothers hurried to her side and formed a protective shield around them.

Bone deep shivers wracked his body while the blood boiled within Steinar's veins. His vision clouded with sickening agony, and his wolf rose on a growl with only one thought. Vengeance. Ripping his tunic in half, Steinar flung the material outward. Unable to control the beast, Steinar shifted in a blur of gray and silver into the wolf. He had become the blood thrall of the beast.

The wolf howled in fury as he lunged across the shore to the Goddess, intent on seeking revenge, even if it meant his death.

Rán swung her power at him. "How dare a beast of Odin charge at me!"

Continuous blows struck man and beast in the chest, but their rage so great, they kept charging onward. When another blow struck the wolf's head with blinding force, the animal tumbled over the sandy ground, coming to a stop against a large boulder. Pain seared like a thousand blades into their bodies.

Steinar fought the temptation to succumb to the darkness snaking a path through his mind. His wolf snapped and snarled, unable to stay focused—both man and beast slipping into the dark sleep.

"Stop!" Inga's screams snapped Steinar from his weakened condition. His wolf shook his head in an attempt to clear the dizziness and lifted his sight outward.

"Nae, nae, my pirate," choked out Inga, stumbling

over the shore while clutching Leif's arm. Slumping down next to him, she buried her fingers into the wolf's fur and pressed her cheek against the side of his head. "For our love, I *beg* you not to strike out at her. You will surely lose this battle. You will die. Hear me—pirate *and* wolf."

Storm clouds descended over the ocean, snaking a path in their direction, followed by a deafening crash of thunder. The ground heaved and rumbled beneath them. A bolt of lightning seared a path through the sky before striking the ground, leaving a scorched trail to the edge of the water.

Rán lifted her hand upward in defense. "Do not interfere, Odin! This is all *your* fault! Be grateful I have not ended his life!"

Tears spilled down Inga's face and into the wolf's fur. She stroked a hand over his back, soothing the beast with her touch and words. "Forgive me, Steinar. There is only one solution." Carefully, she removed the sunstone from around her neck and slipped it over the wolf's.

Rising slowly, Inga regarded her brother. "Watch over them."

Leif grabbed her arm. "Give me a plan."

"Do not let Steinar come after me." She paused and drew in a shallow breath. "And this last order is meant for all of you. Do not follow me. I must grant my mother—the *Goddess* what I vowed to her weeks ago."

The wolf gnashed his teeth in warning, attempting to sit up.

Slowly, Leif released his hold. "This is not finished. We will find a way to release you."

Inga held out her hand to her mother while walking away from him. "My life I give freely in exchange for the man you saved for me. A life given as payment by the laws of the sea kingdom. In this bargain, you will consent to cause nae further harm to Steinar MacDougall and his wolf."

Her mother lowered her arms. The wind settled to a light breeze around her. "You would give your life in exchange for the wolf's?"

On a choked sob, Inga replied, "I'd give up my life to save the man I *love*—the man who holds my heart. The man *and* wolf I saved from your clutches."

"Accepted. I shall await you in my chambers." Rán lowered herself into the water, disappearing from their view.

With each step Inga took, Steinar's dread grew. Turmoil knotted within him, and with great effort, he shifted from wolf to man. An anguished cry wrenched from his throat. "Do not go, Inga! *Nae*! 'Tis my life she should take!" Standing on shaking limbs, he gasped for air.

Leif blocked him with an outstretched hand.

Steinar roared as one—man and wolf. A warning to the man in front of him. If any attempted to stand in his path, death would be swift. Blind rage overcame all rational thought, except one. Save his beloved.

Lowering his hand, Leif took a step aside and pleaded, "You will gain nothing, MacDougall. The Goddess has taken her payment. From the moment Inga rescued you from the siren's song, she sealed her fate. We warned her, but she refused to listen. In the end, we thought she could bargain for her freedom *and* your life. But the edicts—*the laws* of the sea kingdom are firm."

Steinar shoved past the man, watching his beloved step into the water. He clenched his fists, battling between the pain in his heart and seeking the blood of those who would take her. "*Inga!*"

Slowly, she turned around. Tears streaked down her face, leaving a shimmering trail over her skin. Placing her hand over her heart, Inga's voice remained calm, her gaze steady. "I shall carry my love for you always. It beats inside my heart. Even when I take my last breath, my love for you will continue to the depths of the oceans, until they are nae more. Remember our love, Steinar. I am yours, until the end." On a final sob, she managed, "You are mine, *Pirate Wolf.*"

While keeping her attention fixed on him, Inga bent and dipped her fingers into the water. "I love you, always."

In a soft blur of light and stars, she vanished into the sea.

Steinar's grief so raw, he roared out his agony and stumbled across the shore. When he reached the water's edge, he bellowed her name over and over again. Dropping to his knees, he let the waves crash over his body. The pain of her loss ripping his heart to shards of steel.

He bent his head, pouring out his grief. Soon, fury—dark and dangerous—entered his mind. With one final cry, he shifted from man to beast.

The wolf howled in frustration, digging his paws into the gritty sand. After long moments, he retreated from the water. He yearned to leave a place where the pain was too unbearable. The salty brine of the sea sickened them both. Turning away, the wolf tore across the shore, seeking refuge far away—banishing all that had once brought them immense joy and agonizing torment.

And both man and wolf made a silent promise to never set sail onto the seas again.

Chapter Twenty-Three

Ignoring the summons to appear in the Goddess' royal chambers, Inga dismissed the guard with another stern reply. Upon her arrival, she'd stormed away from her mother, vowing to never speak to her again. Thankfully, her mother permitted Inga access to her old chambers in the royal palace. She half-expected the Goddess to hand her over to the sirens who prepare those for the warriors' tomb inside the dark caverns.

Days had slipped by in suffering anguish since she had agreed to spend the rest of her life in the sea kingdom. Nights were spent in tears, rants of shouting, pounding on the walls, or in sorrowful silence. She wept for the passionate love that blossomed inside her heart, only to be ripped apart by an ancient edict.

When sleep finally came, her dreams were filled with him. Her pirate invaded her with his love, sweeping back into her arms. She'd wake to find his touch and breath lingering over her skin as if the dream were real, recalling the smoldering passion Steinar had ignited in her.

Inga realized no amount of time would lessen the ache of loss. Each day it bloomed anew.

In the end, the Goddess Rán had won a valuable prize—her daughter.

"If you do not appear at the royal court within twenty-four hours, all your privileges shall be stripped, and you'll be confined to this chamber." The guard's terse tone did not go unnoticed with Inga.

"Remind me how slowly time passes here, Rolf? And when you say confined, do you mean chained or locked?" She fidgeted with the armbands denoting her lineage around her forearms, twisting and turning them. She waited for his answer while the sea animals pressed their noses in greeting against the crystal chamber. Placing one hand against the cool surface of the pale crystal wall, she welcomed them back within their minds.

Yet they sensed her somber mood and swam away within the floating seaweed.

"For every hour above, equals several minutes here. Or so the ancients profess. As for your confinement, I am unsure. But this makes the tenth time the Goddess has summoned you."

She muttered a curse and kept her back to the man. Eventually, Inga wanted to roam the vast kingdom without a guard at her side. Grieving inside her chambers would not be allowed to continue. Would her mother consider sending her away to another part of the kingdom? If she had to spend her life below, Inga wanted to live it out beyond the reach of her mother.

"Are you coming?" asked Rolf, his tone becoming impatient.

Unable to find a spark of kindness in her words, she asked, "Afraid the Goddess will strip you of your service if I send the same message?"

Rolf spoke with quiet, but desperate firmness. "Banishment to the outer kingdom for me and my family."

Inga bit her lip to stifle the outcry. *How cruel to*

leave his fate in my hands, Mother. The day of reckoning could no longer be delayed. She wiped her hands down her gown of deep blue and turned around.

"Then I have nae choice. Guilt would plague me if I never saw your face again." Though sadness engulfed her, Inga offered the man a smile. "You may tell my mother I will greet her in one hour."

The guard shifted his stance. "If I might suggest, ten minutes instead of an hour?"

Inga arched a brow, though his message was clear. "Aye, an hour here moves slowly. For your sake, I have nae desire to stir her wrath any further."

Rolf dipped a slight bow. "My thanks, *Princess*."

Inga winced but remained silent. How she despised the formality.

After the guard departed her chambers, Inga took a comb and brushed it through her hair. Adjusting the silver armbands around her forearms, she reasoned she would be acceptable to her mother.

Crossing to the door, she flung it open and proceeded to stride with purpose along the coral and amber corridor. Muted colors reflected back to her in all directions from the enormous sea kingdom. Raising her head, she marveled at the shimmering glow. She'd forgotten the beauty here. Inga paused and whispered, "You would have loved viewing the sea from this vantage, my pirate."

Inga tried to ease the distress with deep calming breaths. Minutes ticked by, but the pain remained—a constant reminder of what she'd lost.

Straightening her shoulders, she marched onward through the corridor and down a set of marble stairs, opening to the garden of sea flowers. Their petals seem to wave in a gentle greeting in the light warm breeze. Ignoring their heady scent, she made haste, winding and twisting her way to her mother's chambers.

The guards noted her arrival and opened the double-doors.

Inga strode inside and halted. She'd also forgotten the expanse of her mother's chambers. The green crystal floor dipped in places, leading to other hidden alcoves and rooms. The view of the sea beyond, immense.

Rising from her chair at her coral desk, her mother reached outward with her hand, beckoning her daughter to her. A smile creased her features. "The beauty of the sea kingdom cannot compare to the world above in the human realm—Odin's land."

Inga struggled to find the words to respond. Hurt, anger, shock—all straining for control. She remained rooted in her position, unable to take a step forward.

The Goddess laughed and bent her head to the side, studying her. "You have forgotten the splendor of the sea kingdom and palace."

Her mother appeared to enjoy Inga's struggle to capture her composure. Clasping her hands in front of her, she responded, "Greetings, Mother. You summoned me here."

A frown replaced the humor across her mother's face. "I called you here because I have missed you. Since your home is now with me, I wanted to speak to you about your duties and show you the additional learning chambers in the palace."

Doing her best to keep her voice steady, Inga responded, "I have been grieving. Surely, you can understand what it's like to lose someone you love."

Rán's expression was one of pained tolerance. "Do

not speak of the comparison."

"But nae God or Goddess forbade your union with my father, did they?"

Her mother struck her hand on the table, sending several sheets of golden parchment onto the floor. "I met him on Torvay's shore. I did not rescue him from the siren's song. There is a stark difference!"

Inga's courage and determination were like a rock inside her. She finally moved toward her mother. "Love strikes, regardless of the circumstances."

"This is not why I have asked you here. This discussion has ended."

She dared to stir her mother's anger further. Inga pressed her palms upon the smooth surface of the desk. "Did you conceive me as part of your plan to seize back what you had lost? The chance meeting with my father merely an opportunity to bear a child who would retrieve the stolen relic for you?"

Rán's mouth opened in stunned silence, then she snapped it shut. Fury infused her words. "You have gone too far in your cruelty, Inga."

"Cruelty, nae. Questions I have considered asking you since my arrival." Inga shoved away from the desk. "I am confused, hurt, and in pain. Without considering your actions—*your demands*, you drew me, Steinar, and those around us into your feud with Odin. You gave nae thought to the havoc you and Odin would cause in our lives. And you have not answered my question."

Her mother's features softened. "The moment I saw your father standing on the shore, my heart opened to love." She settled back into the chair with a sigh. "I disregarded all the laws of my world and stepped onto the land, hoping he'd feel the same for me. There was never a plan, Inga. I conceived you out of love. As far as I am concerned, Steinar heard the call—"

"Nae! He fell overboard and your sirens tried to lure him below. You knew who he was, and you also knew about the prophecy between me and a wolf!"

Rán nodded her head solemnly. "He will bring death or destruction. Aye, I had heard the words of the seers. But the sirens took their prize. There are rules here, which even I cannot go against."

"Rules can be amended," snapped Inga. "Did you not once spout this to me in a heated argument over the leadership of the Serpents? You disregarded all discussions, even those of my own people—the seers who again advised against making me the leader. You disregarded the law above the sea."

"But I did listen," corrected her mother.

Furious with the direction of the conversation, Inga argued, "You bend the laws to suit your needs but will not consider listening to mine."

Rán spread her arms wide. "What do you expect from me? To go against this one edict would bring about destruction."

Without hesitation, Inga answered, "Find a way to send me back to the man I love. If not, then you doom us both to a life of pain and suffering. Until then, I am leaving the royal palace and shall seek shelter with the healers who dwell in the far north of the sea kingdom. I forfeit all privileges as the daughter of the Goddess. You started this and I shall end it!"

Her mother's gasp surrounded Inga as she hastily fled the chambers.

****

Islay—August 1207

Tossing aside his wrap, Steinar lifted his head to the bleak sunlight filtering through the canopy of trees. Though a warm morning breeze drifted over his skin, a sudden chill coursed within his body and seeped into his bones. He scrubbed a hand over his face, trying to banish the dream of holding his beloved in his arms. Raising his fist, he shouted, "Why do you torment me with dreams of her? Why, Odin?"

Leaves circled in a dance around his feet before sweeping past him. A raw and primitive grief overwhelmed Steinar.

"Always the same," he muttered in contempt when no answer came forth from the God.

Steinar rested his head on his bent knees. Weariness settled inside his body like a lodestone. Sleep became elusive, and he avoided everyone.

When he returned to Islay, he acknowledged his right to stand by his uncle and become his heir upon his death, surprising his uncle when he immediately signed the parchment. Never again would Steinar venture out on the sea—so he declared to Rangvald, even sending a message to the Brotherhood. In his document to Magnar, he requested a task to take him away from the isles and far into Scotland. While he loathed traveling across the land, he had no desire to view the ocean, knowing his beloved dwelled far below without him.

And each day, each night, his wolf howled in utter agony. Unable to soothe the beast, Steinar relented and permitted him to continue with his sorrowful, tortured cries.

Lifting his head, Steinar twisted around and reached for the aleskin. He finished what remained in one long gulp. After wiping his mouth with the back of his hand, he tossed it onto the ground.

A bird flew down from a tree limb, eager to catch any scraps of food. His chirping appeal became louder as he searched through bits of dead leaves and dirt.

Steinar regarded the feathered friend. "I have nothing left to give."

"When was the last time you had a meal?" demanded the man behind him.

Silent and lethal, the leader of the Brotherhood had approached without Steinar's awareness. "How long have you been standing there, *Magnar*?"

"Too long. Get up."

"I prefer the ground."

A great growl filled Steinar's mind. Cupping his hands over his ears, he tried to stifle the brutal command from the man's wolf. Yet the more he fought, the more persistent the demands became. Several moments passed before the pain lessened. He blew out a frustrated breath.

"Do not make me ask you again," warned Magnar, moving to one of the trees in front of him. He leaned against the bark and folded his arms over his chest.

With great effort, Steinar made to stand and glared at his leader. He dared the man to utter the first word, for he would not.

Silence grew like an oncoming storm.

Magnar flashed him a dangerous look. Pushing away from the tree, he stormed to stand directly in front of him. "Are you *challenging* me? You dare to show your beast to me within your eyes?"

The bitter words Steinar craved to lash out at the man lodged firmly in his throat. Did Magnar not understand his message? Did he not fathom the anguish that consumed him and his beast? Furthermore, why was the leader of the Brotherhood on Islay? In an attempt to harness any thread of control, he clenched his hands and looked away.

Steinar's wolf silently retreated.

"Even though I have allowed my wolf to make the journey here and *we* have not rested, I can wait all day *and* night for you to speak. I am not leaving," declared Magnar with cool authority.

Keeping his gaze steady on the trees, Steinar coughed to clear his throat. "I am astonished you would leave your wife and new bairn."

"Elspeth's pleas and urging left me nae choice. She is the one who reminded me of my duty, not only to her and my son, but also to those brothers in need."

Slowly, Steinar relaxed his hands and turned toward his leader and friend. "I must thank her on my return," he managed softly.

"And she would welcome seeing you," encouraged Magnar. "Especially from one she holds in high regard."

"Why me? I have done nothing to deserve this praise."

His friend gave an exasperated snort in good humor. "You protected her on more than one occasion, even though you had your own doubts about her loyalty to me."

"I did so even with Rorik's wife, Ragna," admitted Steinar, embarrassed by his previous misgivings with both women.

"Regardless, she grew concerned after I spoke with her about your decision. If you have not learned by now, Elspeth loves all of those in the Brotherhood. They are now her family and protectors."

Concerned, Steinar asked, "Which wolves did you

leave protecting them?"

"Ivar and Bjorn. They are the strongest and keen observers. However, they were insistent on coming with me. All grew concerned with the content of your message."

Steinar exhaled, allowing some of the tension to subside from his body. "How is your son?"

Magnar beamed, fisting his hands on his hips. "Thomas is strong, healthy, *and* loud. The Gods have blessed us. I marvel at his growth each day."

"Good, good…"

"Let us speak out in the sun. 'Tis a warm summer day and my journey was fraught with storms," suggested Magnar, gesturing for Steinar to proceed him.

Hesitating for a brief moment, Steinar walked out into the sunlight. He shielded his eyes from the sun's intensity. The warmth seeped into his weary body as he kept walking toward a clump of wildflowers. Lowering himself onto the ground, he waited for Magnar to join him.

When the man settled next to Steinar, he glanced sideways at him. "Why are you here?"

Magnar settled his arms over his bent knees. "Tell me about Inga the Ruthless."

The pain intensified inside Steinar's chest, and he fought the urge to rub his hand over his heart. "She is my wife, was the former leader of the Serpents, and who also happens to be the daughter of the Goddess Rán."

"By the Gods, you *claimed* her?" Magnar let out a groan.

"Do I sense disapproval?" Steinar narrowed his eyes, preparing for another argument.

His friend laughed. "From me? Nae. If you recall, I

found love with a woman who follows the new religion. The Fates destined us to be together. Rangvald has given me the account of the battle but left out any knowledge he had of the woman. When Gunnar returned and we received an urgent message from a falcon regarding Odin's magical isle, we all grew worried." He waved his hand dismissively in the air. "But Inga is the daughter of a Goddess—a Goddess who has power over the seas."

"Which I didn't ken until weeks later," Steinar shot back.

"Give me your account," ordered Magnar, leveling his attention on him.

After brushing a hand down the back of his neck to ease the tension, Steinar leaned back on his hands and stretched out his legs.

For the next couple hours, Steinar gave in great detail how Inga stormed into his life, bringing her strength, wisdom, beauty, and love. And for the second time since they had met, the daughter of Goddess Rán bargained for his life, leaving his heart destroyed.

Watching as the sun began its descent in the sky, Steinar lamented, "In our brief time together, my heart found love—I found the woman destined to be by my side. Never did I accept this fate. Now…" He sighed heavily before continuing, "With her loss, there is an emptiness filled with harsh bitterness. I mourn each day—each night. I cannot venture onto the seas again."

Rising from the ground, Magnar raked a hand through his hair. "I propose a new plan for the return of Inga."

Steinar's brow furrowed. He stood abruptly. "Did you not hear what I have said? If the Goddess refused to listen to her daughter, what makes you deem she'd hear any other idea? The laws of their world are firm."

His reaction seemed to amuse Magnar. "Will you fight for her—for the woman you love?"

Unable to fathom the spark, hope surged forth inside Steinar. "Aye, until my last breath!"

Magnar wrapped an arm around his shoulders and shouted, "Did you hear that, Rorik and Gunnar? Our Steinar is going to battle the Goddess of the sea for the return of his wife!"

Both men emerged forth from the trees, smiling.

"Better him than me!" shouted Rorik, coming to stand in front of him.

"You'd probably seduce her," remarked Gunnar, nudging the man with his elbow.

Rorik pointed a warning finger at the man. "I am nae longer known as the *Dark Seducer*."

Gunnar chuckled low. "I forgot, you are now married, and Ragna would not tolerate you bedding another woman, especially a Goddess."

Steinar choked on his own laughter. "By the hounds, 'tis good to see you both."

Leaning slightly forward, Rorik said, "We traveled as wolves through rough weather and terrain to assist you."

"Aye," acknowledged Gunnar, adding, "And we will journey with you to Torvay."

Wariness settled within Steinar. Unsure how to respond, he remained silent.

Magnar released his hold and walked forward. He halted before a clearing, exposing the view of the sea. "This is our proposal, *Pirate Wolf*. We all return to Torvay, and *you* meet with the wise women and present *your* plan to them."

Steinar flung his hands out in frustration. "What plan?"

Magnar glanced over his shoulder at them. "First, you must present your idea to another. If he is in agreement, then I'm almost certain these women who dedicate their life to Rán would be agreeable to deliver your request."

Intrigued, Steinar crossed to stand beside his leader. "There is only one I can think of who could persuade or tempt Rán with an offer, though I fear she might consider him as a threat."

Magnar nodded slowly in understanding. "*Odin* loves his wolves, and you, Steinar, love Inga. Are you prepared to speak with All Father? Are you ready to reclaim your treasure—*your wife*?"

"With all my heart," declared Steinar, smiling outward toward the sea.

Chapter Twenty-Four

Torvay—Late August 1207

Steinar shifted his position outside the gates leading to where the priestesses lived. The women had kept him waiting for five long days. And on this fifth day, the sun began to slip away over the horizon without an appearance of a single woman.

Once he had presented the gilded parchment detailing his plan to them, Eira explained it might take time to request an audience with the Goddess. Frustrated, Steinar had snarled his response. Not pleased with his behavior, Eira banned him from further speaking with them or entering their enclosure until they judged he could talk without his beast growling. She then proceeded to slam the gates on him without taking the parchment.

"Irritating women," he bit out through clenched teeth.

Pacing in front of the iron gates, Steinar considered shifting to his wolf. The wolf could easily manage the tall gates. He halted, lifting his gaze to the iron structure. What would they do if they saw the huge beast lumbering across the path toward them? Either swords would be drawn to slay him, or worse, they'd collapse in sheer terror. Resuming his pacing, he banished the idea.

Steinar halted when he heard the humming from a

certain lass. He tempered his anger while he waited for Alvilda to appear.

"There is another way to deliver your message," she announced, carrying a large bundle of wildflowers in her arms.

He arched a brow skeptically. "Is your wisdom greater than those inside the temple?"

The lass giggled. "Bend down and I'll tell you a secret."

His lips twitched in humor. After complying, he waited for her to impart this news.

Leaning forward, she whispered into his ear, "Aye, far greater. I contain the wisdom of the ancients, but do not share this with anyone. 'Tis only for you." She touched his shoulder. "Your wound has healed."

Blowing out a soft whistle, Steinar nodded slowly. "Aye, you did warn me about the hidden danger. I am honored you have shared this with me. So, what else can you impart?" He tapped his fingers against the parchment tucked inside his belt.

Alvilda tilted her head to the side. "Walk with me, and I will show you."

Rising, he offered, "May I carry your bundle for you?"

The smile she returned lit her entire face. "Gladly."

After transferring the lush flowers into his arm, she took off skipping along the path heading through the trees and into the meadow while singing a song. The wild grasses so tall, the lass disappeared from Steinar's view. He made long strides, grateful for the distraction and hoping the lass proved correct.

When the meadow dipped and curved along the edge of a cliff, fear seized Steinar, Swiftly, he darted after her. "Take my hand!"

"There is nae danger here," she responded calmly.

Regardless of what she stated, he looped his other arm around her waist and lifted her tiny body against his side. Rocks, bits of shells, and pebbles bounced over the side. Steinar swallowed the curse he longed to fling out.

Alvilda's peal of laughter surrounded him. "Is this a game?" she asked.

"Aye," he lied, grateful when the path widened, leading them downhill to the shore.

No sooner did he bring her to the ground, than she wrapped her arms around his leg. "You are a true warrior, Steinar MacDougall! Now hand me my flowers."

Her joy infused him, giving him hope.

Pressing the bundle into her small arms, he asked, "Now what?"

"We present our gifts and your parchment to the Goddess."

Stunned, he watched as she danced to the edge of the water. *Could it be so simple?*

Alvilda beckoned him forward with one hand. "The sun sets. The first star approaches. Come!"

Eager to do her bidding, Steinar hastened to her side.

The lass rose her voice in an ancient song of welcoming. On the last word, she tossed the wildflowers into the water. Alvilda lifted her gaze to him. "Now drop your request on top of my gift."

Uncertainty filled him. Odin had sealed the parchment himself. If only he had reassurance his beloved would be allowed to return.

"Trust me, Steinar. The Goddess will receive your message." Her voice spoke of old wisdom, not the young lass who stood beside him.

Carefully, he removed the parchment but held it firm in his hands.

"The time soon passes," she whispered, tugging on his trews.

Steinar swiftly closed the door to all his doubts. Taking a cautious step forward, he threw the parchment outward, where it landed on top of the flowers. Watching as they drifted farther out into the sea, he clasped his hands behind his back.

When the last ray of sunlight dipped beyond the horizon, the lass let out a sigh.

"'Tis done." She turned and started walking away from him.

Frowning, he asked, "Do I wait here?"

Hesitating, she blinked. "If you so wish. She has heard your request."

Steinar wanted to ply Alvilda with more questions, but he realized no answer would satisfy him. As with any God or Goddess, one had to be patient. Except his patience had worn fragile and filled with annoyance.

"I thank you for your assistance. Are you returning up along the cliff?" he asked, concerned for her safety.

"Do not fear, my mother waits for me in the other direction. Be well, Steinar. May the Gods and Goddesses favor you with long life."

He dipped her a slight bow. "And the same to you, fair lass."

After Alvilda slipped from his view, Steinar crossed to a set of large boulders and settled against the largest one. Determined to keep his trust and hope alive within his heart, he maintained a watchful position along the coast. "If only I had brought food and ale," he uttered softly.

The sound of approaching footsteps had him instantly standing. "Snorri," he acknowledged.

"How fortunate I have found you here. 'Tis good to see you have not given up hope for Inga's return." The skald dumped his satchel onto the ground. Taking a seat beside him, he said, "Let us discuss other matters. Before I read you my saga of the great Pirate Wolf, I require your precise account of the battle."

Steinar folded his arms over his chest. "Did I not give you every detail? In truth, I told my version on more than one occasion."

The man dug into his satchel, producing an aleskin and bundle of food. "Aye, aye, you did. I am grateful for all your accounts. Nevertheless, *you* did not provide details of the treasure."

"I would have thought you had many versions from the Olafssons," replied Steiner, dryly.

Snorri laughed, smacking the ground next to him. "When the brothers have plenty to drink, they tend to embellish their tales even more. We shall eat first, then you'll build a fire so I can read you the tale."

"Is that slices of boar meat?" Steinar unfolded his arms, staring at the food the skald began to unwrap.

"'Tis a feast for man and wolf." Snorri licked his fingers.

"Are you tempting me with food and drink?"

The skald raised an eyebrow. "I have yet to see your wolf. And since I depart tomorrow on a ship back to Iceland, I had hoped to encounter you this evening. We had not concluded our business we spoke of the first day we met on the ship."

Steinar sat down, resuming his position against the

boulder. "Has my absence been noted by the others?"

"Truth?" he asked, spearing a slice of meat with his blade.

Removing his own dirk, Steinar shook his head. "Nae need. I am certain with the arrival of the other wolves, especially Magnar, the Olafssons are eager to discuss new trading and have not missed my appearance. I reckon they grew weary with my foul mood."

Snorri snorted with unrestrained laughter. Finally recovering, he belched and shoved the meat into his mouth.

Eager to savor the small fare set before them, Steinar dug in with relish. The sound of the waves became their companion, while each man ate in silence. Steinar watched the crescent moon surrounded by the brilliance of the stars, and his mind eased.

Reaching for the aleskin, Steinar drank fully and returned it near the food. "Odin's treasure was beyond any I could have imagined," he began, brushing his finger over his nose. "Jewels the size of my fist. Weapons whose hilts were imbedded with gems. The riches would have sustained us all, including the king. However, we did not judge it right to take what was not granted to us."

Snorri lowered his blade. "'Tis what the others confirmed, as well. A test of honor. Will your king be content that you have not secured the treasure for Scotland?"

"As far as I ken, King William was not made aware of my quest. If anything, I merely had been aiding the Serpents. Considering his belief in the new religion, the king would have rejected any right to claim the riches. Especially those created by a *heathen God*—King

William's words, not mine."

"Still your loyalty is to this king."

"As mine is to him," remarked Steinar, removing his boots. Rising from the ground, he shed his cloak and tunic from his body.

"Are you thinking of taking a swim in the ocean?" asked Snorri between bites of meat.

Steinar regarded the man with a wry smile. "Did you bring your writing tools? Parchment? Before I build a fire, my wolf is longing to run across the shore. He grows anxious waiting."

The skald choked on his food. He held up his hand. "Aye, wa...*wait* a moment while I prepare."

"Do not worry, my friend. He will return once I let him roam." Steinar stripped from his trews. In a soft shimmer of gray and silver, he shifted into the wolf.

Snorri gasped. "By the Gods, you are a magnificent beast," he muttered, digging through his satchel for his writing items.

The wolf stretched, and then sniffed the moist ground. Giving one final look at the man, he lunged across the shore in contentment.

****

Steinar cracked open one eye, then promptly shut it. The sun had begun its ascent on a new day and still nothing from the Goddess. Drawing his cloak over his shoulder, he yearned to go back to sleep. Yet the birds' constant shrills with their morning song filled his head.

On a groan, he flung the garment aside and moved to a sitting position. He yawned and stretched his arms over his head. After brushing the sand from his clothing, Steinar stood. Recalling the night spent with the skald, he smiled. When the night hours had drifted on, he finally changed back from wolf to man. The Icelander had filled much of his parchment sheets with drawings of his beast and several more tales worthy of talking about around the fires. They continued to talk about their lives until Snorri resolved to seek his bed. His ship would depart early at dawn.

Fisting his hand over his heart, Steinar whispered, "Safe journey, Icelander. Long life to you."

His hand encountered Inga's sunstone beneath his tunic, and he drew it over his head. Light danced in an array of colors as he spun the stone. He swallowed. "I miss you, *my kærr*. Return to us."

Clutching the sunstone in his hand, he turned away from the ocean. Once more, he held the stone up to the sunlight. "Without you by my side, I have nae need for this but 'tis all I have left to remind me of our time together."

Steinar lowered his head and dropped his arm. For weeks he'd battled his emotions—from fury, despair, loneliness, and utter rage. "Enough!" Steinar shuttered them all. Determination clawed at him. *I'll continue to fight for the woman I love, regardless of any God or Goddess.*

"Would you discard a gift given with love, *Pirate Wolf?*"

Steinar froze, unable to draw in a breath. Thick emotion clouded all rational thought. Was his mind addled? Could the voice be his beloved? Slowly, he risked a glimpse over his shoulder. Unprepared for the vision behind him, he muttered, "Are you real? Or is this another dream?"

Tears slipped down Inga's cheeks as she moved from the water onto the shore. Reaching for a portion of her gown from the bottom, she lifted the material and started running to him.

"Praise Odin." He dropped the sunstone to catch his beloved into his arms. Steinar crushed her to his chest, almost lifting her up against him. "*Inga*," he breathed her name against her lips.

"My pirate," she returned, wrapping her arms around his neck.

The blood pounded in his veins—hammered against his chest. Her scent filled him, and her touch soothed the anguish consuming him. Steinar captured her mouth in wild, savage hunger. His tongue thrust deep, demanding all she had to give. In her kiss, Inga banished the darkness within him.

"*Steinar*," she moaned, threading her fingers into his hair.

With great effort, he eased back. Tenderly, Steinar kissed the salty tears from her cheeks. Rocking her gently against him, his own vision blurred. "You are indeed here."

She choked on a laugh, and then hiccupped. "Better than a dream, aye?"

He grunted a curse. "Do not speak to me of dreams, *my kærr*. You haunted me each night, leaving me in burning agony when I woke."

Her expression turned somber. Inga cupped the side of his face with her warm hand. "As you did mine."

Steinar lifted her into his arms and strolled over to a flat boulder. After easing them both down, he cradled her in his arms. Bringing a handful of her stunning locks against his face, he inhaled deeply. "It has been far too long."

"Less than a week," she declared softly.

His eyes widened. "*Nae*. 'Tis late August."

"Truly?"

Steinar nodded.

Inga's voice trembled. "For every hour that passes here, only minutes in the sea kingdom." She pressed her hand against his chest. "It must have been torture for you."

"You are now here—in my arms. Your mother got my message?"

Sighing heavily, Inga rested her head on his shoulder. "Her cry of outrage could be heard throughout the sea realm before she even read the document. However, her mood softened when she read the last line of the document. How could she object to Odin's offer of a warrior from the halls of Valhalla?"

Steinar stroked his fingers through her glimmering locks, trailing a path down to her bottom. "He asked for a warrior among those at his table. Many came forth when they heard the daughter of Goddess Rán had chosen one of Odin's wolves for her husband."

She shifted within his arms. "Though she was displeased with my departure, I did agree to return once a year during the time of the great gathering. All those who dwell in the sea kingdom come on midsummer for a celebration and the games."

Steinar's mouth clenched as he digested the information. The thought of his beloved returning, even for one day, settled inside him like a swarm of bees.

His wolf snarled in protest.

Inga shook with quiet laughter. "Of course, you will accompany me to the gathering. I told my mother to extend the invitation to my *husband*."

"And her reply?"

"She'd be honored to welcome the Pirate Wolf to her kingdom. After our last conversation, my mother feared never seeing me again. She is desperate to forge a relationship as a mother and daughter, not as the Goddess spouting out orders. It will take time to mend the rift between us, but I am hopeful."

"Time will reveal her intentions. Forgive me if I am wary of her."

Leaning back, Inga studied him with a glint of wonder in her eyes. "Your hair is longer. Where is your braid?"

"There was nae one to do the deed."

She touched his chin. "And the full beard?"

Steinar shrugged, though a smile tugged at the corners of his mouth. Unable to take his gaze from her face, he realized how much he had missed his beloved. "Never found the time to take a blade to my face."

She was the moon to his sun. The calm to his storm. His wife.

"I love you, Inga." Desire—hot and powerful—rushed into his body.

"As I love you," she avowed, resting her forehead against his.

Rising from the boulder, Steinar set her feet on the ground. Swiftly retrieving his cloak and the sunstone, he grabbed her hand. He proceeded to move away from the shore, taking the path to the one place they had called their own weeks ago.

"Must we go see my brothers?" complained Inga, attempting to pull free from his grasp. "I had hoped to spend more time alone with you."

Steinar's grip tightened. "I am not taking you to see your brothers."

"Then where are we going?"

He gave her a wink. "Did you ken there is this ancient oak tree beyond the standing stones up on the hill?"

"If I recall, I spent the most *passionate* night of my life with a man near this tree."

A hint of seduction teased with her reply, and Steinar quickened his pace. "So this man pleased you? Brought you pleasure?"

"The passion he stirred inside me took me beyond the ocean's depths and then to the stars. I have thought of nothing else but to have him touch me there again."

Steinar's cock swelled painfully against his trews. He slowed their progress, stopping at the bottom of the hill. His mouth grazed her earlobe. "Do you think you could show me when we get there? Or is there a secret desire you have yet to explore—one which *I* might be able to fulfill?"

Inga's voice lowered, along with her gaze. "Oh, aye. I have not *tasted* all of the man. Would he be hard or soft when I licked a path from his broad chest down across his muscled stomach to—"

"Sweet Goddess," he choked out. The blood raged in his veins. Eager to strip the gown from her body and plunge his aching cock into those sweet folds, Steinar released her hand.

Inga took swift advantage and darted ahead of him. "I shall race you to our special haven."

He cursed and then laughed in disbelief. "In a gown? With nothing to protect your feet?"

She looked affronted. "By the hounds of Odin! I am not a weak lass!" Retrieving the small blade at her side, Inga made a deep slash around the material, starting at her knees. After she sheathed the blade, she proceeded to rip apart the gown around her body, letting the scraps fall to the ground.

Inga lifted her gaze to meet his. Her smile spoke of desires yet to be fulfilled, but it was those long, bare legs Steinar yearned to have wrapped around him.

He stripped his tunic from his body. "Should I give you a fair start?"

"Steinar, Steinar, you have never seen me run," she taunted, wagging a finger in front of him.

Arching a brow, he challenged, "But the wolf is faster."

Without giving her a chance to respond, Steinar changed from man to wolf.

Inga's deep, joyful laughter filled him as he took off sprinting toward the ancient tree.

Chapter Twenty-Five

Sweeping her gaze beyond the huge gathering of people, Inga searched for the one man who made her knees weak, her heart beat faster, and filled her life with complete happiness. The numbing helplessness when they had parted weeks ago, now replaced with joy.

Steinar left her without breath each time she glanced his way. All sensible thought left her. And when he held her in his arms, she became unbridled in the passion he aroused within her body—always demanding more from the man.

Would her warrior side confess this to him? Nae. But the woman, constantly. Inga adored both—the man and the wolf.

She grew restless waiting for him while she chewed on her bottom lip.

Eira approached near her side. "You look splendid in your gown. The pale blue reminds me of the ocean and the seed pearls woven around the hem are a symbol of the water's white foam."

"A gown worthy of the daughter of a Goddess *and* wife of the Pirate Wolf," added Helka, coming to stand on her other side.

Inga dipped a bow in greeting to both women. "I am honored to have you witness this formal joining between me and Steinar. The gown was a parting gift from my mother."

"We are the honored ones who were chosen by the Goddess to oversee this union," stated Helka, pressing a kiss on her cheek.

"Agreed." Eira smiled. "The other women from the temple send their blessings. Each has blessed the ring of shells by the stones where you shall say your vows."

Placing a hand on the woman's shoulder, Inga mentioned, "Before we depart for Islay, we shall visit the temple. Rangvald is holding a feast for us. We travel there soon."

"So, the Pirate Wolf and his warrior lady will govern both islands—Torvay *and* Islay?" asked Helka. "You are certain this is what you want?"

"Leif is not ready, nor does he seek to claim rights over Torvay. All he wanted was to lead the Serpents," Inga reassured, lifting her hand outward. "His home is on the seas, and my brothers are united in this decision. Furthermore, Steinar's uncle is relieved to have us assist him in overseeing duties on Islay. Am I certain this is what I want? With all my heart. The sea will always be in our blood, but we are also a part of the land. My father told me this once, many, many moons ago. His wisdom is one I value, even now."

"We were blessed to have known him," murmured Eira. "And the people of Torvay welcome you and the wolf to watch over them. Your father banished all other laws years ago and created a new one giving you and your brothers the right to lead and govern this island. Sadly, with his death, you were unaware of this knowledge until recently."

"Aye, aye," acknowledged Helka softly.

Eira tucked her hands within the folds of her cloak. "The wolf has yet to make amends for his rude actions at the temple."

"Now, Eira, you ken there was a good reason. Steinar was in a foul mood on that day. Who could blame his wolf for growling at you with threats," chastised Helka, glancing around Inga.

Eira bristled. "Nevertheless, an apology would be welcomed."

"You could ask him right now," suggested Helka, giving a firm squeeze to Inga's hand before departing to join the others.

Eira clucked her tongue in obvious disapproval and followed after her friend.

Inga slowly turned around. Steinar gave her a smile from across the crowd that set her heart racing. His deep blue tunic, etched with silver threads around the edges of the sleeves couldn't begin to rival the color of his eyes. They shone even from a distance, along with the silver of his torc. She returned his smile with one of her own.

Inga clutched her hands in front of her in anticipation. *You are finally here!*

He arched a brow seductively. *Miss me?*

She shivered from his one look. *You're late.*

Steinar stroked a hand over a slightly bearded face. *You're early. The sun has barely made its descent.*

Arrogant wolf. The first star has already appeared, therefore you're late.

She watched in a haze as his powerful strides bridged the distance between them.

Depends on which star we were discussing the other night. As I recall, my hands and mouth were savoring your lush breasts while you suggested—

Sweet Freyja! All right! I shall concede this once!

Never concede, my kærr, for I enjoy sparring with

you.

Steinar reached for her hand. While keeping his focus on her, he gently kissed the vein along her wrist. "*Kærr*, your beauty steals the breath from my body." He linked his fingers through hers and took a step back, raking a gaze over her. "Where did you get this gown? The material flows over your curves like water."

"Then you approve?" she responded softly, tugging him closer. She'd confess later who had bestowed the gift.

"Aye." He breathed the word against her lips.

Inga became lost in his scent, his taste until loud coughing and cheers resounded behind them. Reluctantly, she parted from him.

Steinar leaned near her ear. "I shall enjoy slipping this gown from your soft skin. For now, those from the Brotherhood, including my leader, Magnar, will pledge their vow to you. When each man claims a wife, all make this oath of protection."

Turning to the group of men, she smiled fully. "You honor me with this gesture."

Magnar stepped forward. He placed his sword on the ground in front of her and knelt on one knee. In a loud voice, he proclaimed, "From the power bestowed upon me from Odin, my sword and strength are yours to protect and defend, Inga MacDougall, daughter of Olaf, and the Goddess Rán. As leader of the Wolves of Clan Sutherland, you are now under our protection."

Rising, he gave a curt nod to Rorik and stepped aside for Gunnar. Tears smarted her eyes, overwhelmed with gratitude.

When the other two men had sworn their oaths, Magnar approached her and Steinar. He placed a hand on each of their shoulders, saying, "Before the first snow falls, you appearance is required at Castle Steinn. There, you shall meet with King William, along with Bjorn and Ivar, who will also make their oaths to you."

"The king?" mumbled Inga with uncertainty.

Steinar chuckled softly, taking her hand. "If you can battle a Goddess, then surely you can meet with the King of Scotland."

Her eyes widened. "As long as he doesn't give us a quest on the seas."

All the men roared with laughter. Inga was not amused.

Tucking her hand in the crook of his arm, Steinar gently moved her forward. "Do not fear, beloved, the king merely wants an audience. I do not think he is aware of your lineage with a Goddess."

She tilted her head to the side, staring intently at him. "Is that a promise he won't give us a task away from the isles, Pirate Wolf?"

"Aye." His mouth twitched, exposing the untruth.

Inga fought the smile curving her lips. "We shall see."

He led her along the pebbled path to the standing stones. A circle of seaweed, assorted sizes and colors of shells, and coral had been placed on the ground before the middle standing stone.

A symbol of the sea and the land. A bond of their union.

After they stepped over into the center, Steinar wrapped his arms around Inga's waist, loving the feel of her.

The crowd gathered below them, bringing the light of their torches.

Overcome with emotion, Steinar cleared his throat. "From the moment you rescued me, *kærr*, my heart opened to love. A feeling I never sought nor desired. The sea was my mistress, and I thought this to be enough. Until you stormed into my life like a tempest. My wolf acknowledged you first, but I remained slow to accept the challenge to allow love into my life. Your beauty, strength, and love are now woven into mine for you. I am your shield of protection, my axe to defend you, and my body to love. Until my last breath, Inga—my warrior, my wife."

Placing her hands on his chest, she whispered, "Oh, my *Pirate Wolf*, I nae longer care if this was fate, the Gods, or the Goddesses which brought us together. We make our own destiny, aye?"

"*Aye*," he growled in affirmation, bringing her closer to him.

Inga laughed softly as the tears slipped down her cheeks. "I never wanted a man in my life. Feared the chains of marriage would weaken me. From the instant I saw you plunge into the ocean, my heart beat truly for the first time. Time stood still for me, and a change occurred inside my soul. I did not fear your wolf, but feared the man who could shatter my heart."

She visibly swallowed. "From this life to the next, from the seas to the stars, with all I possess, Steinar MacDougall, you have my love. When storm clouds threaten your days, I shall banish them with my love. When there is nae hope, I will conquer the darkness with you. I stand beside you as a warrior, lover, and also your wife. You are my *sunstone*, Pirate. Never forget."

"And you are my moon, *my kærr*—from the first rising star to the last. I love you." His lips descended over hers, kissing her passionately. Her moan filled Steinar, and he responded with one of his own.

The crowd broke out into boisterous laughter and shouts of approval. Jugs of mead were passed in celebration, and some began to make their way to the longhouse.

Steinar nuzzled the soft spot below her ear. "What would happen if we didn't go to the feast tonight?"

Inga groaned, inciting his desire further. "This one is important," she pleaded.

Steinar disagreed. He pressed a finger to her lips, flushed from his kiss. "We have spent the last three days feasting, and drinking games—"

She bit down on his finger. He growled.

"My brothers seek another game of *skinnleikr*."

Laughter burst forth from Steinar. "Have you seen their faces? I reckon Brant has a broken arm. Even with assistance from Rorik, they lost."

She looked beyond him and scowled. "Aye, aye. But they'd like to challenge you again for a fifth time. They soon depart for Ireland."

"Nae," he demanded. "Tonight is for us. Let us join them tomorrow."

"Stubborn wolf," Inga scolded. Though a smile creased her luscious mouth. "Feasibly—"

Steinar kissed the pulse at the base of her throat. "Nae."

"Then where shall we go?" she murmured softly, rubbing her cheek against his.

He leaned back and stared at his beloved. He tugged on the soft curl resting against her full breast. "Show me," encouraged Steinar.

Inga's eyes darkened to pools of desire. "There's a

lush waterfall and stream that feeds into the ocean. 'Tis deep in the forest, but I'm certain we can manage to find the narrow path with the aid of the moonlight and your wolf."

"Should we get food and drink?" he asked, releasing his hold on her.

Inga gave him a wink and started to walk away. "We can pick up the satchel I prepared near the oak tree."

"Hmm...this was your plan? You were simply teasing me with your brothers?" Steinar peered over his shoulder. Magnar gave him an abrupt nod as he turned to lead Inga's brothers down the hill.

He saluted his leader and friend.

Contentment filled Steinar, and he ran toward the woman he adored. Within moments of finding her, he swooped her into his arms, spinning her in all directions. Inga's laughter filled him as he lowered his head and poured all his love into a searing kiss—one filled with a lifetime of promises and adventures.

Epilogue

Late September 1207

Steinar remained silent. He understood the difficulty for Inga to part from her brothers. They had journeyed the seas and fought battles together. Yet the Serpents' true leader had finally emerged.

"Are you certain Brant's arm is healed?" asked Inga. Skepticism reflected in her tone.

Leif gave a quick glance over his shoulder at the ship, and then resumed his attention on his sister. "He heals. Even so, our brother would not be swayed to remain behind. We must journey before the good weather changes."

She embraced her brother. "The Goddess will guide you. If you need anything, call for the great whale with the ancient words I've taught you. She will carry a message to me and my mother." Drawing back, Inga wiped away the moisture on her face.

"All will be well," reassured Leif, placing a kiss on her forehead, adding, "We are the feared Serpents, aye?"

Inga nodded while a smile twitched at the corners of her mouth. "With Leif the Bloody Spear, you'll continue to incite terror on land *and* seas."

"Possibly, respect?" Steinar suggested, believing anything was likely.

"Why not both?" Leif laughed, extending his arm

outward to Steinar.

Grasping the man's forearm, Steinar replied, "A good plan."

"Be well, MacDougall. While my sister is a warrior, I trust you shall let nae harm come to her."

"A warning?"

Leif smirked, releasing his hold. "You ken my meaning."

Steinar's wolf let out a low rumble.

Inga laughed. "*Men.* How I love you both."

"We shall return in the spring. Be well, *little sister*," remarked Leif, turning to make his way toward the ship.

"May the Gods and Goddesses favor you with good weather and safe passage, my brothers," whispered Inga, reaching out for Steinar with her hand as she kept her sight fixed on them.

Instantly, Steinar wrapped his arm around his wife's waist, drawing her near his side. Silently, they watched until the ship sailed far out onto the sea. Birds drifted beyond them, and Steinar smiled as they gracefully glided over the waves.

Inga leaned into him, tilting her face toward his. "When do we depart for Islay?"

He wiped away a tear streaking down her cheek. "With the fair weather, I judge it wise we leave within the next few days. From there, we'll travel to Steinn."

"Will you be content dividing our time between the two islands?"

"My quest is here with you," he returned. Her question surprised Steinar. Not once did he regret his decision to govern the isles with Inga by his side. He exhaled slowly, stroking his thumb over her bottom lip. "Contrary to what you may believe, my heart—my life belongs with you. The ocean greets us each morning and night. We can travel to the other islands by ship, satisfying our need to be on the water. Will you miss the adventure, *Inga the Ruthless*?"

"You are my greatest adventure. And I prefer *Inga the Brave*. Who else would dare to rescue a man and his wolf from a siren's song?" Her tongue slipped out along her lower lip, enticing him.

Steinar lowered his hand to her breast. "Brave, aye, *my kærr*. Care to explore more daring adventures this day?"

Inga's lips parted on a sigh. "What were you thinking? Is this a game of skills? Shall I gather my shield, sword, or axe?"

"*Pleasure*," he returned, squeezing the pert nipple through her gown. His cock strained against his trews.

"I have a confession," she uttered in a throaty whisper.

"Do tell."

"Your skills in pleasure are highly pleasing. I'd like to learn to do the same to you."

Steinar bent his head and gently bit her lip. "Inga, you give me pleasure each morning and night—from the sound of your voice, your husky laughter, and the sounds you make when I am loving your body. Never doubt your skills, ever."

Inga slipped her fingers into his hair. "I love you, *my* Pirate Wolf."

His lips seared a path down her neck while he murmured the words against her skin. "Forever, my beloved, my wife. I love you with each breath I take. Let me show you the moon and the stars."

"Can we swim in the stream again?" Inga arched

against him.

"Ah, you enjoyed the pleasures there? The feel of the water while I thrust slow and steady inside you?"

Her indrawn breath surrounded Steinar, giving him his answer.

Drawing forth her moan into his body, he answered with one of his own—kissing her passionately. In his silent vow, Steinar promised to cherish and love Inga until the last star faded from the night sky.

Note from the Author...

I hope you've enjoyed Steinar and Inga's epic sea adventure and journey to find love. Trust me, dear readers, I was unprepared for the surprising twists, mysteries, and betrayals while I wove their tale. As an author, I like to plot out my stories. Each chapter has a theme. Yet I found myself arguing with all my characters over various *shifts* in plots and scenes. When I finally relented, the story poured out of me in waves of writing.

Let me share a *wee* bit of historical information about the real Snorri, the *Icelander*. While during my Viking and Norse research, I came across an important historical person by the name of Snorri Sturluson (1179-1241). Born in western Iceland, Snorri was the son of an Icelandic chieftain. Snorri ascended to become Iceland's richest and powerful leader. He has long been assumed to be the author of medieval Iceland's greatest works, including the *Prose Edda*, which is one of Scandinavia's vast source for Norse mythology, and the *Heimskringla Saga* about the history of Norway's kings. I could think of no one better qualified to pen the fictional tale of the *Pirate Wolf* than Snorri Sturluson.

What's next in this author's world? I believe I've teased you enough with his presence in this story. As a thief, Gunnar MacKinnon is highly praised for his skill in retrieving any object required by the king. A skill which has left this one believer of Christ seeking penance at every holy shrine he encounters. Conflicts arise when he's tasked to kidnap a certain Highland lass—one who wields the old magic and is also the daughter of Lord Sutherland.

In addition, I'm outlining a future Dragon Knight's

story. I cannot forget the most powerful Dragon Knight. James MacKay MacFhearguis is stirring up embers in the background. As I've stated in my 10-year anniversary tour for *Dragon Knight's Sword* last summer, I'm not finished telling their tales.

Until then, may your dreams be filled with Irish charm, Highland mists, and the Wolves of Clan Sutherland!

Other Books by Mary Morgan

Order of the Dragon Knights ~
Dragon Knight's Sword, Book 1
Dragon Knight's Medallion, Book 2
Dragon Knight's Axe, Book 3
Dragon Knight's Shield, Book 4
Dragon Knight's Ring, Book 5
~* ~

Legends of the Fenian Warriors ~
Quest of a Warrior, Book 1
Oath of a Warrior, Book 2
Trial of a Warrior, Book 3
Destiny of a Warrior, Book 4
~*~

Highland Holiday Romances ~
A Magical Highland Solstice
A Highland Moon Enchantment
To Weave a Highland Tapestry
Wishes Under a Highland Star
~* ~

The Wolves of Clan Sutherland ~
Magnar, Book 1
Rorik, Book 2